FAER...

They came from all si... ...est and through the field, ...iver behind them, dozens of stra... ...eings, not one quite the same as the other. There were little men no taller than his knee, with twigs and leaves in their hair, their arms and legs like spindly roots. Pale-skinned women with wet-green hair, dark eyes, and sinuous bodies. Rounded little men with grey beards and wrinkled faces. A woman with the face of a fox and a long bushy tail. . . .

CHARLES de LINT is one of the major pioneers of the modern "contemporary fantasy" novel—stories that bring ancient folk tales, themes, and characters into modern settings. His acclaimed novels *Moonheart, Mulengro* and *Yarrow* are, like *Jack, the Giant-Killer*, tales of fantasy set in the Canadian city of Ottawa, where de Lint makes his home. He is also the author of *Greenmantle, Svaha*, and numerous works of short fiction.

DRINK DOWN THE MOON

CHARLES DE LINT

ACE BOOKS, NEW YORK

Grateful acknowledgment is made to Robin Williamson for permission to use a portion of "By Weary Well" from the album *A Glint at the Kindling* (Flying Fish, FF 096); copyright © 1979 by Robin Williamson. For further information on Robin Williamson, write: Pig's Whisker Music Press, P.O. Box 27522, Los Angeles, CA 90027; or Pig's Whisker Music Press, BCM 4797, London WC1N 3XX, England.

This book is an Ace original edition,
and has never been previously published.

DRINK DOWN THE MOON

An Ace Book / published by arrangement with
the author

PRINTING HISTORY
Ace edition / June 1990

ISBN: 0-441-16861-2

Ace Books are published by The Berkley Publishing Group,
200 Madison Avenue, New York, New York 10016.
The name "ACE" and the "A" logo
are trademarks belonging to Charter Communications, Inc.

PRINTED IN THE UNITED STATES OF AMERICA

10 9 8 7 6 5 4 3 2 1

for
Donna & Doug

Sun & fire & candlelight
To all the world belong
But the moon pale & the midnight
Let these delight the strong.
—Robin Williamson,
from "By Weary Well"

Where the wave of moonlight glosses . . .
We foot it all the night,
Weaving olden dances,
Mingling hands and mingling glances
Till the moon has taken flight. . . .
—W. B. Yeats,
from "The Stolen Child"

CHAPTER
1

The King of the Fairies was abroad that night—in a fiddle tune, if not literally.

He slipped through the darkness in the 4/4 tempo of a slow reel, startled an owl in its perch, and crept through the trees to join the quiet murmur of the Rideau River as it quickened by Carleton University. At length, he came to the ears of a young woman who was sitting on the flat stones on the south bank of the river.

The fiddle playing that tune had a mute on its bridge, substantially reducing the volume of the music, but it was still loud enough for the woman to lift her head and smile when she heard it. She knew that tune, if not the fiddler, and yet she had a sense of the fiddler as well. There was something—an echo of familiarity—that let her guess who it was, because she knew from whom he'd learned to play.

Every good fiddler has a distinctive sound. No matter how many play the same tune, each can't help but play it differently. Some might use an up stroke where another would a down. One might bow a series of quick single notes where another would play them all with one long draw of the bow. Some might play a double stop where others would a single string. If the listener's ear was good enough, she could tell the difference. But you had to know the tunes, and the players, for the differences were minute.

"There's still a bit of you plays on, Old Tom," she

1

whispered to the night as she stood up to follow the music to its source.

She was a small woman with brown hair cropped short to her scalp and a heart-shaped face. Her build was more wiry than slender; her features striking rather than handsome. She wore faded jeans, frayed at the back of the hems, sneakers, and a dark blue sweatshirt that was a size or so too big for her. Slipping through the trees, she moved so quietly that she found the fiddler and stood watching him for some time before he was aware of her presence.

She knew him by sight as soon as she saw him—confirming her earlier guess. It was Old Tom's grandson, Johnny Faw. He was a head taller than her own four foot eleven, the fiddle tucked under his clean-shaven chin, his head bent down over it as he drew the music from its strings. His hair was a darker brown than her own, an unruly thatch that hung over his shirt collar in back and covered his ears to just above his lobes. He wore brown corduroys and black Chinese rubber-soled slippers and a light blue shirt. The multi-coloured scarf around his neck and the gold loops glinting in each earlobe gave him the air of a Gypsy. His beat-up black fiddle case lay beside him with a brown quilted-cotton jacket lying next to it.

She waited until the tune was done—"The King of the Fairies" having made way for a Scots reel called "Miss Shepherd's"—and then stepped out into the little clearing where he sat playing. He looked up, startled at her soft hello and sudden appearance. As she sat down facing him, he took the fiddle from under his chin and held it and the bow on his lap.

With the tunes stilled, a natural hush held the wooded acres of Vincent Massey Park. The quiet was broken only by the sound of distant traffic on Riverside Drive and, closer to where they were sitting, Heron Road, both thoroughfares hidden from their sight by the treed hills of the park. What they could see from their point of vantage, through a screen of other trees, were the lights of Carleton University across the river.

They sat regarding each other for a long while, each one trying to read the other's expression in the poor light.

He was as handsome as Old Tom, she thought, studying the strong features that were so familiar because, like the fiddling, they reminded her of his grandfather. Some might say he was a bit too thin, but who was she to talk?

"I didn't think anyone would come," he said suddenly.

"I didn't know I was invited."

"No. I mean . . ."

She took pity as he grew flustered.

"I know," she said. "The tune was supposed to call me."

He nodded.

"And it did—for here I am. I'm sorry about Old Tom, Johnny. We all loved him. I know he stopped coming to see us, but some of us didn't forget him. We went and saw him, once in a while, but it was hard to do."

"I hated that place, too," Johnny said, "but it got to the point where I couldn't take care of him anymore. I wanted to, but he needed more than I could give. A nurse on twenty-four-hour call. Somebody to always sit with him. I couldn't afford to hire anyone. I have trouble just paying the rent as it is."

"We asked him to stay with us," she said, "but he wouldn't come."

"He could be pretty stubborn."

She smiled. "I'm not stubborn," she said in an excellent mimicry of Old Tom's voice. "I just know what's *right*."

"He used that argument on me, too," Johnny said with a grin.

They were both quiet for a long moment, then the woman stood. Johnny quickly put his fiddle and bow in their case and stood with her.

"Wait," he said.

"I have to go. I only came because . . ." Her voice trailed off and she shrugged. "For old times' sake."

"You can't go yet."

"But I can't stay."

"Why not? I mean, it's just . . . Who are you? How did you know Tom? How do you know *me*?"

She smiled. "I've seen you with Old Tom—and he talked to me about you."

"Before he died, he told me to come here and play that tune—'The King of the Fairies'—but he wouldn't say why. 'They'll come,' he said, and that's all he'd say. So I played the tune and now here we are, but I don't know why."

"You miss him, don't you?"

Johnny nodded. "I went to see him just about every day."

"We'll miss him, too."

As she turned to go, Johnny caught her arm, surprised at the hardness of her muscles.

"Please," he said. "Just tell me: Why would you come here when that tune's played? Who are you?"

"We knew each other a long time ago," she said. "Old Tom and I. That's what I always called him—even back then— because he never seemed young. But he and I didn't wear our years the same and it bothered him. We didn't see him much for a while and then, when he married your grandmother, we didn't see him at all—not for years. Not until she died. Then he came back, looking for what he'd lost, I suppose, and we were still here. But it wasn't the same. It's never the same."

"You're not making any sense," Johnny said. "How could you know him before he met Gran? You don't look any older than I am."

A strange uneasiness was settling in the pit of his stomach. The feeling of being lost that had come over him since his grandfather had died intensified, leaving him with the sensation of being cut off from the rest of the world, from history, from everything that was, except for this moment.

"I know," she said. "It bothered Old Tom, too."

"You're confusing me. How can . . . ?"

But his voice trailed off. He wasn't sure what he wanted to ask anymore.

"I'm sorry," she said. "I don't mean to confuse you." She loosened his fingers from her arm. "You can call me Fiaina."

His hand fell limply to his side when she let it go. She reached up and brushed his cheek with the backs of her fingers.

"It's hard for me to ignore the music," she explained, "but I can't go through it all again, Johnny. Be well. Be good at everything you do. And especially keep the strings of your fiddle ringing—that keeps Old Tom alive, you know. He's in your music, because it's from him that you learned it."

She dropped her hand and stepped back.

"Now I do have to go."

Johnny took a half-step towards her, but kept his distance, not wanting to scare her off.

"What . . . what sort of a person are you, Fiaina?" he asked.

A look came to her face that was both merry and sad. She reached into her pocket and took out a small object that gleamed white in the starlight before she pressed it into his hand.

"We call ourselves sidhe," she said. "But you know us better as faerie."

And then she was gone.

She didn't step away into the trees. She never moved. One moment her fingers were light on his palm; the next she had disappeared.

Johnny stared at the spot where she had vanished, not sure what had happened. He took a step or two forwards, moving his hands through the air, half-expecting to come into contact with her, but the little glade was empty except for him. The feeling in the pit of his stomach grew stronger. The sense of dislocation intensified. He looked down at what he held in his hand.

It was a small piece of flat bone, no longer than an inch and a half, carved into the shape of a fat fiddle. He turned it over in his fingers, feeling its smoothness. There was a tiny hole where the fiddle's scroll would have been if it was a real instrument—to hang it from a thong, he supposed.

He closed his fingers around it and slowly sat down. She couldn't have just vanished. It had to be this weird feeling he had—like he had the flu or something. Because people didn't just vanish.

We call ourselves sidhe . . . but you know us better as faerie. . . .

Faerie. Right.

It had to be a joke, only how had she pulled off that vanishing trick? For a moment he thought of picking up his fiddle and playing the tune again, but he knew without trying that it wouldn't work a second time.

Not tonight.

It might never work again.

He swallowed dryly and gave the bone fiddle another look. The sense of dislocation was beginning to fade, finally, but he didn't feel any better. Something had happened here, something strange, and it left him uneasy. If it had been a trick, then what was the point of it? And if it hadn't . . . what did it mean?

Faerie. We call ourselves . . .

But that was even more preposterous.

His hand started to tremble. He thrust the little carving into his pocket. She'd been touching his hand, and then she'd just vanished. How could she have done that? Nobody could move that fast.

Nobody human, he thought, but firmly pushed that thought away.

He studied his surroundings, the dark trees, the empty glade, waiting for someone to jump out and cry, "April fool!" Except it wasn't April. Though maybe he was a fool.

A shiver went through him and he put on his jacket. Picking up his fiddle case, he gave the spot where his mysterious visitor had vanished a last quick glance, then hurried off down the paved bike path that would take him by Billings Bridge Plaza to Bank Street.

They stood in Faerie—a half-step sideways from the world as Johnny Faw saw it—and watched him go. The woman who had named herself Fiaina had been joined by two others.

One was a small old man, shorter than her by a few inches, bewhiskered and thatch-haired, with a dried apple of a face. He wore a blue jacket over brown trousers and shirt, small leather boots that laced up, and a large, wide-brimmed hat with a three-cornered crown. His name was Dohinney Tuir.

The other was taller than either of them—a stocky, muscular woman with a blue-black mane of hair. There was a certain equine set to her features, accentuated by her broad flat nose, the wide set of her dark eyes, and the squareness of her jaw. Her name was Loireag and there was nothing but the wind between the night air and her ebony skin.

"You answer to 'Fiaina'?" Loireag asked the first woman. There was a bite of gentle humour in her voice as she spoke. "There's a new one."

"You're not the only one can claim that name, Jenna," Dohinney Tuir added.

Jenna shrugged. "It wasn't a lie. I've been called wild before, and worse. I wasn't about to give him a true name—not even a speaking one."

"And if he goes out some night calling for Fiaina?" Tuir asked. "Arn knows what'll come in answer."

Jenna looked up to where Arn hung in the sky—a round full moon, deep with mystery.

"I gave him a charm," she said.

"Oh, yes!" Loireag broke in with a whinnying laugh. "And Arn knows what *that'll* call to him."

"Nothing unsainly—that much I can guarantee."

"Nothing evil, perhaps," Tuir agreed, "but maybe the Pook of Puxill?"

Jenna sighed and looked away from her companions.

"I've had too many tadpoles in my pond," she said. "I've neither the time nor the heart for yet another."

Tuir nodded knowingly. "It's no comfort watching them wither away and die in the blink of an eye—I'll give you that."

"I still can't understand why you bother with them in the first place," Loireag added. "They've no stamina."

"They shine so brightly," Jenna said. "It's that light in them that always draws me. They're here and gone so quick that they have to burn brightly, or not be seen at all."

"How can you miss them?" Loireag asked. "Set a pair of them down any place and quicker than you can blink, you'll be up to your ears in them. They breed like rabbits."

"They *are* a lusty race," Jenna said with a smile.

Loireag snorted. "Give me a hob any day. At least they last the whole night."

She grinned at Tuir, who was puffing up his chest at her words.

"When they're not too old, that is," she added.

The little man lost his breath, chest sagging, and scowled at her.

"If he comes again," he said, turning to Jenna, "will you answer his call?"

She shook her head. "I won't be here to answer any calls. I gave him the charm, the same one Old Tom had before him, only Tom returned it to me. Johnny Faw can either follow where it will lead him, or not—it's his to choose."

"You're still going, then?" Loireag asked.

"Someone has to—if there's to be a rade at all this year."

All three of them were quiet then, thinking of how long it had been since the fiana sidhe had gathered for the luck rade.

The fiana sidhe were solitary faerie, not aligned with either the Seelie or Unseelie Courts, and got their luck in ways different from those of their gentrified cousins. They gathered, once a moon, to ride a long and winding way through the land, following old straight tracks and other moonroads in single file. This was how they got their luck. There was something in the long winding file of faerie, following those roads with the full moon shining above them. . . . Some combination of it all made the luck grow strong in them, recharging them like batteries.

Without it, they diminished. Their magics weakened. They faded.

Last autumn there had been a struggle between the two Courts, a struggle that the Seelie faerie won. The Wild Hunt had been freed from centuries of bondage, the Gruagagh of Kinrowan had given his Tower to a Jack, and the Unseelie Court was cast to the winds—many of them slain. The weeks following that time, from Samhain into Midwinter, had been a period of change. The Seelie Court settled back into its old familiar ways, the Wild Hunt was gone—Arn knew where— and the Unseelie Court slowly began to regroup and gather into new alliances.

The fiaina sidhe, never ones to join either Court, had stood back and watched it all.

The closest they came to a communal effort was their rade, for solitary or not, all faerie followed the Moonmother Arn and she had imbued even the fiaina with a certain sociability—even if it was only realized once every four weeks when Arn turned a new face to the world below. So they had gone about their own ways until they realized that something was taking advantage of the upset in the balance between the two faerie Courts to make inroads into the Borderlands that the fiaina claimed for their own.

Old haunts were found deserted of their inhabitants. Here a hob was found slain, stripped of his blue coat and stitcheries. There a derrie-down was taken from her river holt, lying stretched out and dead on the shore. And the rade was disrupted, time and again.

When they gathered for their rade, a foul wind with the smell of old graves would rise to hang about them. Clouds would cloak the moon's face. Whisperings and ugly mutterings could be heard all around them, but nothing was seen. And Jenna Pook, the Pook of Puxill who led the rade, who alone knew the

twists and turns of the old tracks and moonroads, would find
her mind fogged and clouded until she was too confused to take
a step.

As their luck faded, many of the fiaina sidhe fell back from
their old haunts in the Borderlands, faring deeper into their
secret territories to come no more to the gatherings. Where the
Courts would band together in a time of crisis, the fiaina
withdrew as though it was a disease that beset them and they
might catch it if they came too close to each other.

Too proud to go to their cousins for help, and unwilling to
pay what that help would cost them, there were still a few
fiaina who were determined to stand up to whatever it was that
threatened them. Foremost of them was the Pook who led the
rade.

As though sensing that she was its greatest danger, the
enemy concentrated on her. More nights than one she'd spent
fleeing . . . something. She had no clear picture of what it
was that chased her. Sometimes she thought it was a black dog,
other times a black horse. Sometimes it came upon her so
quickly that she barely escaped. Other times it merely crept up
on her like a mist, or a tainted smell. It was only constant
vigilance that kept her free of its clutches.

So it was that she made her decision to look for help—not
from the Courts, for like all the fiaina, she wouldn't pay their
price. The Laird of the Seelie Court would demand allegiance
in return for his help, and the fiaina would never give up their
independence. As for the Unseelie Court, no one knew if they
had a new chief to approach in the first place, and if the Laird's
folk would demand allegiance, the Host of the Unseelie Court
would take their souls.

So it was to their own that the fiaina must turn—a skillyman
or wisewife of the sidhe. The first that had come to Jenna's
mind was the Bucca who'd taught her the way that the rade
must follow, who'd untangled the skein of old tracks and
moonroads and given her their proper pattern.

"A Fiddle Wit would help us," Dohinney Tuir said after a
while.

"If we had one," Jenna said. "But Johnny Faw's a tadpole,
not a Fiddle Wit."

"He could learn."

"He could," she agreed. "If he wanted to. He has the

music—I won't deny that. But wit takes more than music, more than luck and a few tricks as well. From what little I've seen of him, I don't know if he has what's needed."

"It's hard to learn something," Tuir said, "when you don't know it's there to learn."

"But if we led him every step of the way, it would mean nothing. He'd be no closer. The wit needs to be earned, not handed to any tadpole who looks likely—*if* it even was the sort of thing that could be handed out."

"Still. You gave him the charm."

"I did. I owed him that much—for Old Tom's sake."

"So you'll go off, looking for the Bucca," Tuir said, "while—"

"It's not my fault the luck's gone!"

"No. But only a Pook can lead the rade, and the closest we have after you is your sister, who—"

"Half-sister."

"It doesn't make that much difference. She has fiaina blood and—"

"Not to hear her tell it."

"—she's the closest to a Pook we'll have if you don't come back."

"I'll be back."

"Yes, but—"

"Don't forget," Jenna said a little sharply. "We have no rade as it is—whether I go or I stay."

"I think it's the Gruagagh that's to blame," Loireag said firmly. "It's always a gruagagh that's to blame when there's trouble in Faerie. A wizard never knows to leave well enough alone. They're as bad as humans—always taking a thing apart to see how it works."

"The only gruagagh we've had near here was Kinrowan's," Jenna said. "And he's gone now."

Loireag frowned. "It's a new one then—one who hasn't made himself known yet."

"What I want to know," Tuir said, "is this: Gruagagh or whatever, it has your scent. When you go, will it follow you, or will it chase down your sister, or some innocent like your tadpole whose only crime is that you gave him a charm with your scent upon it?"

"You're too soft-hearted," Loireag told the little man before

Jenna could reply. "It's just a human we're talking about. Better the enemy goes sniffing after him than follows our Pook. At least *she's* doing something to help us."

"Johnny Faw will be in no danger," Jenna said. "The charm will sain him from evil influences. And as for my half-sister, she goes her own way—as we all do."

Tuir nodded and kicked at the turf with the pointed toe of his boot.

"I just wish you didn't have to go," he said.

"Or that you'd at least not go alone," Loireag said.

"The Bucca will be hard enough to track down as it is," Jenna said. "I'll never find him with you in tow. He's never been one for company—two's a crowd, so far as he's concerned. I don't doubt he's hiding away in an Otherworld of the manitous and I'll have a stag's own time chasing him down."

There was nothing the other two could say. They'd been through this argument before—too many times since Jenna had announced her intentions to leave a few days ago.

"When do you go?" Tuir asked.

"Tonight. Now. Johnny Faw's calling-on tune strikes me as a sign of sorts. Giving him the charm was like completing the last piece of unfinished business I had. So I'll go now with my own calling-on tune . . . for the Bucca."

Loireag nodded and stepped close to her, enfolding Jenna in a quick embrace.

"Luck," she said gruffly, and stepped back.

Jenna found a smile, but Loireag had already turned and was making for her home in the river. Halfway between the water and where Jenna and Tuir still stood, the running figure of the ebony-skinned woman became a black-flanked horse. She reared at the edge of the river, hooves clattering on the flat stones, then the water closed over the kelpie's head and she was lost from sight.

"Don't worry so much," Jenna said to her remaining companion. "I'll be back before you know it, and then I'll lead us all on such a rade as we've never seen before—high and low, we'll follow more roads than a spider has threads in its web."

Tuir nodded, blinking back tears. In his eyes, Jenna could see the same foreboding that had been in the kelpie's. She watched him swallow uncomfortably, his Adam's apple bobbing, as he obviously tried to think of something cheerful to say. Finally, he gave her a quick kiss and a tight hug, then hurried away, following the bicycle path that Johnny Faw had taken when he'd left earlier.

Alone now, Jenna stood for long moments, breathing the night air. Everything had a clarity about it in the moonlight, a sharpness of focus that kept her standing there, drinking in the sight of it, the smells, all the sparkle of the moment. Then she shook herself, like a person who'd caught herself dozing. Fetching a small journeysack from where she'd left it by Loireag's river, she shouldered it and set off, crossing the river and heading north.

It was the quest itself that was as much to blame for what happened, as anything else.

After long weeks and months of fretting and danger, of losing the rade and its luck, of being hunted but not being able to strike back . . . to finally be *doing* something . . . Jenna let her guard down as she ran at a pace-eating lope that she could keep up for hours.

She was thinking of the road before her and the Bucca at its end, not about what had driven her to set off on this quest. Her heart felt lighter than it had for a very long time, for she'd always been a doer, not a thinker. She even hummed a tune to herself, a fiddle tune—not one of Johnny Faw's, but one that Old Tom used to play in the old days.

A mile or so north of where she'd left her friends, after speeding through city streets to the landscaped lawns that the National Capital Commission kept neat and trim along the Parkway that followed the Ottawa River, the enemy found and caught her.

It came like a pack of dogs, spindly creatures, with triangular goblin faces, that ran on all fours, but could clutch and grab and tear with fore and hind legs. They made no sound as they came up from behind her, rapidly closing up the distance between them. When they struck, she never knew what hit her. She never had a chance.

Attacking, they were no longer silent. Snarls and high-pitched growls cut across the night as they circled her still body to slash, dance away, then slash again. By the time the brown-cloaked figure arrived to drive the pack from its prey, there was only a heartbeat of life left in her. The figure bent over Jenna, pushed back its hood to look into her eyes as her life drained from her. When the moment passed, the figure rose, its pale eyes gleaming as though it had stolen the Pook's life force and taken it into itself.

Tugging its hood back into place, the figure stood and walked away, leaving the broken body where it lay. Of the pack that had taken Jenna down, there was now no trace, but the sharp sting of magic stayed thick in the air.

CHAPTER
2

Henk Van Roon was sitting on the stairs of Johnny's porch when Johnny arrived home, the octagonal shape of his lacquered wood concertina case on a step by his knee. He was a few years older than Johnny, having just turned thirty the previous week—a tall, ruddy-cheeked Dutchman who seemed, at first glance, to be all lanky arms and legs. His long blond hair was tied back at the nape of his neck with a leather thong and he was dressed in jeans and a Battlefield Band T-shirt, with a worn and elbow-patched tweed jacket overtop.

"How're you holding out, Johnny?" he asked.

Johnny sighed and sat down beside him, laying his fiddle case on a lower step. "Like I've got a hole inside me—you know?"

"You want some company?"

Johnny didn't answer. He looked across the street, thinking of how many times he'd sat on these steps with Tom, playing tunes sometimes, or talking, or sometimes just not doing anything, just being together. He turned slowly as Henk touched his shoulder and found a weak smile.

"Yeah," he said. "I could use some company. C'mon in."

Grabbing his fiddle, he led the way inside. The house was an old three-story brick building on Third Avenue of which he rented the bottom floor. He unlocked the door to his apartment and stood aside to let Henk go in first, closing the door behind them.

15

"You want something—coffee, tea?" he asked.

"You got a beer?"

"I think so."

Johnny left his case by the door and went into the kitchen. Henk stood for a moment, then lowered his long frame into the beat-up old sofa that stood under the western window. There was a fake mantelpiece on the north wall, snugly set between built-in bookcases that took up the rest of the wall. The bookcases were filled with an uneven mixture of tune books and folklore collections, the remainder made up of paperbacks of every genre, from mysteries to historicals and best-sellers.

The mantel was covered with knickknacks, most having something to do with fiddlers or fiddling. There were wooden gnome fiddlers and ceramic ones; a Christmas rabbit complete with a red and green scarf and a pig standing on its hind legs, both with instruments in hand; pewter fiddles lying on their sides; even a grasshopper, playing its instrument like a cello.

Two old Canadiana hutches stood against the south wall, holding Johnny's stereo and record collection. The west wall didn't exist, except as a hall that led from the front door to the rest of the apartment—a kitchen at the end of the hall, two bedrooms, and a washroom. A door at the back led from the kitchen to a storage shed that was set snug against the rear of the house. The walls of the living room and throughout the apartment were covered with posters and pictures of folk festivals, Irish crofters' cottages, Scottish landscapes, and the like.

"All I've got is a couple of domestics," Johnny said as he returned with a can of Labatt's Blue in each hand.

"No problem," Henk said.

Johnny gave him one of the cans and took the other to one of the two chairs that stood opposite the sofa. There was a low coffee table between sofa and chairs, covered with magazines and a coffee mug that was half full of cold tea.

"You going to pick up Tom's stuff tomorrow?" Henk asked. Johnny nodded.

"You want a hand with it?"

"There's not that much—but thanks."

"I was thinking more of some moral support."

"Well, I could use that. Thanks, Henk."

"Hey, no problem."

They sipped at their beer, neither speaking for a while. Just when Henk thought he'd better come up with something to pull his friend out of his funk, Johnny looked up.

"I had something weird happen to me tonight," he said.

"Weird curious, or weird spooky?"

"A little of both, I guess."

He related what had happened to him.

"She was touching my hand," Johnny said as he finished up, "giving me the bone carving, and then she was gone. Poof. Just like that. Now, I know I've been a little out of it lately, what with Tom and everything, but there's no way she could have just slipped away from me. She vanished, and I can't figure out how she pulled it off. Or what it was all about in the first place. Does it make any sense to you?"

Henk shook his head. He picked up the bone fiddle from where it lay on the coffee table between them and turned it over in his hands as he had when Johnny first showed it to him.

"Do you believe in ghosts . . . or fairies?" Johnny asked.

Henk smiled. "Only when I'm stoned."

"Know anybody who does?"

"I'd've figured you—with all those books."

"Those are—were mostly Tom's," Johnny said. "And besides, they're not the same thing. They all talk about old farmers seeing things—country stuff. Old country stuff at that. I mean, some old guy living in the Shetland Islands, maybe, or the Black Forest—who knows what they'd see. But this is the city—or at least a park in the city."

He sighed, staring at the carving in Henk's hand.

"And I don't believe in them either," he added. "I'd like to, I guess. But . . . you know."

Henk nodded. "It doesn't make sense. He laid the bone fiddle back down on the coffee table. "Did she really seem to know Tom?"

"We didn't talk that much, but she seemed to. Except she acted like she knew him when he was young, and she didn't seem any older than you or me."

"And she really just vanished?"

Johnny nodded.

"Somebody's playing games with you, Johnny. I don't know how, or why, but that's what it's got to be."

"I guess."

Talking it over with Henk made it all seem different. When Fiaina had stood there talking to him, when she'd just vanished . . . it had seemed very real. Or very unreal, but actually happening.

He picked up the bone fiddle and rubbed his thumb against it. "This thing's old."

"Seems to be."

"What if she really was what she said she was?"

"Uh-uh. You're setting yourself up for a bad fall there. Somebody's playing a scam on you and if you start taking it seriously, you'll be playing right into their hands. Don't go with it, Johnny. The best thing you could do is put that carving up on the mantel, with the rest of your fiddle collection, and forget about it."

"But I've got a feeling. . . ."

"Yeah. Me, too. And it's a bad one."

Johnny gave him a curious look. "What makes you say that?"

"I don't know. I wasn't there, so I didn't see what happened. But I know you, Johnny. You're a pretty straightforward kind of a guy. You've never chased phantoms. We both know there's no such thing as elves and goblins and all that kind of thing, so why start believing in them now?"

"That's a pretty lame reason," Johnny said. "But I know what you mean."

He glanced at the wall of books, not at the paperbacks so much as the hardcovers that Tom had collected over the years. Douglas's *Scottish Lore and Folklore*. Alan Garner's *The Guizer. The Folklore of the Cotswolds,* by Katharine Briggs. Evans's *Irish Folk Ways*. There were over a hundred of them, all collections of old stories and anecdotes, country customs, and the like. Johnny had read through some of them, liking the connection they made with his music—just liking them for what they were, really. Even those that were a little heavier going, like Graves's *The White Goddess* or Baughman's index of folktale types and motifs.

"But I like the idea of hobgoblins and little people still being around," Johnny said, looking back at his friend. "I never liked the idea that we'd chased them away to some Tir na nOg, you know?"

"If," Henk said, "and remember I'm saying *if* they ever

existed, I don't see any reason why they couldn't adjust to the way the world's changed."

Johnny smiled, his first real smile since he'd got the phone call late one night last week, telling him that his grandfather had died.

"See?" he said. "It's beginning to intrigue *you* now."

His smile widened at the big "Why not?" grin that came to Henk's features.

"Can you see punk elves?" Henk asked.

"Disco dwarves!"

They both laughed.

"We've got to have a plan," Henk went on. "Whoever that woman was, we've got to track her down."

"How are we going to do that?"

"Go back to the park tomorrow night."

Johnny shrugged. "I suppose."

"You've got a better idea?"

"No. It's just that she gave me the feeling that she wouldn't be showing up there again."

He glanced at the books again.

"It's too bad," he added, "that there's no one collecting contemporary folktales. Citylore. There's got to be stories."

"You hear about that kind of thing in a place like New York," Henk said, "but Ottawa? What've we got? Anyway, what good would that do?"

"It'd give us a place to start looking, for one thing. Maybe there's a certain part of the city that's got more weird stories about it than another. We could go check it out . . . ask around."

"If we asked most people about fairies, they'd think we were looking for gays."

"Cute."

"No, really. We can't just go around and do what? Talk to winos and bag ladies?"

Johnny nodded. "Now, there's an idea."

"Oh, come *on*. You can't seriously expect we'll find your mysterious fairy queen by chatting up bums?"

"No. I'm not really thinking about her, to tell you the truth. It's the idea that intrigues me now—of elves and the like living in an urban environment. Not that they *really* are—just what sort of perception people have of them in the city."

"What?"

"You know. What kind of odd little stories or unexplained incidents people talk about."

"Oh. Like the lunatic fringe. UFOs and stuff like that. We'll have to have certain criteria to go by. Everybody we interview will have to have pink hair, say, and—" He paused and snapped his fingers. "Wait a minute."

Johnny rolled his eyes. "Come on, Henk. You're getting out of control—and on just one beer. Think of your rep."

"No. This is something different. I just thought of somebody who fits your bill perfectly. Have you gone to see Greg's new band yet?"

"No, I've just heard of them. What're they called—AKT? I hear they've got a dynamite lead singer."

Henk nodded. "I was thinking of their sax player."

"I don't listen to a lot of R&B."

"You don't have to. You just have to talk to this girl. She's always making up stories about gremlins living in the sewers and stuff like that."

"Oh, yeah? What's her name?"

"Jemi Pook."

It was one of the Laird of Kinrowan's own foresters who found Jenna's body just before dawn. He was a young hob named Dunrobin Mull, somewhat taller than most hobs and beardless, with a dark red stocking cap, and trousers and jerkin of mottled green. He rode a brown and grey speckled pony that was shaggy and short-legged. The pony came to an abrupt halt as it and its rider spied the Pook's torn and battered body.

For a long moment the hob sat astride his mount, staring down, his stomach turning knots as he looked on the gruesome sight. His pony sidestepped nervously under him, nostrils widening. Mull leaned over and patted its neck, then slowly slid from its back and stepped closer toward the body.

Being neither gruagagh nor skillyman, he knew little of magic and so sensed nothing of the traces of it that were left in the air, nothing except a weird tingle at the nape of his neck that lifted the hair from his skin. He put that down to the eeriness of the moment. But he was a tracker, and it surprised him to find only a single set of man-sized tracks leading up to the corpse, and then away again. There was no sign of what had done such damage to the Pook, only the marks of her flailing about as she had tried to fight off her attacker.

"Hempen, hampen," Mull muttered as he sketched a quick saining in the air. "What sort of a beast can do this damage and leave no sign?"

It hadn't been the man, for it was plain by the tracks that he'd done no more than bend down over the Pook before turning away again. Mull looked about in all directions, through both Faerie and the world of men, but saw nothing. There were only the tracks of the man who'd come and gone.

It was a poor neighbor who left a body lying like this after discovery, Mull thought. He'd not treat the dead so poorly himself—none he knew would.

He took a blanket from where it was tied in a tight roll at the back of his saddle and gingerly placed Jenna's body upon it. He folded the blanket around her, tied it shut, then struggled with it to his pony, staggering under its weight. The pony shied at the burden until Mull spoke a few comforting words, but it was still long moments before the beast was calm enough to let him tie the bundle to his saddle. Giving a last look around, Mull spotted the Pook's journeysack where it lay a few feet away. He fetched it and tied it to the saddle as well.

"Come on, Goudie," he murmured to his pony. "It's not so far to the Laird's Court."

The pony whickered, thrusting its nostrils against the hob's shoulders. Mull gave the broad nose a quick comforting pat, then led the pony away, heading eastward to where the Laird's Court stood overlooking the Ottawa River from the heights that men named Parliament Hill.

CHAPTER
3

All Kindly Toes, better known to friends and fans as AKT, were playing a street dance the next night. According to the posters stapled to telephone posts, the dance was being billed as "The Last Days of Summer Tour." It didn't seem to bother anyone that just one gig was being advertised as a tour—it was all in good fun.

The band was already on stage and halfway through their first set by the time Johnny and Henk arrived. The easternmost block of Chesley Street in Ottawa South had been closed off and the stage squatted where the street made a "T" as it met Wendover, speakers racked up on either side. The sound board was set up on the northeast corner and there was a crowd of over a hundred people dancing in front of the stage or standing and watching from the sidewalks. The band was just finishing up a funky version of "Love Potion No. 9" and immediately launched into "River Deep, Mountain High."

"They're good," Johnny said, speaking into Henk's ear to make himself be heard over the music.

Henk grinned and nodded. He kept his gaze on the stage as he led them closer.

On the right side of the stage, Greg Parker, the founder and old man of the band, was playing guitar. He had short dirty-blond hair and was wearing a Hawaiian shirt with a clashing burgundy and white striped tie, blue jeans, and an off-white cotton sports jacket with the sleeves rolled up to the elbows. The bass player, Tommy Moyer, was dressed similarly, if a touch more tastefully, as his shirt and tie matched. He was a big bearish man, the Fender bass he played looking like a toy in his hands. David Blair, a thin black man wearing a UB40 T-shirt, was playing drums. Both he and Tommy, like the rest of the band except for Greg, looked to be in their early twenties. Greg was thirty-eight.

On the far left, Trudy MacDonald was playing the organ. She had short brown hair and a round face, and grinned as she played. Center stage was the lead vocalist, an old girlfriend of Henk's, Johnny remembered as he looked at her. Her name was Beth Kerwin. She swayed as she sang, holding the microphone in one hand, head tilting back as she hit the chorus. Her brown hair was cut short on top, the sides and back long and gathered into a French braid that fell halfway down her back. She wore a short black fifties-style dress that was covered with a design of multi-coloured jelly beans.

As the band went into the bridge between verses and the sax cut in, Johnny turned his attention to the girl they'd come to meet. Jemi Pook was tiny, her tenor sax seeming as huge in her hands as Tommy's bass with diminutive in his. She was wearing a grey and pink minidress, the rectangular-shaped colours arranged in an Art Deco pattern. Her hair was pink, too, a brighter shade than her dress, and stood up in punky spikes—a look that was already passé, but on her it still worked.

Looking at her, Johnny's chest went tight. He knew her, knew that face. With only a late-night memory of it, he still knew her.

There were three more songs before the band took a break, but Johnny hardly heard them. He watched the sax player, trying to understand her. She was relaxed and loose on stage, strutting in time with Greg and Tommy like Gladys Knight's Pips, sharing Greg's mike on choruses, leaning back, the bell of her sax rising up to her own mike when she had a riff to play. There was nothing in what he saw of her on stage during those songs that explained last night.

"Come on," Henk said as the band finished "Baby Love" and left the stage.

He made his way behind the stage to where the band was relaxing with friends on the broad lawn of the tall three-storied

house that towered over the proceedings. Johnny followed, the
tight feeling in his chest still there. He wasn't sure if he was
nervous, or afraid. Maybe a little of both.

We call ourselves sidhe. . . .

There was something weird going on and he was beginning
to have second thoughts about getting involved in it. The last
thing he needed was to get mixed up with a bunch of . . .
what? She'd said nothing last night to make him afraid. All
she'd done was talk about Tom. She'd been nice about it all.
Only why had she come when he'd played that tune? Why had
she given him the carving. *How* had she pulled off that
vanishing trick?"

He thought of just leaving, then and there, but then it was
too late for second thoughts.

"Hey, Jemi!" Henk was calling. "I've got a friend I'd like
you to meet."

She turned at the sound of her name, a beer in hand. She
appeared taller than last night, her hair was a little longer. But,
then, she was wearing black pumps now, and her hair had been
gelled to stand up in spikes.

"Hi, Henk." She glanced at Johnny. "What've you got in
there?" she asked, looking at his fiddle case. "A clarinet?"

"No. It's a—"

"I know. A fiddle. I was just teasing."

Johnny tried to think of something to say, but she was
already looking back at Henk.

"What brings an old hippie like you out of the woodwork?"
she asked, a quick smile taking any possible sting from the
question.

"Thought I'd take Johnny slumming," Henk replied. "You
know—show him what it sounds like when white folk play
black music."

David Blair, the drummer, was standing near.

"This isn't exactly a deep tan," he said, holding out a
dark-skinned arm.

"Well, that's all the band's got going for it, isn't it? Solid
rhythm."

David grinned. "Yeah. And I play great basketball, too."

Greg appeared at David's elbow. "Hey, you guys want a
drink? We've got pop and beer."

"Sounds great," Henk said.

As everyone started to drift off, Johnny touched Jemi's shoulder."

"Fiaina," he said.

She turned towards him, a strange look in her eyes. "What did you say?"

Her eyes didn't seem as big now as they had last night. Eye shadow was dark around them. She wore rhinestone earrings, each with three gleaming strands, and a necklace of fake pearls, tight like a choker around her neck. The thin spaghetti straps of her dress were pale against the brown tan of her shoulders.

"How did you do that last night?" Johnny asked. "How'd you just vanish?"

"Wait a sec—let's back up a minute. Right now's the first time I've met you."

Johnny shook his head. "I played the tune, like Tom said I should, and you came. I'm not about to forget it. And you gave me this."

Jemi had tossed her friends a quick glance and was backing away when Johnny brought the bone carving from his pocket and held it out to her on an open palm.

"I never . . ." Jemi started to say.

Her voice trailed off as she looked at the bone fiddle. She reached out with one finger and touched it.

"Where did you get this?" she asked, her gaze lifting to meet his.

"Last night. You gave it to me."

She shook her head. "It wasn't me—but I think I'm beginning to get an idea of just who it was you did meet."

"It was you," Johnny said.

"Wasn't. We had a rehearsal last night that went on till around two. Ask around if you don't believe me."

"But—"

"You met my sister. Jenna."

"She said—you said your name was Fiaina."

"Fiaina's just a generic term," Jemi told him. "It's not a name. It's like saying a Scotty dog. Or a Clydesdale horse." She took pity on his confusion. "Look, I know what Jenna can be like. Are you planning to stick around for the rest of the show?"

"I guess so. Sure."

"Okay. Let's go get you a beer and relax a bit. I really don't feel up to getting into anything too heavy on a break—I've got to get up and play again in a few minutes, you know? But afterwards, we'll talk."

"This Jenna—"

"Afterwards," Jemi said firmly.

She grabbed him by the arm and steered him to where Henk and some of the others were talking around a cooler.

"Here," she said as she got him a beer. "Your name's Johnny—right?"

"Johnny Faw."

She pointed at his fiddle case. "Are you any good with that?"

"I'm all right."

"Great. Maybe we'll play a couple of tunes together later. Do you know 'Jackson's'? Ever heard it played on a sax?"

Johnny shook his head. "But I've heard Moving Hearts."

"Great band. I jammed with their piper once. Boy. Pipes and sax trading off on trad tunes—you wouldn't think they'd sound so sweet together. Course, they're both reed instruments, so—"

"Okay, kids!"

They looked over to see Greg waving his arms around as though he were leading a cavalry charge.

"Time to go wow 'em again," he said.

The Eurythmics tape that had been playing during the break faded out as the band began to get back on stage.

"Stick around—okay?" Jemi said.

Johnny nodded. "Break a leg," he said.

Jemi shook her head. "In this band," she told him, "it's stub a toe." She grinned when he smiled. "Get out there and dance, Johnny. I'll be watching for you."

And then she was gone, bounding onto the stage and strapping on her sax. Johnny drifted around to the front of the stage as the band kicked into "I Heard It Through the Grapevine."

"She's okay, isn't she?" Henk said as he joined Johnny. "Did she give you any hot leads?"

"Things've gotten a little more complicated," Johnny said.

"How so?"

"She looks just like the woman I met last night, only she says that woman's her sister."

"Go on."

"No, really. She's going to talk to me later."

"So you're going to stick around?"

Johnny nodded.

"Well, I'm taking off. Mountain Ash are playing up at Patty's Place and I haven't seen either of those guys for a long time. Maybe we can meet there later."

"I don't know. It all depends on what Jemi's got to say."

"Okay. Then maybe I'll just call you tomorrow."

"Sure."

As Henk left, Johnny turned back to the stage and met Jemi's gaze.

"Dance!" she mouthed at him.

The Jack of Kinrowan's Tower, formerly the residence of Kinrowan's gruagagh, Bhruic Dearg, was an old three-storied house. It faced Belmont Avenue in Ottawa South, while its backyard looked out on Windsor Park. When the Gruagagh had lived there, the building had always had a deserted look about it. The new owners soon changed that.

Outside, the lawns were mown, the hedges and shrubberies trimmed, the flowerbeds weeded. The backyard held a small vegetable plot now, and if the rear hedge was a little unruly, that was only to ensure privacy from the park beyond. Three tall oak trees, two by the hedge and one closer to the house, stood watch over the yard, throwing their shade over most of it except for where the vegetable garden was laid out, close to the house.

Inside, things had changed as well. Bhruic Dearg had lived frugally. The downstairs rooms had ranged in decor from spartan to bare, for the Gruagagh had only used two rooms on the second floor. Now the downstairs had a homey, if somewhat cluttered, air to it. There were Oriental and rag carpets on the floor, bookcases overloaded with books, two sofas, three fat easy chairs, cabinets for the stereo and records, side tables, funky old standing lamps, and every kind of personal knick-knack and treasure.

The kitchen had a nook with a small table and four chairs in it. There were pots, pans, and utensils hanging from its beamed ceiling and the walls. Pictures of wild animals, English cottages—at least five of Anne Hathaway's, showing the famous garden—and barnyard scenes hung wherever there was room.

Upstairs, there were two bedrooms in constant use, with a pair of guest rooms and a large bathroom. It was on the third floor that the building retained the strangeness of a wizard's tower.

There were bookcases all along one wall here as well, but its books held the lore and histories of Faerie as fact, unlike the books that Johnny Faw's grandfather had collected, which contained only mankind's view of Faerie. Another wall held a long worktable, with a window above it. On either side of the window were hundreds of tiny drawers, each filled with herbs, medicines, and remedies. The table itself was a clutter of jars and bottles, notebooks, quill pens now long dried, various knives, pestles and mortars, and tools. Against a third wall were a pair of comfortable reading chairs with a low table and a reading lamp between them. The fourth wall held a large window. Leaning on its sill and looking out was the Jack of Kinrowan.

Jacky Rowan was a young woman in her early twenties with short-cropped blond hair and a quick smile. She was dressed casually in faded jeans, moccasins, and an old patched sweater. Her eyes were a dark blue-grey, her gaze intent on what she studied through the window.

The curious property of that particular window was that the entire city could be seen from it, every part of it, in close enough detail that individual figures could be made out and recognized. It was a gruagagh's window; an enchantment born of Faerie.

The Tower itself stood on a criss-crossing of leys, the moonroads that the fiaina sidhe followed in their rade to replenish their luck. In this Seelie Court, it was the Gruagagh who had been the heart of the realm, gathering luck from the leys and spreading them through the Laird's land of Kinrowan. As Jacky had taken his place, she was now Kinrowan's heart as well as its court Jack. The realm that the window looked out upon was all under her care.

Her attention was focused on a house in the Glebe, an area just north of Ottawa South that the faerie called Cockle Tom's

Garve. Earlier in the evening she had noticed a greyish
discolouration about the house—a vague aura of fogging that
emanated from every part of the building. As that house also
stood on a crossing of a number of leys—though not so many
as the Jack's Tower—it was a matter of some concern.

Jacky looked down at the book she had propped up on the
windowsill beside her, running her finger down half a page as
she read, then returned her gaze to the house.

"Basically," she said, "it just says it's some kind of
depression."

"How so?"

"Oh, I don't know," Jacky said, feeling frustrated.

She turned and sat on the sill to look at her friend.

Kate Hazel was sitting on a tall stool by the worktable, a
number of other books and one of the Gruagagh's journals
spread out in front of her. She was Jacky's age, a slim woman
with dark brown curly hair that was tied back in a short
ponytail. Jacky envied Kate's natural curls. Jacky's own hair,
if she let it grow out, tended to just hang there.

"Well, according to this," Kate said, tapping one of her
books, "a grey hue on a building or place—especially one
situated on one or more lines of power—means something's
interrupting the flow."

"And that means?"

"That it needs to be fixed, or we'll have a problem. If the
flow of the leys gets too disrupted, or it it spreads out through
their networking lines . . . Dum da dum dum."

Jacky sighed. "How can a house be depressed?"

"I think your book's referring to the flow rate of the current
being depressed," Kate said. "Not that the house is bumming
out."

"Does *your* book say how to fix it?"

Kate shook her head, then grinned and waved at the wall of
books. "But I'm sure it's in there somewhere."

"Oh, lovely. One day we really should take the time and
index them."

"I'll bet one of the wally-stanes would do the trick."

"We've only got six left," Jacky replied. "I think we should
save them for something important."

Jacky had won the wally-stanes in a bargain with another
Jack—nine of them, all told. They were spellstones, the

proverbial wishes of fairy tales, though unfortunately, they weren't quite as all-encompassing as in the stories.

They'd wasted their first one trying to wish Jacky into being a gruagagh. All that had happened was that she'd walked around for a few weeks in Bhruic Dearg's shape until they found a hob skillyman who could take the charm off. The next two had been used for them each to gain a working knowledge of the languages of Faerie so that they could read the books that the Gruagagh had left them. After that, Jacky had hoarded the remaining six stones like a miser might her gold.

"I think an index is of prime importance," Kate said, looking at the wall of books.

She stood up from her stool, stuffed a loose tail from the white shirt she was wearing back into the waist of her skirt, and walked over to where Jacky stood.

"Show me the house again," she said.

Jacky started to point it out when the doorbell sounded downstairs.

"Who's that?" Jacky muttered.

"That was the back door," Kate said.

She had a better ear for that sort of thing than Jacky did. Only faerie came visiting at the back door.

"Maybe it's Finn," Jacky said as she led the way downstairs. "Do you think he knows anything about ley depressions?"

Kate laughed. "You sound like a pop psychiatrist."

"Ho ho."

They had reached the kitchen by then. Jacky flung the door open—a "Hello, Finn," on her lips—but though it was a hob standing there, it wasn't their usual visitor. Instead it was a younger cousin of Finn's—one of the Laird's foresters.

"Dunrobin Mull, if you please, Missus Jack," the hob said. "At your service."

He was nervously turning his red cap in his hand and the two women knew immediately that whatever his reason for coming was, it wasn't to bring good news.

"You'd better come in," Jacky said.

CHAPTER
4

The dance ended at eleven—in accordance with city noise ordinances. Johnny pitched in, helping the band and their friends dismantle the stage and load all the equipment into the van and pickup truck that it had come in. By a quarter past twelve, he and Jemi were saying their farewells and started to walk slowly down Chesley towards Bank Street.

"Wow," Jemi said. "I'm still buzzing."

Johnny nodded. He felt that way himself when a gig went well—all wound up with excess energy.

"What happens now?" he asked.

"Let's walk a bit and take it as it comes—okay?"

"Sure."

Jemi was wearing a silver-buttoned piper's jacket over her dress now, carrying her sax in its case. She refused his offer to carry it for her. Looking at her, Johnny had to shake his head. She certainly knew how to catch the eye. Her whole look— from pink hair to what she was wearing—made him smile, though not in any superior sense. He found himself liking the look, liking her. He'd never known anyone quite the same before.

"Are you hungry?" she asked as they reached Bank Street.

"Some."

She nodded to a Chinese restaurant on their left. "Want to grab a few egg rolls?"

"Sure."

Fifteen minutes later they were sitting inside the South Garden, munching egg rolls that they washed down with Chinese tea. Jemi ate with great gusto, dipping her egg roll first in the little pool of soya sauce on her plate, then in the plum sauce, before each bite. Johnny followed her example at a slower pace. At last he had to ask her as she finished her sixth egg roll.

"How do you stay so small—"

"When I eat so much?" she finished for him. She shook a finger in his face. "That's not very polite, Johnny Faw."

"I guess not," he said with a smile.

She grinned back. "I've just got a quick metabolism—I burn it all off before it has a chance to settle."

They had the restaurant to themselves. Chinese pop songs, sung by a woman with an incredibly high-pitched voice, issued softly from the ceiling speakers in each corner of the room.

"So where do we start?" Jemi asked as she finished her seventh and final egg roll.

She replenished both their teacups from the pot on the center of the table.

The enjoyment in Johnny's eyes clouded as he remembered why he'd looked her up in the first place. He'd been having such a good time, listening to her band, and she was so full of light-hearted energy, that he'd just let the reason fade away.

"Maybe you should tell me just what happened last night," Jemi said softly, seeing the look in his eyes.

She put the teapot down and patted his hand, before picking up her cup and taking a sip.

So Johnny went through the story again. Jemi was a good listener and didn't interrupt. She waited until he was done to ask a few questions.

"That *was* Jenna," she said when Johnny again described the woman he'd met.

"So what's going on?" Johnny asked.

"I knew Old Tom—he used to bring me sweets, but that was a long time ago." There was a far-off look in her eyes. "I've always had a sweet tooth."

"But," Johnny began, then he paused, deciding on a different tack. "Are you twins—you and Jenna?"

"Oh, no. She's much older than I am."

"Well, how old are you?"

"How old do I look?"

"About twenty-one, twenty-two."

"That's close enough."

Johnny sighed. "Look. She said she knew Tom before he met my grandmother. That's a long time ago. And now I'm getting the feeling that you knew him back then as well. But that's impossible. You'd have to be in your forties at least."

"Oh, I don't know about that," Jemi said.

"I'm really not trying to pry," Johnny said. "It's just that I'd like to know what's going on. Why would Tom tell me to play that tune in Vincent Massey Park? Why would your sister come when I played it?" He took out the bone fiddle and laid it on the table beside the teapot. "What's this thing mean? What did she mean by saying she was a fairy?"

"You've got so many questions," Jemi said, "and it's most unfair not to answer them."

"So answer them."

She shook her head.

"C'mon," she said, and stood up.

"Why? Where are we going?"

"To Puxill."

Johnny remained seated. "I'm not going anywhere. I don't know what you and your sister are playing at, but I don't like it. I think I'll bow out now."

"I'm not playing at anything," Jemi said.

"Well, I don't believe in fairies. I suppose you're going to tell me that you're one, too?"

Jemi laughed. "Of course not!"

"Well, then, where are you planning to take me? Where's Puxill? *What's* Puxill?"

"It's what the—it's what Jenna calls Vincent Massey Park."

"And what are we going to do there? Play 'The King of the Fairies' again?"

Jemi shook her head. "No. We're going to talk to Jenna. Now, c'mon."

Johnny stared at her for a long moment, then slowly got to his feet.

"You're not much of a one for whimsy and wonder, are you?" Jemi said.

"It's not been a good week."

Jemi touched his cheek with the backs of her fingers. The gesture reminded him of her sister.

"I know," she said. "I'm sorry about your grandfather. Everybody liked him."

"How come I've never heard of all these everyones before?"

"Maybe your grandfather just liked to keep a secret or two."

"He's not alone in that," Johnny said.

"That's true. Poor Johnny Faw. Did you never have a secret to keep?"

"It's not that. It's just . . ."

He shook his head. He didn't seem able to frame what he wanted to say.

"It all came at a bad time, didn't it?" Jemi said.

Johnny nodded. "And I don't even know what 'it' is."

"Let's find out what Jenna has to say."

They paid their bill and left the restaurant. Outside, the traffic was sparse on Bank Street. They followed the street down to Billings Bridge, weaving their way through the construction on the bridge as they crossed the river, then turned right to follow the water west. Here there was even less traffic on Riverside Drive, just the occasional car. They kept to the bicycle path, with the river and its reeds and its slow-moving water on one side, neatly-kept lawns on the other. Overhead, the sky was thick with stars.

"Does she do this kind of thing often?" Johnny asked.

Jemi shook her head. "But she likes tricks. I don't think she meant you any harm. It's hard to know sometimes—don't you think? I mean the way things can go. You might mean one thing, but somebody might take it otherwise. She probably did just want to see you for old times' sake, to see you and leave it at that. Instead, she just filled you up with questions. I don't think she planned that. You were supposed to just forget about her."

"It's hard to forget someone who comes at the call of a tune and then vanishes into thin air."

"It depends on what sort of a person you are." Jemi glanced at him, a smile touching her lips. "And just how used to that sort of thing you are."

Johnny sighed, but didn't rise to the bait. He was tired of questions, tired of puzzles, tired of not really knowing what was going on.

"Don't be glum," Jemi said. She took his free hand. "Enjoy the night for itself, if nothing else."

With that small hand warm in his, Johnny didn't reply. He kept hold of her hand, almost afraid that if he didn't, she would disappear on him just as her sister had. He tried not to think of what the familiarity meant. There was no denying to himself that he was attracted to her; he got the feeling that she liked him as well. What he wasn't sure of was how he felt about it all.

There was something going on, some undercurrent that lifted goosebumps on his arms when he considered it. He tried to follow her advice and not think about it. He tried to just enjoy the night and her company.

Just when he was beginning to have some success, Jemi began to hum a fiddle tune, very quietly. At least it wasn't "The King of the Fairies," Johnny thought. Then he recognized the tune. It was "The Fairies' Hornpipe." He shot her a quick glance. In the vague lighting, she looked back at him, a guileless look on her face.

"Whatever you're thinking, Johnny Faw," she said, breaking off the tune, "remember this: I don't mean you any harm."

As she spoke, Johnny got the impression that he was walking through some fairyland, hand in hand with a diminutive princess. He blinked, and the moment was gone. The bicycle path was back, Ottawa's night around them. Jemi Pook was still holding his hand, walking at his side, in her pink and grey dress with the piper's jacket overtop and her hair all spiked.

A warmth and closeness grew up between them as they walked, and the empty feeling inside that Johnny had known since Tom's death lost some of its grip. Right then he was happy that he'd gone out with his fiddle last night and called up the sister of the woman who walked at his side.

He wondered, looking at Jemi, if there was such a thing as punk elves. If he ever did put together a collection of city folklore, he didn't doubt that they'd have a place in it.

They listened to the hob's story over herb tea, sitting around the table in the kitchen nook, Dunrobin Mull perched in his seat, sitting arrow-straight, not touching its back, Jacky slouched in hers, only Kate using her chair in the way it was designed to be used.

"What I don't understand," Jacky said when Mull was done with his tale, "is why you've come to us. Shouldn't you go to the Court with this?"

"I've been to the Court," Mull said, "but the Laird wasn't there to see. No one was. Hay of Kelldee sent me to put the matter in your hands."

Jacky remembered then. The Laird and most of his Court had left yesterday afternoon for the Harvest Fair in Ballymoresk. Hay of Kelldee, a Brown Man who was the Court's seneschal, was looking after things in the Laird's absence.

"But still," she said, "isn't this something you foresters should handle? Who's the Chief for that area?"

"What area's that?" Kate asked. "Avon Learg?"

Jacky nodded. That was the faerie name for the whole strip of land along the Ottawa River that ran from the headland of Kinrowan where the Court was kept, all the way west to Britannia Beach.

"Then Shon Buie's the Chief," Kate said.

"And he's gone, too," Mull said. "They're all gone. It's been so peaceful of late since you killed all those giants—"

"Two giants," Jacky corrected, though she couldn't help feeling a little pride still.

"There's been no trouble," Mull continued, "not for all the year. This is the first time in a long while that the Court could go to the Fair, so most of them went."

The Harvest Fair was one of the two big yearly gatherings of the Seelie Courts—one for the harvest, one for the sowing and winter's end. The closest Fair to Kinrowan was in Toronto, what faerie called Ballymoresk, Big Town by the Water.

"Howsoever," Mull said, "being how things are, this is the sort of problem that the Laird would have brought to the Gruagagh anyway."

But I'm not a gruagagh, Jacky wanted to say.

And it was true, even if she *had* accepted a gruagagh's responsibilities and done well enough so far. But that might only be, she admitted in moments of honesty, because a real challenge hadn't come up yet.

She caught Kate's gaze, but Kate only shrugged as if to say, We're stuck with it, kiddo.

"The victim," Jacky asked. "She wasn't a Seelie fey?"

Mull shook his head. "She was the Pook of Puxill. One of the fiaina sidhe. Her name was Jenna."

"Do they fight amongst themselves?"

Jacky didn't know as much about the solitary faerie as she'd like to. She didn't know enough about a lot of things, really. Every day something came up to remind her of how much there was still to learn.

"Oh, they'd quarrel—the same as we," Mull replied. "But not like this. She was butchered, Missus Jack. I'd say it was a bogan or some other Unseelie creature did the deed, only the tracks are all wrong. Whatever she fought, whatever butchered her, it left no sign."

"But you saw footprints . . ."

"Walking up, bending down for a look, walking away again. I didn't know that track, but I do know this: Whoever made it didn't kill the Pook."

"This doesn't make sense," Kate said. "There had to be tracks."

"I saw what I saw," Mull replied somewhat huffily.

"Oh, we believe you—don't we, Kate?" Jacky said. "It's just . . . strange, that's all."

Kate nodded and the hob looked mollified.

"That's why the Hay of Kelldee sent me to you," he said. The two women regarded him blankly.

"Don't you see?" he said. "It was a magic that killed her. So this isn't a matter for foresters—it's for gruagaghs and skilly-folk."

"But . . ." Jacky shook her head as the hob turned to her. "Never mind," she said.

She wasn't about to tell him that she couldn't help him. She might not be a gruagagh, but she *was* the Jack of Kinrowan. She'd taken on the Unseelie Court and won.

"Will you be wanting to see the body?" Mull asked.

"Uh, no. No, that won't be necessary."

She felt a queasiness in her stomach just at the thought of it. Glancing at Kate's blanched features, she knew she wasn't alone.

"You did a real good job describing it," she added.

"Hay of Kelldee was keeping it in case you did. We should see about finding someone from the fiaina to claim it." A bleak look came into his eyes and both Jacky and Kate knew he was seeing the body again. "She'll need a proper cairn, to be laid to rest by her own people . . ."

None of them spoke for a long time. Faeire aged at a different rate from humans. Their birthrate was much, much lower as well. Deaths diminished their ranks far more quickly than they could be replenished.

"I'll have to look at the spot where you found her," Jacky said after a while. "To see if there are any . . ."

She looked at Kate for help.

"Residual emanations," Kate filled in. "Of a magical nature."

Jacky shot her a quick smile of thanks.

"Can you take us there?" she asked Mull.

When the hob nodded, the two women left him to change and fetch jackets.

"Are we getting in over our heads?" Jacky asked.

She stood in the doorway to Kate's bedroom, putting on her jacket while Kate changed into a pair of jeans.

"We pulled out okay the last time," Kate said. She paused, one leg in, the other out, to look at Jacky. "We accepted the responsibility from Bhruic. We can't just back out the first time things start to get a little rough."

"I know. I wasn't saying that."

Kate got her other leg into her jeans and tugged them up. "You just don't want to blow it, right?"

"Something like that. I don't want to make a muddle. I guess I'm scared of making things worse, instead of fixing them."

"We've done fine so far."

"Little things. But—"

Kate joined her in the doorway and laid a finger across Jacky's lips.

"Listen up, kiddo," she said. "If it wasn't for you, there wouldn't be any Seelie Court left in Kinrowan. Remember that. And since then you've kept the luck replenished, just the way you're supposed to."

"Right. So now we're supposed to play detective and figure out who murdered some poor little fiaina sidhe? And what do we do if and when we *do* find out? What are we going to do about something that can cause that kind of damage without leaving any trace of itself behind?"

"Run like hell?" Kate tried. She gave Jacky's shoulder a

light punch. "Just kidding. Don't worry, Jacky. Things'll work out."

"Easy for you to say. You've got a valiant tailor complex."

"While you're a giant-killer—remember? So let's not keep our hob waiting."

She led the way downstairs.

"I only brought the one pony," Mull said when they rejoined him. "I never thought—"

"That's okay," Kate said. "We'll follow on our bikes."

CHAPTER
5

The night was quiet in Puxill.

The only real sound was that of the Rideau River washing across the flat stones by which Johnny and Jemi Pook were sitting. There was a mist on the river, making a blur of the university's lights on the other bank. It muffled the already vague sound of distant traffic until it seemed to Johnny that he and his diminutive companion were the only ones about at this hour.

At first the time passed pleasantly enough. While they didn't talk much, Johnny was content to wait until Jemi's sister came before asking any more questions. But as they continued to sit there waiting, the earlier sense of warmth and closeness slowly drained from him and he grew impatient again.

Why were they just sitting here? For that matter, how did he even know that Jemi had a sister? The whole affair was beginning to feel like another prank—or a part of the same one that he'd fallen for last night.

He stood up suddenly and walked to the edge of the river. Picking up flat stones, he skimmed them across the water, growing more angry with each throw.

"She's not coming, is she?" he asked.

He turned to face Jemi. She seemed tinier than ever—a small bundle of shadow, perched on a rock.

"It doesn't seem so."

"Of course, how could she even know that we're waiting for her? We didn't phone ahead or anything."

"It doesn't work like that."

Johnny nodded. "I know. It needs a fiddle tune. What should I play?"

"That won't work," Jemi said. "She should have known we were here by now. I guess she's just not around tonight."

"*If* she even exists in the first place."

The shadow that was Jemi moved as she looked up from the stones at her feet to frown at him.

"Are you saying I lied to you?" she asked.

Remembering the warmth, the feeling of closeness, even if he couldn't regain it at the moment, Johnny shook his head. But it was too hard to simply set aside his frustrations and forget.

"I just don't know what I'm doing here," he said. "I mean, last night was strange enough. You'd think I'd have learned my lesson. But no. Here I am, back again."

He skimmed another stone across the water, using far more force than was necessary. It skipped all the way across to the other shore.

"What *are* we doing here, Jemi?" he asked as he turned back to look at her once more.

"Waiting for Jenna."

He shook his head. "C'mon. What would she be doing here?"

Now even the memory of the warmth he'd felt with her was fading.

"She lives here," Jemi said.

Johnny looked around.

"Here?" he asked. "Under these stones, maybe? In the base of the train bridge? In a tree?"

"I'm worried," Jemi said, ignoring his questions. "It's not like Jenna to leave like this."

"Leave what?"

"Puxill," Jemi said impatiently.

"Your sister's a baglady?" Johnny asked. "She lives in this park?"

Quicker than he might have thought possible, Jemi was on her feet, closing the distance between them and poking a finger in his chest.

"Don't talk like that about her!" she said. "I said I was worried. I don't need your stupid jokes on top of it."

"Oh, excuse me. How rude of me to not take this all more seriously."

He took a step back as she lifted her finger to poke him again. A wet stone slid under his foot and he would have fallen, except Jemi reached out and grabbed his arm, hauling him erect. As soon as he regained his balance, Johnny moved gingerly around her and onto safer ground. He rubbed his arm where she'd grabbed him. Like last night, the grip had been very strong.

"It *was* you last night, wasn't it?" he said. "Why are you going through with this charade of looking for a sister who doesn't even exist?"

Jemi looked at him for a long moment, then shook her head.

"Screw you," she said, and vanished.

Johnny stared at the spot where she'd disappeared. This time there couldn't be any other explanation. Last night she might conceivably have slipped into the trees somehow—she *could* move fast, he remembered—but there was no place for her to have done the same here.

The stones were bare, pale as bones in the starlight. She couldn't have gone into the mist on the river because he would have heard her in the water. They'd been standing on a slight promontory jutting out into the river. To get to the forest behind him, she would have had to pass by him, and she hadn't.

She'd just disappeared.

"Jemi?" he called quietly. "Jemi! Look, I'm sorry. Please don't take off like you—uh, like your sister did last night. I thought you were just having me on again—pulling my leg."

There was no reply.

He turned slowly, head cocked slightly as he strained to hear her move. He caught sight of their instrument cases and hurried over to them, staking claim to them with either hand. She wouldn't just take off and leave her sax behind, would she?

"Okay," he said. "I'm going. I'll leave your sax with Greg, or you can come and get it now."

He looked around some more. Maybe she'd fallen into the river, he thought suddenly. The water could have taken her under before she had a chance to call out. He just hadn't heard her fall—that was all. The water wasn't running fast, but all it needed was a slip on a mossy stone—he'd slipped himself a moment ago—maybe crack your head on a rock as you fell . . .

He started for the river, alarmed now, then stopped dead in his tracks. Like a magician's rabbit, pulled from an empty hat, Jemi was suddenly standing in front of him. They studied each other, neither speaking. Johnny swallowed, his throat unaccountably dry.

"Look," he began. He cleared his throat, started again. "I don't know how you're doing that, but—how *are* you doing that? Wait. Don't tell me. I know you don't like questions. So how about if I just leave your sax here"—he set the case down on the stones between them—"and I'll just go, okay? No hard feelings, right?"

He began to back slowly towards the bicycle path, trying not to think about what she might do next. If she could just pop in and out of existence the way she did, who the hell knew what else she could do? Best not to find out. Best just to get out while he could.

"Don't go," she said.

He stopped moving immediately. She'd asked him, not told him, but he wasn't taking any chances.

"You've got nothing to worry about from me," Johnny told her. "I won't tell anybody about you. Well, I told Henk, but I won't tell anybody else, okay? And even Henk doesn't know that you . . . that you're . . . what you can do . . ." He looked helplessly at her. "Christ, I don't even know what I'm talking about."

"I'm sorry," Jemi said. "I really am worried about my sister, but I never stopped to think about what this must all seem like to you. Since she got you into it, I was going to let her explain it, but now I don't know where she is and . . ."

She sighed.

"Hey," Johnny said. "It's no problem. Really. I'll just go and you won't have to worry about—"

Jemi stamped her foot. "Would you *stop* acting like I've got three heads and I'm about to take a bite out of you with one?"

"Well, it's just . . ."

"I know. You thought I'd just disappeared on you like Jenna did last night."

"Well, you did."

"But it's not disappearing—not really. It's just sort of . . . stepping sideways. I'm still here, but you just can't see me."

"That might not seem unusual to you," Johnny said, "but it doesn't make a whole lot of sense from where I stand."

"I want to show you something," Jemi said. "And after I've shown it to you, I'll answer your questions. Okay?"

"Ah . . . sure."

She picked up her saxophone case with one hand and took his with the other.

"It's up the hill a bit," she said.

"Puxill?"

She smiled briefly and nodded. They crossed the bicycle path and plunged into the woods on the other side of it, angling in a southwesterly direction, which took them to the park's steeper slopes. In a small clearing, Jemi paused.

"Now, don't get all weird on me again," Jemi said as she let go of his hand.

"Me go all weird on *you*? Hey, I'm not the one that—"

"Whisht!"

Obediently, Johnny fell silent. He closed his mouth and concentrated on what Jemi was doing. She bent over a granite outcrop and tapped it with her finger. Once, twice, quickly. After a pause, a third tap. Giving him another quick smile, she stepped over to him and took his hand again. Her grip was very tight.

"That's starting to hurt—"

But then he knew why she was holding him so firmly. Given his druthers, he'd have preferred to simply bolt.

A large piece of sod was slowly lifting from beside the outcrop. As it moved to one side, Johnny could see a short tunnel that led into something wider which was dimly lit.

"What . . . what is it?" he managed.

"This is my home—where Jenna and I live," Jemi said. "Though I spend more time in the city itself lately, this is my real home, Johnny."

Johnny stared down the tunnel. "So you . . . you're a fairy, too?"

"A halfling, actually. And we're not exactly faerie—not Court fey, at any rate. We call ourselves fiaina sidhe."

"A halfling?" Johnny asked. "Like a hobbit?"

"No. I'm just half fiaina—the other half's as human as you."

"And Jenna's really your sister?"

"Half-sister. She's pure fiaina."

"Right. And you live in this hill."

"Well, not so much lately. But Jenna does."

"And you can step sideways, which is like disappearing, but isn't."

"It's stepping into Faerie, actually. The Middle Kingdom. Not everyone can see into it."

"You need special glasses, right?" Johnny tried.

Jemi smiled. "Do you want to come inside?"

Johnny looked down at the short tunnel, then back at her.

"Why are you showing me this?" he asked. "Why are you telling me your secrets?"

"I'm not sure. Partly because of Old Tom, I suppose, and partly because Jenna's been a little unfair to you. But mostly because I have a feeling . . ." A look Johnny couldn't read came into her eyes. "I've a feeling that I'm going to need a friend and I'd like you to be it."

Jemi's explanation put Johnny through another mood shift. The puzzled anger he'd been feeling earlier was gone as though it had never existed. He felt like he had to be dreaming, but he couldn't deny the tangible evidence that lay before his eyes. The hill was hollow and Faerie existed. If he accepted that—he had to accept it, it was lying right there in front of him—then by the same token he should be willing to believe that Jemi meant him no harm.

He wasn't sure how the logic of that worked; it was just the way it came to him.

"I'd like to be a friend," he said, "but I've got to admit that my head's still spinning."

"Duck that head," Jemi said, and she led him into the tunnel.

Without looking into Faerie, there didn't seem to be anything out of the ordinary in the place where Dunrobin Mull had found the Pook's body, but in the Middle Kingdom, it was plain to see the scene of the butchery for what it was. The sod was torn up where the Pook had struggled, the grass still stained red with her dried blood. Jacky and Kate laid their bikes on the ground nearby and walked gingerly forwards to look around. Behind them, Mull slipped from Goudie's back and followed.

"It wasn't bogans?" Jacky asked after having taken a slow turn around the disturbed ground.

"No bogan tracks," Mull said. "Just what the Pook made in her struggling."

Jacky nodded, deciding that a forester would know. She couldn't even see any tracks made by whoever had looked at the Pook after she'd been murdered.

"What about the sluagh?" she asked, unable to suppress a shudder just thinking of the restless dead.

"They would have left a bog scent," Mull said.

"And there was none of that," Jacky said thoughtfully.

"But there is something," Kate said.

Both Jacky and the hob looked at her.

"What do you mean?" Jacky asked.

Kate shrugged. "There's just a feeling in the air—like when Finn works his stitcheries. It's not strong, but I can feel it. Just a tingle."

"Magic," Mull said.

"You can really feel that?" Jacky asked.

"You can't?"

Jacky shook her head.

"Can you tell what sort of magic it was?" Mull asked. "A gruagagh's or a skillyman's or what?"

"No," Kate said. "I'm sorry. But it reminds me of something. Sort of like . . ."

Her voice trailed off and the other two waited for her to finish. Finally Jacky spoke up.

"Like what?"

"Look," Kate said, instead of replying. "Over there."

She pointed towards the downtown skyline behind them. Standing on a rise, watching them, was a huge black dog. Because of the distance and poor lighting it was difficult to see it properly, but they all got the impression that it was very large—at least the size of a Great Dane, but bulkier, more powerfully muscled, with shaggy hair.

It studied them for a long moment after Kate had spotted it, then abruptly turned and sprinted away. The shadows below the rise upon which it had been standing immediately swallowed it.

"What was that?" Jacky asked in a small voice.

She was suddenly very aware of the fact that they were standing in the open, unprotected. Mists clouding the surface of the Ottawa River nearby did nothing to lessen the sudden attack of the creeps that came over her.

"An unsainly beast," Mull said, and he quickly shaped a saining in the direction it had vanished.

He looked to Jacky, to Kate, then mounted his pony and rode to where the dog had stood watching them. The women fetched their bicycles and walked them to the top of the rise where Mull was poring over the ground.

"You see?" he asked when they joined him. "There's nothing. No track, no sign it was ever there. There's something new haunting Kinrowan."

"You think it was that dog that killed the Pook?" Jacky asked.

Mull nodded.

"Then why didn't it attack us?" Kate asked.

Mull shrugged. "I don't know. Perhaps its bloodlust is sated for the moment. Perhaps it has a master and it was only spying out the lay of the land for now. Oh, I don't like it."

He stood slowly, a frown wrinkling his brow.

"I think it's time we talked to Hay of Kelldee," Jacky said.

Mull nodded and mounted his little hob pony. He followed his companions as they walked their bikes to the parkway. When they reached the pavement, Jacky and Kate pedaled downtown, going slowly so that Mull could keep up, Goudie bearing him at a brisk trot.

CHAPTER
6

Jemi kicked off her shoes as soon as they were inside and turned to Johnny.

"So what do you think?" she asked.

All Johnny could do was stare out the big window that was set in the wall. Through it he could see the trees and slopes of Vincent Massey Park. The window, reason told him, could not exist. It was impossible. He *knew* there was just a hillside out there.

"This . . . this window," he said slowly. "It's . . . when we were outside . . ."

"We're in Faerie now."

"Just a step sideways. Right. Only . . ."

He shook his head and turned to look at the rest of the room.

At first glance it reminded him of his own apartment. There was a wall of books—old leather-bound volumes and paperbacks evenly mixed. A sofa and two easy chairs stood near a large stone hearth—the chairs were wooden frames filled with fat comfortable pillows. A pair of battered wooden cupboards on either side of the room held a clutter of knickknacks and the like. The floors were polished oak, islanded with thick carpets. Tapestries hung from the walls. A door at the far end of the room led off into darkness.

The room was well lit with the light coming through the window. Johnny got the impression that there was something about the window that heightened the light. He wondered if it

51

dimmed it accordingly during the day. A pair of oil lamps stood on the mantel above the cold hearth, neither of them lit.

Jemi leaned her sax case up against a wall and settled down on the sofa.

"There's more rooms through there," she said, pointing to the door.

Johnny nodded and slowly crossed the room to where she sat. He lowered himself into one of the easy chairs across from her and held his fiddle case between his knees.

"It's . . . not quite what I expected," he said, looking around the room.

"What did you expect?"

"I don't know. Piles of gold and jewels lying around?"

"We're not rich faerie."

"There's rich faerie?"

She shrugged. "Some. You should see the Court of Kinrowan sometime. There's treasure there. Do you want something to drink?"

"Ah . . ."

"Oh, don't worry. It's just some beer that Jenna brews. It won't keep you here for a hundred years or anything—that's just in the stories."

"Sure. A beer'd be great."

She got up and went through the door that led deeper into the hill, the darkness obviously not bothering her. When she returned, Johnny was standing in front of one of the three tapestries that hung in the room. It showed an old-fashioned schooner anchored off a rocky shore. Pines grew near the beach and a longboat was being lowered onto the water. All around the men lowering the boat and standing at the ship's rail, faerie were depicted, perched on barrels, riding the longboat as it was lowered, swinging from ropes—a whole crowd of little folk.

"My father wove that," Jemi said as she handed him a mug of beer.

"Thanks," Johnny said. He took a swig, foam mustaching his upper lip. "Hey, this is good."

Jemi nodded. "Jenna brews the best beer this side of Avon Dhu—the St. Lawrence."

She went back to the sofa. After a few moments of studying

the tapestry, Johnny returned to his own chair. Jemi leaned forward.

"You're probably wondering why I've gathered you all here tonight," she began with a smile.

Johnny laughed. "That's how faerie came here, right?" he asked, pointing his mug at the tapestry. "You hitched a ride with the early settlers."

"Not all at once," Jemi replied, "but that's about it."

She told of the migrations then, of the two Courts, the Seelie and Unseelie, and of the fiaina sidhe, who were aligned to neither.

"Were you around back then?" Johnny asked.

What the hell, he thought. If he was going to accept part of it, he might as well go the whole route.

"Oh, no. I'm just a babe compared to most faerie. I'm probably not much older than you are."

"Thirty-one."

Jemi shrugged. "Okay. So I'm a little older."

"How'd you end up playing sax for AKT? I mean, it's not exactly what I'd picture a faerie to be doing. And neither's, well, the way you look."

"You don't like my look?" Jemi asked, running her fingers through her short pink hair.

"I didn't say that. It's just . . ."

"I know. We're all supposed to be little withered dwarves, or these impossibly beautiful creatures. Sorry." She shot him a dazzling smile. "But as for AKT, I just love that sound. I like our music, too—faerie music, which is more like what you play—but there's something about the excitement of an electric sound. . . . Everything seems more alive these days—music, fashion, everything. I like being a part of it, that's all.

"Jenna says it's my human blood coming out in me, but I don't know. I'm a Pook, and we just like to have fun. Jenna does, too, but she finds hers in other ways."

"Are you the only one that . . . I guess you'd say, mixes with us mortals?"

"Oh, no. But you wouldn't know a faerie to look at one—we're good at wearing shapes that don't set us apart if we don't already have an appropriate one."

"And you . . . ?"

"This is all there is to me, Johnny." She touched her hair. "I don't even have to dye this brown or blond anymore to fit in."

Johnny smiled. "Natural pink hair?"

"What can I say?"

Her gaze drifted to the tapestry that he'd been looking at.

"It's a funny thing," she said, more seriously. "The old folk say that we depend on you, on your belief, to sustain us. I don't know if that's true or not, but with the current upsurge of interest in fantasy and make-believe, our luck *is* getting stronger. I've always wondered about that dependence faerie are supposed to have on mortals, myself."

"You don't think it's true?"

"I don't know. But if it is, then it doesn't affect me so much as a pureblood—only that confuses me more. It's like, we don't exist unless some of you believe in us, but at the same time we can crossbreed. How can that be possible if we're just born from your imagination? Imagoes brought to life."

"Are you?"

She shrugged, troubled. "I don't know. It's mostly the older sidhe like Jenna who feel that way. The younger ones figure the world turns around them—but I guess that's what everybody thinks when they're young. What I do know is that we keep our luck by our rade—that's a night the fiaina sidhe get together and follow the moonroads to wherever they'll take us.

"There hasn't been a rade for a while, though. I guess I've ignored it, living mostly with mortals, but I know it was worrying Jenna. But even in the city I've heard rumours, of hobs leaving their holdings, derrie-downs dying. . . ."

"Hobs? Derrie-downs?"

"Hobs are like gnomes, I guess you could say. Little men. Brownies. And derrie-downs are like . . . selchies. Only they live in fresh water—rivers and lakes and the like—and they're otters in the water, instead of seals. This far from the ocean, only those with Laird's blood can take a seal or a swan's shape."

She fell quiet then and they sat for a while, neither speaking. Johnny regarded her and felt very odd. Rationally he knew that none of this could exist. Everything she was talking about— this house inside a hill, for God's sake—but at the same time, it all wound together inside him to form a sensible pattern. One that fit within the boundaries of its own rules—not the ones he

wanted to impose upon them. That left him feeling that he was
either going right off the deep end, or it was all real.

He preferred to think it was real.

Looking at Jemi, ensconced in her sofa, he sensed her
spunkiness falling from her. She looked tiny still, but frail
now, too. He could almost see the tears sitting there behind her
eyes, just waiting to be released.

"What's the matter?" he asked softly.

She looked at him, eyes shiny. "Oh, I'm so worried,
Johnny. I think something terrible's happened. I wasn't sure
before—it was just a vague kind of a feeling—but now I know
something is wrong. Something's happened to Jenna and I
don't know what to do."

"Isn't there someone we could go ask? One of her friends?"

She bit at her lower lip and shrugged. "I suppose."

"Where does the closest one live?"

In a tree? he thought. Under a mushroom?

"Down there," Jemi said, pointing to the window. "In the
river."

Johnny followed her finger with his gaze. Right. In the river.

He sat there and stared out the window, wondering just how
deep into this he wanted to get. But then he looked at Jemi,
remembered her saying she was going to need a friend, and
what he'd said to her then.

"Come on," he said, standing up. "Let's go talk to him."

"Her," Jemi said. "It's a her. Her name's Loireag and she's
a kelpie."

The Parliament Buildings—housing the Senate, the House
of Commons, and numerous members' offices and committee
rooms—stood on a headland in the Nation's Capital, overlooking the Ottawa River. They were originally built in the 1860s,
partially destroyed by fire in 1916, then rebuilt thereafter in
their original Gothic Revival style, the final work being
completed on the Peace Tower in 1933.

While the federal government went about its business above,
underground in the limestone cliffs that made up the headland,
the faerie of Kinrowan kept their Court and Laird's Manor. The
hollowed cliff contained a bewildering complex of chambers,
halls, and personal residences, all the while remaining hidden
from the eyes of various groundkeepers and RCMP patrols.

Jacky and Kate chained their bicycles to a street sign on Wellington when they arrived, then followed Mull on his pony around the wall fronting the Hill to the bottom of the cliffs in back of the buildings. The mists gathering on the river were thicker here, drifting to land and making visibility difficult. But Mull knew the way. Jacky and Kate walked with a hand on either flank of his little hob pony until they reached the entrance to the Court. Hay of Kelldee was waiting for them at its stone doors.

The Brown Man was a dwarf, brown-skinned with red frizzled hair and beard, and dark glowing eyes. As befit his name, he was dressed in various shades of brown, from the dark of forest loam to the mottled brown of a mushroom. He took one look at their faces, then ushered them away from the curious eyes of those faerie who hadn't accompanied the Court to Ballymoresk. Not until they were in his private rooms would he let them speak.

"Oh, that's bad," he said when they told him about the dog.

He paced back and forth across the room, stopping to stare out a broad window overlooking the river, before turning back to them.

"What's to be done?" he asked Jacky.

"Ah. Well . . ."

"We'll have to study this in the Tower," Kate said. "It's not a simple thing."

"No," Hay agreed, nodding his head slowly. "It's not simple at all."

He studied them sharply from under thick red brows.

"I've heard rumours," he said finally, "that there was trouble amongst the fiaina—but nothing like this."

"What sort of trouble?" Jacky asked.

"Oh, the usual sort with such solitary folk—or so it seemed. This hob's not been heard from for some time, the rade was not so good this moon. . . . Even some talk of mysterious deaths. Nothing that any of us saw personally, but even the rumour of such is disturbing. We should have looked into it sooner, I suppose, only things being as they were—with no word of the Host abroad, save for the odd troll or bogan—we've grown lazy. It's a bad time for the flower of the Court to be away."

Jacky didn't say anything, but she found it hard to stay quiet.

The last time there'd been trouble in Kinrowan, the "flower" of the Court had been noticeably absent as well—at least from taking a part. They'd hidden in their halls and in the Court, while Jacky and her friends had taken on a host of giants, bogans, and other Unseelie folk.

"We should go," Kate said.

Jacky nodded. "We'll be in touch. If you hear from Finn, could you ask him to come to the Tower?"

Hay nodded. "If you need any help . . ."

"We'll let you know," Kate said before Jacky could speak.

Jacky waited until they were outside again and making their way back to their bikes before saying anything.

"Why didn't you want to take him up on his offer of help?" she asked.

"Oh, think for a moment," Kate replied. "The Laird's gone and while Hay means well, what's he going to do on his own? The only ones left behind are those too weak to make the trip to Toronto—and of course a few foresters to patrol the borderlands. If and when we know something, then we can ask them for help—or we can ask the foresters, at least. But until then, they'll just get in our way."

"Lovely. And in the meantime, we're going to take this thing on by ourselves?"

"Don't be silly. We're going to go through the Gruagagh's books and find out just what it is that we're up against. *Then* we'll call in the cavalry."

"I suppose. I'd like to talk to some of these fiaina—see what they know. Do you think Finn could introduce us to any?"

"It won't hurt to ask." Kate shot her a quick look. "This time we've got to use another of the stones—you do know that."

"To do what?"

"Index all those books!"

"We'll need to think that through carefully. I don't feel like walking around looking like a mobile file card system, or changing the Tower into a computer or something. Anything's liable to happen."

"We did okay learning the language."

"Yes, but—shit."

They'd reached their bikes and were unlocking them when Jacky froze. Kate didn't say anything. Taking her cue from her companion, she followed Kate's gaze. The black dog was back, sitting on its haunches not a half-block from where they stood.

"Jacky?" Kate began.

Jacky shook her head. "I'm not even wearing my stitched shoes."

They each had a jacket and a pair of shoes into which Dunrobin Finn had stitched a skillyman hob's enchantments. The jackets made the wearer invisible to mortals—and to faerie as well, if you stayed very still. The shoes gave you quickness. They were both wearing their jackets, but not the shoes.

"If it comes towards us I'm going to scream," Kate muttered.

The black dog chose that moment to rise to its feet and move in their direction.

"Jacky!"

"I'm thinking, I'm thinking."

Fingers fumbling, Jacky continued to work on her bike lock. When the lock sprang open, she stuffed it into her pocket and tugged the chain free. She felt like a bad actor in some biker B-movie, but the weight of the chain in her hands was far more comforting than facing the dog empty-handed.

The beast continued its approach, a low rumble of a growl starting up deep in its chest. The hackles around its neck rose thickly. It drew back its lips, showing sharp rows of teeth that made Jacky's knees knock against each other. Her throat was dry and felt like sandpaper when she tried to swallow.

About three yards from them, the dog crouched down. By now its growl was like the constant revving of an engine without a muffler. Still feeling weak-kneed, Jacky took a step towards the beast, the chain held awkwardly in her hands. The chain was cold iron—not much good against urban faerie who had grown so accustomed to its sting that it no longer hurt them, but still a powerful enough weapon against those creatures that hadn't yet acquired an immunity to it. If she was lucky, the dog was one of the latter.

She could see it tense, getting ready to lunge. She stared into its eyes, then remembered someone had once told her something about not trying to stare down a dog, it just made them madder. She didn't need monstrous Fido here any madder, but she couldn't look away.

"Get on your bike, Kate," she said over her shoulder.

"Jacky, what are you—"

"Kate, just get on your bike! I'll try to scare it off."

"No way. I'm not going to—"

The dog leapt.

Jacky screamed and flung the chain at it, only just remembering to hang onto one end of it. Before the chain could hit it, however, before the dog was upon her, a tall shape moved out of the shadows from beside the wall separating the Hill from Wellington Street. Jacky caught a glimpse of a pale face inside a dark hood before the newcomer turned on the dog. Grabbing it by the scruff of the neck, the figure started to haul back on its massive weight. But at his touch, the dog simply dissolved.

The hooded figure took a step back, obviously surprised. Jacky, her own mouth gaping, started to pull the chain back to her in case the beast appeared again.

"What in the Moon was that creature?" the cloaked figure asked.

The voice was a man's, deep and resonating. He turned towards the two women, pushing back the hood of his brown cloak.

"One moment I had Laird knows how many pounds of some black monstrosity in my hands," he said, "and the next nothing but smoke."

"I . . . we're not sure," Jacky said.

She was happy to see that she'd kept most of the tremble from her voice.

The man's features, revealed by the streetlight now that he was fully out of the shadows, proved to be strong and not altogether unhandsome. The brow was smooth, eyes somewhat wide-set, cheekbones high, chin firm. Under the brown cloak, he wore a simple shirt and brown trousers.

"Thanks," Jacky said.

She left it at that. Rescuer or not, she wasn't about to give him their names. Finn had taught her that much caution long ago.

The man nodded. "My name's Cumin," he said. "Of Lochbuie. That creature . . ." He frowned. "Have you ever heard of such a thing before?"

"It killed a Pook last night," Jacky said.

"Did it now."

Kate stepped to Jacky's side. Her nostrils flared as she caught a scent, sensed a tingle of magic in the air.

"Are you a gruagagh?" she asked the stranger.

"The Gruagagh of Lochbuie," he said. "At your service."

"Boy," Jacky said with relief. "Could we use a gruagagh right about now."

Cumin's brows rose quizzically. "Surely Kinrowan still has its gruagagh? He's an old friend of mine that I haven't seen for a very long time. Bhruic Dearg. Do you know him?"

Jacky nodded. "But he's not around anymore. I live in his Tower now. I'm the Jack of Kinrowan," she added, feeling it was safe to give their names to a friend of Bhruic's, "and this is my friend Kate."

"I'm pleased to meet you both. But Bhruic—he's left Kinrowan?"

"Maybe you should come back to the Tower with us," Jacky said. "It's a long story. Do you have a place to stay?"

"I'd thought to stay with Bhruic."

"We'll give you the hospitality that he would have—it's the least we can do after you chased off that dog for us. Right, Kate?"

"Sure," Kate said with a nod.

But she wondered at the scent of magic that she could still sense in the air. Jacky was wrapping her chain around the seat post of her bicycle now, locking it in place, chatting to Cumin the whole time. Kate looked at the place where the gruagagh had stepped from the shadows. How could they have missed seeing him there? And why would the dog disappear when he grabbed it? It had killed a Pook. . . .

"Coming, Kate?"

She started guiltily and hurried over to her own bike.

"Sure," she said again, and fell in behind them, walking her bike as Jacky was.

What she wanted to do was jump on hers and leave this gruagagh far behind, but she didn't know why she felt that way. There was no real reason for her nervousness, except that once it had turned into an unpleasant night, why should it necessarily change at this point?

She listened to Jacky talk about the Pook and how she wouldn't like to be the Hay of Kelldee, who was taking the body to Puxill right now in hopes of finding a fiaina to claim it, and wasn't it a shame . . .

Oh, don't tell him too much, Kate wished at her friend.

She stepped up her pace so that she was walking abreast of them.

"So where's Lochbuie?" she asked in a pause of the conversation, speaking quickly before Jacky could launch into something else.

Cumin's eyes appeared to narrow for a moment, but then he smiled and Kate wasn't sure if he'd actually looked angry just then, or if she'd projected that on him because of the way she was feeling.

"Far east of Kinrowan," he said. "Though not so far as the sea itself. I'm on a trip to Gormeilan, you see. . . ."

The rest of the way back to the Tower, Kate kept the Gruagagh talking about himself. Jacky didn't interrupt, but whether that was because she understood what Kate was doing, or because she was simply interested in what Cumin had to say, Kate didn't know.

CHAPTER
7

Leaving their instruments in the hollow hill, Johnny and Jemi returned to the riverbank. The mists were thicker now. The night had grown still quieter. The flat stones shifted underfoot as they walked, the rattling sound loud in the stillness. When they paused by the water's edge, the sound continued. Johnny wasn't aware of it immediately, but Jemi turned her head quickly to look behind them.

"Faerie," she murmured.

Johnny turned then as well to see three small ponies soft-stepping across the stones. Two had riders, the third a long bundle tied across its back. Jemi's hand crept to Johnny's arm, her fingers tightening painfully as she clung to him.

A half-dozen yards from where they stood, the ponies stopped and their riders dismounted. The foremost was a fat dwarf with a dark beard and darker hair. The other was taller and smooth-shaven. The dwarf cleared his throat.

"Are you friends to Puxill's Pook?" he asked.

"I am," a voice said from behind them before Jemi could reply.

The tall, ebony-skinned figure of a naked woman stepped around them to face the dwarf. Water glistened on her skin. This'll be Loireag, Johnny thought. Before the woman could speak, Jemi let go of his arm and pushed her way in front of the woman.

"I'm Jenna's sister," she said.

She shot the kelpie a quick glance. Loireag briefly touched Jemi's shoulder with the long dark fingers of one hand—a feathery touch that was gone almost before it was made—then returned her attention to the two Seelie faerie.

"My name's Hay of Kelldee," the dwarf said. He frowned, then cleared his throat again. "Oh, it's bad news I have for you tonight."

While he spoke, the other faerie was loosening the bundle from the third pony. Tenderly he laid it on the ground and Johnny had a sudden premonition. He started to move towards Jemi, meaning to comfort her, then froze, abruptly aware that there were more than just the five of them abroad tonight.

They came from all sides, slipping from the forest and through the field, sidling from the river behind them, dozens of strange beings, not one quite same as the other. There were little men no taller than his knee, with twigs and leaves in their hair, their arms and legs like spindly roots. Pale-skinned women with wet-green hair, dark eyes, and sinuous bodies. Rounded little men with grey beards and wrinkled faces. A woman with the face of a fox and a long bushy tail.

Some were tiny, others taller than Johnny. Some he could see clearly and wished he couldn't; others were hidden in shadow allowing him only brief glimpses of narrow pretty faces, and those he wished he could see better. Towering over them all was a nine-foot-tall troll, his hands hanging below his knees, his back stooped, his eyes glittering.

Johnny found it hard to breathe. His chest was a tight knot and there was a sour taste in the pit of his stomach. The crowd of creatures pressed closer, encircling them. They filled the night with strange smells and a hushed whispering. Johnny could feel himself trembling, but couldn't stop it.

He felt like he had the one time he'd tried acid—years ago, and never again. That same sense of dislocation from reality pressed on him now. The sensory overload made it difficult for him to maintain any semblance of balance. He flinched when a small twiggish creature touched his leg, tugging at his trousers. Moving back, he bumped into a tall man, so thin he seemed skeletal, just bones and skin, without flesh. The man grinned at him, flashing rows of sharp teeth, and Johnny stumbled away from him.

He lost Jemi in the crowd. He was aware that the dwarf was

still speaking, but couldn't hear what was being said. He tried to push through the press of bodies, to get away. When he came upon a sudden opening, he slipped into it only to find himself standing by the third pony. Jemi was bending over the bundle, opening it.

A dead Jemi stared up from the blanket—skin alabaster, bloodied and torn, eyes bulging, but the features still all too recognizable. Jemi's sister. Jenna.

Jemi lifted her face to the sky and howled her grief. The sound was a wailing shriek that froze the blood in Johnny's veins. This was what a banshee's scream would sound like, he thought. This despair. This grief. This anger underlying both.

His vision spun and he staggered back into the crowd, flailing his arms, trying to get away from that sound. Hands—little hands, big hands—shoved and pushed him out of the way. Jemi's wail burned through his mind. He fell to his hands and knees on the stones, scrabbling for purchase, trying to stand, to flee.

His limbs gave out from under him and he went face down on the ground. He cut his lip, tasted blood. His vision still spun, but the sound was finally gone—not faded, just abruptly cut off. Slowly he raised his head and looked around.

He was alone on that beach of flat stones. The river mist was ghostly and writhing on one side of him, the forest dark on the other, while he was crouched on the pale strip between them.

A nightmare, he thought. I've freaked out. Somebody slipped me something in a drink. A Mickey.

Jemi. Jemi Pook. She . . .

It all became a blur. He fell forward on the stones once more, only this time he didn't rise.

It was late when they finally got back to the Tower. While Jacky sat the gruagagh down in the kitchen nook and fussed about getting tea ready, Kate excused herself and went upstairs. Ostensibly, she was going to bed, but instead she made her way up to the third floor where she took down a familiar book from its shelf and sat in a chair to leaf through it. The fat leather-bound volume bore the title *The Gruagaghs, Skillyfolk and Billy Blinds of Liomauch Og* and, like everything else pertaining to Faerie and Kinrowan in that room, had belonged to the original Gruagagh of Kinrowan.

Bhruic Dearg's books had a peculiar property Kate and Jacky had discovered very early on in their residence. Their content tended to change so the various reference volumes remained up-to-date all the time. It was Kate who had first discovered this one day, looking through the very book she was holding now. She'd come to a heading for Kinrowan and discovered that under the Court, rather than Bhruic's name being listed as its principal magic-worker, it now had Jacky's name, with her own underneath, listed as an assistant.

The book called her Kate Crackernuts, but that didn't stop her from getting a little smile of pleasure every time she turned to that page. She knew that in Faerie the hazel tree was often called the crackernut.

She went straight to the index tonight, looking up Lochbuie. Surprisingly, for all her suspicions, there was such a place listed in the book. From the map she was directed to, she realized it was a part of Gaspé. But there was no Cumin listed as its gruagagh, in fact no gruagagh listed at all. There were two hob skillymen in the area—one named Scattery Rob, the other Dabben Gar—a wisewife named Agnes Lowther, and a longer list of Billy Blinds for the various faerie holdings in and about the immediate vicinity.

There was a Court mentioned as well, but it appeared to be a small one. Not big enough for a gruagagh, it seemed, though there had been one at the turn of the century. According to the book, his name was Balmer Glas, which, even by a long stretch of the imagination, didn't sound a bit like Cumin.

Kate frowned. She turned to the index again, this time looking under the C's for Cumin's name. When she found the listing, it referred her to "Comyn." That listing sent her to a brief paragraph that told her that the Comyns were an old family of Billy Blinds and gave her various other references to turn to, none of which helped her with her present search.

Sighing, she laid the book aside and went to stand in front of the wall of bookshelves. There were just too many titles. What they needed—as she kept telling Jacky—was a proper index. A file system like in a library, or even a general index book that could send them looking in the right direction. Kate knew that it wasn't important how much you knew so much as that you knew where to look for what you wanted to know. Anyone could keep a clutter of information in their head—after all, people were supposed to remember, somewhere inside them, everything that they had ever experienced. The trick was accessing that information.

She replaced *The Gruagaghs, Skillyfolk and Billy Blinds of Liomauch Og* on the shelf and went to stand by the window. Kinrowan lay spread out before her. She checked on the house with its grey aura and found that while the aura was still present, its greyness didn't seem as pronounced at the moment.

A thought came to her, and she looked at where the Pook's body had been discovered. She shivered at the small smudge of grey she saw there as well. It wasn't near a moonroad, so she probably wouldn't have noticed it if she hadn't been looking for it. The spot where the black dog had attacked them had a grey smudge about it as well.

She turned her back on the window and leaned against the sill. They were connected. Whatever had sent the dog after them and killed the Pook was connected to that house on the criss-cross of leys. Had something terrible happened there as well—something really bad, she realized, for the aura to be so dark—or could that even be where the black dog and its master were? It was worth looking into.

She sighed again. This was their first real crisis in the year or so since they'd taken over the Gruagagh's responsibilities in Kinrowan.

Normally, they did a daily check on the various leys, making sure that the luck flowed properly. There really wasn't much to the task. Since the Gruagagh hadn't been all that well liked or trusted, and the faerie had gotten out of the habit of coming to him for advice, they hadn't had to deal with very many requests for help beyond that duty. The few times they had, long hours of going through the Gruagagh's books—with the help of Finn—had pointed them to a solution. But now . . .

It wasn't just the house's aura, or the Pook's death, or even the dog's attack, Kate realized. It was that man downstairs. She didn't trust him one bit.

Jacky had the unfortunate habit of being impressed with important people. She liked hobnobbing with the Chiefs of the Laird's Court when she could. Liked to spend time with the Laird and his daughter. She had an on-again, off-again relationship with Eilian, the Laird of Dunlogan's son.

There was no real harm in any of that so far as Kate could

see, because Jacky didn't lord it over anybody just because she knew some highborn folk. But it was just like her to latch onto a strange gruagagh without so much as a thought to the possible consequences. There was something about Cumin, supposedly of Lochbuie, that told Kate he was far more dangerous than anything they could deal with. He was a gruagagh, after all. He had magics that they couldn't hope to match. If he should turn on them . . .

Her gaze went to the door, then to the secret hollow in the worktable's leg where the six remaining wally-stanes were hidden. The wally-stanes could be a problem. After Jacky and her first failure . . . It had been disconcerting to see Jacky walking around looking like Bhruic Dearg, and a little funny to hear her woman's voice coming from the tall shape of a man.

After that, they'd waited to use any more of them until they'd found some working instructions in one of the Gruagagh's books—a long process with Dunrobin Finn translating for them. The next two spells had worked out fine. The stones just took a lot of concentration. You had to fill all your thoughts with what you wanted, keeping them crystal clear in your mind as you broke the wally-stane.

Kate knew what she wanted right now. She knew it very clearly.

She argued it out with herself for a few moments longer—weighing her need against the unfairness of using one of Jacky's stones without asking her—then made her decision. She crossed the room quickly, locked the door, and fetched the wally-stanes from their hiding place. She took out one of the crystalline spheres and replaced the others. Taking it in hand, she pulled a blank book from the bottom shelf—these were the books that Bhruic had been using to keep his notes and journals in—and brought them both over to the worktable.

She needed a general index and this was going to be it. The blank book, when she opened it after using the wally-stane's magic on it, would answer all her questions. It would tell her where to look for what she needed so there wouldn't be any more of these marathon expeditions through the hundreds of books that made up the Gruagagh's library. She just hoped that Jacky wouldn't be too mad at her. But there was no way she was going downstairs to ask her—not with that gruagagh sitting there, listening.

She held the wally-stane between her hands. It was hard and smooth against her palms. It was odd how the stones worked. They were virtually unbreakable. But when you held it between your hands and worked the spell, pressing your hands together, the stone just dissolved, like candyfloss did in your mouth.

Keeping the book in front of her, she held the stone over it and concentrated for all she was worth. A fierce scowl wrinkled her features. She breathed slowly. Not until she was absolutely sure she had it perfect in her mind—that the book would answer her questions, that it would tell her where the information she needed lay—did she press her palms together.

The feeling of the wally-stane breaking sent a pleasant tingle up her arms. She grinned as she opened her hands and looked at the sparkle of crystal dust that filled her palms. She counted to ten slowly. When all the crystals had dissolved, she picked up the book and opened it to the first page.

Blank.

Quickly she flipped through the book.

All the pages were blank.

Now she'd done it.

She went through the book carefully a second and third time, holding the pages up to a lamp in case the words were written very, very lightly in it.

Still nothing.

She went over her thoughts. Had she kept them absolutely focused? The book was supposed to answer her—

I've got marshmallows for brains, she thought.

Oh, she'd been so clever. She'd concentrated on what she expected the index to do for her, but faerie magic, like the denizens of Faerie itself, were a capricious lot. They were fair. A bargain made was a bargain kept. But you had to spell it out so bloody carefully. . . .

She looked at the book. Clearing her throat and feeling somewhat foolish, she spoke aloud.

"Will you answer my questions?"

Nothing.

She riffled through some more pages, but they were all the same. Blank.

"Oh, come *on!*"

The leather-bound cover of the book looked back at her. She

flipped through the pages some more, shook the book. She was so sure that she'd figured it out. But the book wasn't obliging her. Jacky was going to kill her for wasting a wally-stane on an empty book. . . .

A grin touched her lips again. Quickly she found a pen and opened the book to the first page. What was a book? Pages bound together with words on them. If a book was going to answer her questions, how would it speak? With words. On a page. and how would it hear her questions?

Will you answer my questions? she wrote at the top of the blank page.

As she lifted the pen, words began to form under her question. They were in a neat script, the letters rounded. In fact, she thought, it looked a lot like Bhruic's handwriting, which she knew from the journals he'd left behind.

What would you like to know? the words said.

Kate gave a sharp sigh of relief. Picking up the book and pen, she went to her chair and sat down, the book open on her lap.

Do you know a gruagagh named Cumin? she wrote. *He claims to be from Lochbuie, but he's not in the book of wizard-folk listings.*

Did you look under his name?

Of course. She underlined "course."

There was a moment's pause.

Touchy, the words finally said. After another moment, they continued with, *If this Cumin is not listed in the Annals, he will be a rogue gruagagh and should be considered dangerous.*

But what should I do about him?

Avoid him.

Lovely. She could have figured that out by herself. She reread what was on the page so far, then wrote again.

Who are you?

I am your answer book.

I meant do you have a name?

Only if you give me one.

There was something that Kate had read in one of the Gruagagh's books about the indiscriminate giving of names—a warning. Once named, a thing began to have power of its own. Like all things dealing with faerie magic, that too could be dangerous. But it didn't seem right to Kate that the book should be without one.

How about Caraidankate? she wrote, which meant "friend of Kate" in faerie. *Caraid for short?*

Now that is a gynkie choice, the book replied, meaning a well-thought-out trick.

Kate smiled and looked at the spine of the book. Embossed in the leather now was the word "Caraidankate."

How can I find out more about this gruagagh? she wrote.

Catch his reflection in a mirror and show it to me, the book replied. *Perhaps I will recognize him.*

How will I show it to you?

Catch his reflection, then hide it quickly before that of another is reflected in the glass. Place the mirror face down on one of my pages and I will see him.

Are you Bhruic Dearg? Kate wrote next.

I am his wisdom. I am the friend of Kate Crackernuts.

Kate smiled. *Goodbye for now, Caraid,* she wrote.

Goodbye, Kate.

She closed the book and held it on her lap. She sat thoughtfully for a long moment, then went to the worktable. Amongst the litter of paraphernalia, she found a tiny mirror, which she put in her pocket. With the book in hand, she went to her own room and dug about in her closet until she came up with a small shoulder bag that just fit the book properly. She didn't mean to go anywhere without it from now on.

With the book safe and bouncing against her side, she tiptoed down the front stairs and slipped out the front door. Once outside, she made her way to the back of the house.

She hugged the wall when she got near the windows of the kitchen nook. Underneath the closest one, she took the mirror from her pocket and held it over the ledge of the window, hoping that the gruagagh was sitting in the same place as he had been when she'd gone upstairs. She held it there for a few moments, then quickly covered it with her free hand and shoved it back into her pocket. Ten minutes later she was back on the third floor, carefully taking the mirror from her pocket and laying it face down on the page under where the book had written, *Goodbye, Kate.*

With her usual method of measuring time, she counted from one to ten, then just to be sure, did it again before she took the mirror away. On the page, like an ink drawing, an image of the kitchen nook began to appear.

Kate stared at it in fascination. The picture formed like a developing photograph. When the image was clear, she could clearly make out the gruagagh, the nook around him, and even the back of Jacky's head. She studied the gruagagh's face. There was a bit of a haze around his head. As she turned the book this way and that, she realized that it was a vague image superimposed over his—that of a dog's head.

She shivered and quickly put the book down. It was a few moments before she could pick up her pen again to write.

Do you know him now, Caraid?

The book's reply was slow in coming.

No, it wrote finally. *But I know what manner of gruagagh he is. He steals the luck of faerie for his magics, rather than using the luck that the Moon would give him. Beware of this creature, Kate.*

Does he mean us harm?

He means every living thing harm.

How can we stop him?

You must find where he has hidden his heart—when you find it, you must destroy it.

Kate stared at the words. The gruagagh had hidden his heart? That was something that just happened in fairy tales. She no sooner thought that than she realized how ludicrous a thought it was. As if she hadn't been living in the middle of a fairy tale for the past year or so.

Where can I find his heart? she wrote.

I don't know, the book replied. *But it will be in a place that he considers very safe. To find his heart, you must understand him. But be careful that he doesn't steal your own luck first.*

Kate swallowed nervously. Oh, Jacky, she thought. What have we gotten ourselves into this time?

CHAPTER
8

By about one-thirty, Patty's Place was empty except for Henk and the restaurant's employees. He sat at a small table by the stage, which consisted of a space in the corner of the room where the tables had been slightly pushed aside for the two musicians who had been playing there that night. The members of the duo Mountain Ash had finished packing up their gear and joined Henk for a last pint before heading home.

Mick Cully, the guitarist and bouzouki player, was a short, dark-haired man, more burly than fat, with a quick easy smile. His partner, Toby Finnegan, had a thick mane of light brown hair and a full beard that hung below his collarbone, giving him the look of a leprechaun. He played the fiddle mostly, with a little tin whistle on the side.

"Looks like Johnny's not coming," he said to Henk. "Too bad. I was in the mood for a bit of a session with another fiddle."

Henk nodded. "Johnny's going through some hard times right now, what with his grandfather dying and all."

"We'll miss Tom," Toby said. "He was a grand fiddler."

"Hope Johnny remembers his tunes," Mick added. "It'd be a shame for them to be lost."

"Oh, Johnny's got the tunes," Henk said. "A head full of them—don't doubt it. But he's acting a little strange lately."

"That'll happen," Toby said. "Your man Tom—he was Johnny's only family, wasn't he?"

"Yeah. And Johnny's taking it hard. I wish he'd just, oh, I don't know . . ."

Henk realized that he'd been about to talk about Johnny's strange ideas of the previous night. Not a good idea.

"Pull out of his slump?" Mick asked.

"Something like that."

"Not everyone wants to sit around here all night," a voice said from behind them.

They turned to find the waitress Ginette giving them a hard stare. It wasn't very successful. Blue-eyed and blond-haired, with features that looked as though they'd been filmed through a soft focus, it was difficult for Ginette to look firm, little say cross.

Toby grinned at her and finished off his pint. "Give you a lift?" he asked Henk.

Henk shook his head and finished his own drink. They left chorusing farewells, Mick and Toby heading for Toby's car while Henk stood outside on Bank Street and thought for a moment. He knew that Johnny probably hadn't been in the mood to come up to the pub after All Kindly Toes finished playing and he'd talked to Jemi, but Henk didn't like the idea of leaving him on his own to brood. Johnny's apartment on Third Avenue was on the way home to Henk's own downtown apartment, so he decided to walk up and see how Johnny was doing. When he got there, however, the ground floor of Johnny's building was dark.

Johnny could be asleep, Henk thought. It was almost two-thirty now—but going to bed before three or so just wasn't like Johnny.

He went around to the back and fetched the front door key from under the brick by the rhubarb and went inside. A quick walk through the place told him that Johnny wasn't home. Was he still with Jemi? Maybe getting interested in something more than little hobgoblins living in the sewers? That'd be nice. Johnny hadn't had a regular girlfriend for at least a couple of years. Though, with what Henk knew of Jemi, he wasn't all that sure that she'd be the right one for Johnny. She was a little wild—loved to party—where Johnny was a bit of a homebody, staying in except for when he had a gig.

Henk returned outside, replaced the key, and was about to go on home when another thought struck him. Johnny could also have had his talk with Jemi, and then gone back to Vincent Massey Park, waiting for his mysterious visitor to show up again. Now, *that* sounded more like something Johnny would do.

He opened Johnny's apartment again, stashed his concertina inside, then wheeled Johnny's five-speed out onto the street. He sure hoped Johnny didn't come home in the meantime and think somebody'd walked off with his bike. But Henk doubted that would happen. The more he thought of it, the more sure he was that Johnny had gone to the park.

It took him fifteen minutes to pedal to where the bike path started to incline up into the park. He got off and walked the bike, listening for fiddle music, footsteps, looking for some sign of his friend. It was a nice night to be out. The mist on the river was pleasantly eerie and the park was so quiet. Almost magical. He could see now how Johnny had got the impression that there was something otherworldly about the woman he'd met here last night.

He went the full length of the bike path, taking his time. When he reached Hog's Back Falls, he turned back again. It was getting on to four o'clock now and he was having second thoughts about Johnny being here. And even if Johnny *had* come . . . For all Henk knew, they could have passed each other while he was cycling down from the apartment.

He almost missed the figure sitting on the beach of flat stones on his way back. He was riding the bike, coasting down the hills, using the brakes a lot because of the darkness. When he saw the figure, he stopped and called out.

"Johnny?"

There was no answer. Putting the bike on its kickstand, Henk left it on the path and walked towards the figure. Stones crunched underfoot and there was a dampness in the air, a wet smell that came from the mist.

"Johnny?" he tried again.

The figure finally turned. "Is that you, Henk?"

"Yeah." He made his way to Johnny's side and sat down on the stones. "What're you doing, Johnny?"

"I think she drugged me."

"What? Who drugged you?"

"Jemi. She took me inside a hill, Henk." Johnny turned to look at his friend. "Right under the ground. She tapped on a stone and this sod door opened and down we went. And then we came here and there were more of them—all kinds of them. Little stickmen and trolls and you name them, they were here. Jemi's sister was dead, you see, so all these creatures from Faerie were gathered around. It was Jemi's sister I met last night. But she's dead now. And Jemi wailed. . . . I never heard a sound like that before, Henk. Christ, I hope I never hear it again. . . ."

Henk touched his shoulder. "Why don't you let me take you home, Johnny?"

"She had to have drugged me, right? When she gave me the beer inside the hill? Because those things couldn't have been real. They sure weren't human. And then when she cried—it was like a banshee, Henk. When that happened, everything got muddy. I think maybe I blacked out, just for a second, and then they were all gone. So it had to be drugs, right?"

"Jeez. I don't know, Johnny. Why don't you get up and I'll get you home?"

"But it couldn't have been the beer," Johnny said, looking out into the mist again. "Because she gave me that inside the hill, and the hill couldn't be real either, right?"

"If you say so. Look, Johnny—"

"So I guess it was in the restaurant. Or maybe it was all real. Christ, I just don't know."

He let Henk help him to his feet. When they reached the bike, he drew back.

"My fiddle," he said. "I left my fiddle inside the hill."

Henk looked back to where he'd found Johnny. He couldn't see the instrument down there. The black case would have showed up easily against the pale stones.

"You sure you brought it?"

"Sure, I'm sure. I bring it everywhere."

That was true. Henk couldn't remember ever seeing Johnny go somewhere without it. He'd had it when they went to see AKT earlier this evening.

"Tom gave me that fiddle," Johnny said. "It was really old. It was a great fiddle. And Tom gave it to me. I'm not going to let her keep it."

He started off up the hill, shrugging off Henk's hand when Henk tried to stop him. Henk put the kickstand up and quickly walked the bike up behind Johnny.

"It's okay," Johnny said. "I remember the place."

They entered a small glade and Johnny paused. Henk laid the bike on the grass. Turning, he could see the lights of Carleton U vaguely through the mist on the river.

"I've just got to remember which stone it was that she knocked on," Johnny was saying. He crawled around on his hands and knees in the damp grass. "Two quick raps, then you pause, then another rap. But I can't remember which stone it was."

There were a number of outcrops in the glade and Johnny went to each, rapping his knuckles sharply on each one. Henk followed him, really worried now. He wondered if someone *had* given Johnny some kind of drug, because he sure was acting weird.

"That hurts," Johnny said as he rapped on another stone. "I guess that means I'm not dreaming," he added, and sucked on his knuckles.

Henk checked the glade out quickly, but he couldn't spot the fiddle case.

"Look," he said. "If Jemi's got your fiddle, I'm sure she'll hang onto it for you. Tomorrow we can give Greg a call, find out where she lives, and go pick it up. Okay?"

"She lives here," Johnny said. He hit the sod with his fist. "Inside this hill."

Right, Henk thought. In the hill.

"We'll try the other place that she lives. She does have an apartment in the city, doesn't she?"

"Yeah. At least she said she did."

"C'mon, Johnny," Henk said gently. He got an arm around Johnny and hauled him to his feet. "Let's go home."

Johnny let Henk lead him away with further protest.

"I know I sound crazy," he said, "but it's been a really weird night."

"We all have 'em." Henk shot him a sharp look. "*Did* you take any drugs tonight?"

Johnny shook his head. "Not unless she slipped them to me in the tea."

"Where'd you have tea?"

"In the South Garden."

"And then you came here?"

"Yeah." Johnny rubbed at his temples. "I know it had to have been a dream," he added, "but it sure did seem real."

"Maybe things'll make more sense in the morning."

"Christ," Johnny said. "I sure hope so."

"You let them go?" Dunrobin Finn said, his voice almost a shout. "With trouble abroad, you let them go and gave them no escort?"

The hob was taller than Hay, though a half-head shorter than his cousin Mull. He stood over the seated Hay, his craggy face pressed close to the Brown Man's, a knobby finger poking Hay in the chest. His quick feral eyes glared at the dwarf over the top of a nose that had a curve in it like a hawk's beak.

He'd woken earlier this evening with a bad feeling about Jacky and Kate and made his way to the Jack's Tower, only to find them gone. A passing hob he met in Cockle Tom's Garve mentioned that he'd seen them in the company of his cousin, Dunrobin Mull. The night was alive with odd rumours and an uncomfortable sense of foreboding, sharpening his fears. When he'd learned of the Pook's death, and the black dog that had been spying on his friends, those fears spilled out in anger.

"Oh, damn," he muttered, turning away. "Weren't you all so clever."

"She *is* the Jack," Hay said.

"And what is that supposed to mean?" Finn demanded.

"Well . . . she's killed giants. She fought the Host and won."

"With no help from you."

"You shouldn't talk like that, cousin," Mull said. "Hay is the Laird's seneschal and—"

"More like the Laird's senseless arse," Finn said.

Hay rose angrily from his seat, but Finn stepped closer again and pushed him back onto its seat.

"Understand," he said. "She's not faerie—neither she nor Kate. She's done a grand job, keeping the luck of Kinrowan—being our heart and all—but there's far more that she doesn't know than what she does."

"There's not much we know either about how the Pook died," Mull said. "Or about that black dog either."

Hay nodded. "She took on Bhruic's responsibilities. That's what we feed and clothe a gruagagh for—for times like these."

"And besides," Mull added, "we had to bring the Pook to her kin. With the Court in Ballymoresk, we're stretched very thin."

Only between the ears, Finn thought. But he supposed he wasn't being altogether fair. No one in the Court knew Jacky and Kate the way he did. They all thought the pair were skillyfolk at least, if not gruagaghs. They had never seen the pair of them fumbling about, trying to work something as simple as Kerevan's wally-stanes. They didn't know that for each decision or bit of advice the Jack gave to the Court, Kate and she spent hours poring through Bhruic's library to find the right thing to do or say.

Better the Court didn't know, he supposed. Better things stayed as they were or perhaps the Laird would have second thoughts about leaving a pair of mortals in the Gruagagh's Tower. He only hoped that they had managed to get back to the Tower in one piece.

"There are no new gruagaghs in and about Kinrowan?" he asked finally.

Hay shook his head. "None the Court knows of."

"But you did see a black dog?" This question he directed at Mull.

His cousin nodded. "And it left no sign—the same as around the Pook's body."

Oh, damn, Finn thought. And that hound would have their scent. Now he was really worried.

He pulled his red cap from his pocket and stuck it over his thatch of brown hair. With a quick nod to his cousin and the seneschal, he left the Court through a passage that let him out near the Rideau Canal. He looked around, sniffing the air. The dark bulk of the National Arts Centre loomed over him. He crept out, still cautious, and slipped by the open-air restaurant that overlooked the canal. The chairs were all stacked and chained together in a corner of the patio.

A minute or so of brisk walking brought him under the MacKenzie King Bridge, where he paused again. When he was sure he was alone, he gave a sharp rap on the stone supports.

"Hey, Gump!" he called, and rapped again.

On the third rap a bulky trow stepped out of the stone wall, blinking at the little hob. He stood a good seven feet tall, with long black hair that fell to his waist like a Rastaman's dreadlocks. There were bits of twigs and shells wound up in the locks. His features looked as though they'd been chiseled by an apprentice stoneworker, just learning his trade. Two uneven gouges for eyes, a fat thick nose, square chin, huge ears.

Most trows were aligned with the Unseelie Court, but there were some, like Gump, who didn't have the heart for the Host's evil ways. Such trows lived in the middle of Seelie realms, not quite a part of them, but not quite fiaina sidhe either.

"I was sleeping," Gump grumbled in a deep voice. He squatted down so that his head was more level with the little hob's.

"It's not so late," Finn said.

"It's not so early either, skillyman. Why did you wake me?"

"Well," Finn said. "You know what they say. There's those that look, but don't see; and then there's those that no one pays any attention to, who see everything. Like you."

Gump grumbled a bit more, but he was obviously pleased.

"And what I'm wondering," Finn continued, "is whether you've seen a new gruagagh in Kinrowan—one who might have a black dog for his familiar, or perhaps one who wears the shape of a black dog himself."

Gump thought about that for a moment.

"There's been a thing," he said at last, "that has taken on the task of disrupting the fiaina's rade—you know of that?"

Finn shook his head. Like most Seelie faerie, he had little commerce with the fiaina sidhe.

"Don't know what it is," Gump said, "but I've heard them talk of it. A black dog was mentioned."

"Then that's what killed the Pook earlier this night."

"Jenna's dead?" Gump asked. "Oh, that makes me want to hit something, Finn. She was a good Pook."

"Why would anyone want to disrupt the fiaina's rade?" Finn wondered aloud.

"It's their luck," Gump said.

Now Finn understood. If the Pook's killer was the same one who was disrupting the fiaina's rade, it didn't take a great deal of cleverness to know that it would soon be turning its attention to the heart of Kinrowan—the Jack's Tower, where Kinrowan's luck was stored. The evening's premonitions grew stronger.

"Oh, damn! I'm off, Gump, to the Jack's Tower. Keep an eye out for me, would you, and pass on anything you learn?"

"Which eye?" The trow's face split with a great gap-toothed grin, then he looked serious again. "I'll watch for you, Finn. Spike him once for me when you catch him. I liked Jenna."

"I'll do that," Finn said.

It was best to talk brave around a trow—they understood things like bravery and jokes. It wouldn't do to have Gump know that he was shaking in his hob-stitched shoes.

Gump faded back into the stone wall, for the dawn was coming and while he might hide in stone, he didn't particularly care to become stone, which is what would happen if the dawn's light caught him. When he was gone, Finn set off for the Tower at a run.

This was the problem, he thought, with knowing important people like gruagaghs and Jacks. Trouble was drawn to them like a magnet and it didn't stop to differentiate between the important folk and the odd hob who might just be standing around them.

But I don't stand around anymore, do I? Finn thought.

Not since he'd gone up against the Unseelie Court with Jacky and the others and lived to tell the tale. No, he'd become a doer now as well. But why was it that being a doer only felt good afterwards, when you could sit around and chat about, maybe boast a little? Why couldn't you feel all brave and sure of what you were doing *while* you were doing it?

He wondered if the answer to that was in one of Bhruic's books.

Kate spent the remainder of the night poring over books.

She made a quick foray into her own room, gathering up all the fairy tale books she'd kept since she was a child, and then went into Jacky's room. Jacky had never been one for fairy tale collections when she was young, but ever since the events of last autumn, she'd taken to collecting them with a vengeance.

With her arms full, Kate returned to the third floor, wincing at every creak of the wooden stairs going up. Once there, she dropped her tottering load beside her reading chair. The area was already filled with piles of books she'd taken down from Bhruic's shelves. Slumping in the chair, she picked up a book.

The first reference she'd run across in one of Bhruic's books when she had started to read had a footnote directing her to human literature. In the thematic indexes of folklore, what she

was looking for was listed under Tale Type 302—"The Ogre or
Devil's Heart in an Egg." There were over two hundred and
sixty versions of the story, collected from around the world—
Irish, Indian, African, Native American. That was what had
sent her down to the second floor for the fairy tale collections.
Now she went through the books, searching for the stories in
question. She was looking for hints—for the "understanding"
of her foe that Caraid had told her she'd need to deal with the
gruagagh Cumin.

Most of the versions she found were similar to the Scandinavian story "The Giant Who Had No Heart in His Body." In
that one, the giant's heart was hidden far away from the giant's
castle. In a lake there was an island, on the island a church, in
the church a well, in the well swam a duck, in the duck was an
egg, and in that egg was his heart.

Lovely, she thought as she put it aside. In other words,
Cumin's heart could be just about anywhere.

After a thorough search, she found only two more versions
of the story in the books she had on hand. One was Russian—
called "Kostchi the Deathless"—the other was Italo Calvino's
Italian version, "Body Without Soul." She read them both
through, then turned to the faerie books she'd pulled from
Bhruic's shelves.

She put her feet up on a stack of books, the spines facing
towards her. Gwyn Jones's *Scandinavian Legends and Folk-
tales*. Books by Stith Thompson, Jane Yolen, and William
Mayne. *The Giant Book,* by de Regniers. Asbjornsen and
Jorgen's *East of the Sun and West of the Moon and Other Tales*.
Even classic nontraditional books that collected stories by
Oscar Wilde and William Dunthorn and contemporary titles
like Christy Riddle's *How to Make the Wind Blow.*

I could be at this forever, she wrote in Caraid.

Understanding is like wisdom, the book replied. *Not easily
acquired, but the endeavour is nevertheless worthwhile.*

"Easy for you to say," Kate said aloud, and picked up
another of Bhruic's books.

The faerie versions of the same stories tended to be either
much plainer or wildly exaggerated. In one, an evil gruagagh
carried his heart in a pouch at his belt. In another, it had been
reduced to the size of a pea and hidden in a gem that the ogre
wore dangling from his ear. Then there were complicated ones

that echoed "The Giant Who Had No Heart" story that she'd read a little earlier. But there were few facts that were prevalent in the histories of faerie that the human books hadn't touched on.

The branch of faerie magic that beings such as Cumin followed was far different from that usually followed by Seelie gruagaghs or skillyfolk.

Whereas the luck gathered from the moonroads that a gruagagh tended in a Seelie Court, or was called up by the rade of the fiaina sidhe, was more a borrowing of the Moon's luck, the droichan—as such beings were called—stole their luck. Borrowed luck returned to Arn, where she rode the night sky in her moon house; stolen luck was gone forever. Borrowed luck returned the gift of its giving, twice and threefold, making a circular pattern so that both giver and gifted were strengthened and sustained; stolen luck pierced the fabric of Faerie like a disease and left only sickness and death in its wake.

It was because droichan were more often human that the various tales of the diminishing of Faerie came to be. The less luck there was—it took a very long time for Arn to make new luck to replace that which had been stolen—the fewer faerie could exist. So it wasn't so much a lack of belief in faerie by humans that diminished them, as the amount stolen by droichan.

Droichan were next to impossible to kill—naturally enough, Kate thought with a heavy sigh. You had to find their heart first, and the mystery of their hiding places would tax the greatest of riddlemasters. The only hope that the books could offer was that a droichan had to repeat a spell over his heart once every three months, in the same phase of the moon that he had worked the spell to set his heart free from his body in the first place. This was invariably on the darkest night of the new moon.

Kate sighed again and set aside the last book. It was almost dawn and her eyes were bleary from too much reading and a lack of sleep. As she leaned back in her chair, she was suddenly aware of how quiet the Tower was.

Had Jacky and the gruagagh gone to sleep? Did she dare tiptoe to whatever room the gruagagh was sleeping in and try to find his heart before he woke up?

She shivered and hugged herself. She wasn't feeling that brave right now—not by a long shot.

She'd better not do anything, she decided—not until she'd had a chance to talk to Jacky. And if not her, then perhaps someone like Finn. They'd left a message at the Court for him to come to the Tower. How long would it take him? Oh, why couldn't things have stayed the way they were—just a day or so ago?

I'm finished for tonight, she wrote in her book. *Goodnight, Caraid.*

Wear a sprig of rowan, the book replied.

What for?

To protect you against the gruagagh's spells. Wear it under your jacket—close to your heart.

Does it matter how big a piece it is? Kate asked.

She glanced at the top shelf above Bhruic's worktable where a number of cylindrical containers held bunches of twigs. Rowan. Birch. Yew. Oak. Ash. There were dozens of them.

Rowan, lamer, and red threid, Pits witches to their speed, the book replied.

What's lamer? Kate wrote.

An old word for amber. They are all reddish, you see—like a hob's cap. The size doesn't matter. Goodnight, Kate.

Kate went over to the worktable. She had to get right up onto it to reach the containers. Once she'd chosen her piece of rowan wood, she searched about for a safety pin to fasten it to her jacket, then realized that the iron in the pin might negate the rowan's protection. Many faerie had acquired an immunity to iron, living in cities as they did, but iron still undid many faerie enchantments and glamours. She found a needle and a piece of red thread instead, and sewed the little twig to the inside of her jacket.

She stowed Caraid away in its pouch. We should have got ourselves a book like this ages ago, she thought.

Leaving the mess behind, she headed downstairs, being as quiet as possible so as not to wake sleepers. But when she got downstairs to the kitchen, all set to make herself a cup of tea before going to bed herself, she found Jacky still sitting at the table in the nook.

"Morning, Jacky," she said.

She went on to get the kettle, pausing only to turn back when there was no reply from her friend.

"Jacky?"

She walked back to the table. Jacky's gaze had a glassy look about it. When Kate moved her hand up and down in front of her friend's eyes, there was still no response. She shook Jacky's shoulder. Nothing.

She's been enchanted, Kate realized. The gruagagh's gone and enchanted her.

She started to pull her rowan twig from her jacket, hoping that it could undo the spell Jacky was under with its touch, when she felt another presence in the kitchen. Turning, she saw Cumin standing in the doorway.

"I need her to show me a thing or two of Bhruic's ways," he said conversationally. "Unfortunately, the same doesn't apply to you."

It hurt Kate to do it, but she knew she had no choice. She had to leave Jacky behind.

Before the gruagagh could step into the kitchen, she grabbed the half-full teapot from the table and hurled it into his face. He lifted his arms to ward it off, stepping back into the hall. That was all the time that Kate needed to get to the back door. She heard the gruagagh shout something in a language she didn't understand, and felt a tingle run all through her body, but whatever spell he'd tried didn't take hold.

Kate didn't look back. She just hauled the door open and bolted outside.

The sun was peeping over the horizon and everything was in a haze of early morning light and tendrils of mist that had drifted up from the river. Kate didn't spare a moment to take in the eerie beauty of the sight. She ran headlong for the gate at the back of the yard that would let her out into the park beyond—glad that she was wearing her hob-stitched shoes that lent her their extra speed.

She reached the gate, jumped over, and ran smack into somebody. They fell in a tangle of limbs.

"Kate?" Finn asked, recovering first. "What's the—"

But Kate's attention was on the backyard where the gruagagh was coming after her.

"We've got to run!" she cried, and jumped to her feet.

She dragged Finn to his feet beside her and set off, pulling him along. It wasn't until they'd crossed the park and were standing by the river, partly hidden by the trees there, that she dared to pause and look back. The gruagagh stood at the gate of the Tower's backyard, staring at them across the trimmed lawn.

"Stag's heart!" Finn complained. "What's possessed you, Kate?"

Kate just pointed back across the park.

"He's a droichan, Finn," she said. "He's got no heart. He's captured Jacky and the Tower and we can't kill him unless we find his heart."

Finn stared numbly in the direction she was pointing. With a skillyman's sight he could see the ghostly shape of a black dog that hung about the gruagagh like an aura.

"Oh, damn," he said.

He'd come too late.

CHAPTER
9

"I can't get her out of my mind," Johnny said.

He picked at the mushroom and zucchini omelette that Henk had set before him. Disjointed images from the previous night were still floating through his mind, leaving him with the disconcerting feeling of coming down from the effects of a hallucinogenic drug.

Everything, from his familiar kitchen to Henk's face across the table, had edges that were too sharp, then wavered when he moved his head. There was a curious metallic taste in his throat and his eyes stung. When he closed his eyes he saw, in amidst the swirl of strange creatures that his memory called up, Jemi Pook. Sometimes she was as she'd been in the South Garden, sitting across from him, putting away egg rolls like they were her first meal in a week. But mostly she was lifting her head from her dead sister's body, screaming into the sky, neck muscles stretched taut, eyes closed to slits, her pain like a raw file rasping against his nerves.

That wailing. . . .

He shoved the plate away. Henk pushed it back.

"Eat," he said. "If you were fed some drug last night, you're going to want something in your stomach. It'll flush your system quicker."

Henk had stayed over last night. He'd put Johnny to bed, wondering as he did if he shouldn't have taken him to the hospital instead. But he didn't think Johnny had been drugged.

There was a bump on Johnny's head and his lip was split, but Henk didn't think he had a concussion either.

What Johnny was suffering from was a trauma of some sort. Henk couldn't quite sort out exactly what had happened to his friend last night—the things Johnny babbled about were just too unreal—but something had happened to him. He was sure of that much.

"We'll go see Greg," he said as Johnny finally took a few more bites.

He noted that this time, Johnny, after mechanically taking the first few mouthfuls, was now finishing the omelette. Henk poured them both another cup of coffee.

Johnny pushed the plate away again, but this time it was empty. He rubbed his temples, his hand drifting to the back of his head where it gingerly felt the bump there. He could remember falling face down on the stones, but he couldn't remember getting a knock on the back of his head. All he could remember . . .

The crowd of alien creatures swirled through his head again.

He drank his coffee, then stood up from the table, waiting for a moment to see if he felt woozy.

"Let's go," he said when everything stayed put. "I want my fiddle back."

Henk nodded. He took the dishes to the sink, then followed Johnny outside.

Greg Parker lived in the Glebe as well, on Fifth Avenue, just a few blocks over from Johnny's apartment. His eight-year-old daughter, Brenda, opened the door when they pushed the buzzer and studied them for a few moments before allowing that, yes, her daddy was in, and yes, she'd go get him. They waited outside on the porch, listening to Brenda shouting for her father. Greg appeared a minute or so later, wiping his hands on an apron.

"Making cookies," he explained. "Larry's helping me."

There were smudges all over the apron, the most recent of which looked like chocolate chip batter. Some of the handprints were very small. Larry was Greg's four-year-old son. His head, topped by tousled blond hair, peeked around Greg's leg.

"Henk!" he squealed when he recognized who was there, and threw himself forward.

Henk caught him up and swung him around in the air.

"How's it going, tiger?"

"We're making cookies!"

"Sounds great."

"You guys want a coffee or something?" Greg asked.

Henk shook his head. "No. We just wanted to get Jemi's address from you. Johnny left his fiddle with her last night, but he forgot to find out where she lived so that he could pick it up today."

Greg gave them the address.

"We've got a rehearsal today," he added, "so if you don't catch her at home, I'll let her know that you're looking for her."

"What's her phone number?" Henk asked. "Maybe we should give her a call before we drop by."

"She doesn't have a phone."

"So how do you get in touch with her?"

"Oh, you know Jemi. She's always around. Are you coming to see us this weekend? We're playing the Saucy Noodle—three nights."

"We'll definitely make it." Henk put Larry down and gave him a pat on the rump. "Better get back to those cookies, tiger."

Larry looked fiercely at him and growled. Henk laughed and pretended to back off from him.

"Listen, thanks, Greg. If we don't see you sooner, we'll catch you at the Noodle."

Greg nodded. "I'll tell Jemi you're looking for her if I see her first."

"That'd be great," Henk said. "Stub a toe—okay?"

Greg laughed and waved them off.

They took a #1 bus downtown and walked over to the Sandy Hill address that Greg had given them. It proved to be a three-story wood-frame rooming house on Sweetland, near the corner of Laurier. The building stood at the top of a hill, the street dropping sharply down the remainder of its three-block length. They tried the front door and it was open, so they

walked in. Jemi's name was on the mailboxes in the foyer—
room 11.

"Anybody here?" Henk called.

They waited a moment or so, then, just before Henk called
out again, a large woman came from the back of the building.
She wore a tent-like pinafore over a T-shirt and faded overalls.
Her face was like a full moon—big and friendly—and she wore
her hair in a long braid that hung over one enormous breast.

"Can I help you?" she asked.

"We're looking for Jemi," Henk said.

"I don't think she's up yet—at least I haven't seen her. Come
to think of it, I don't remember her coming in last night. My
room's just beside hers and I was up late last night reading the
new Caitlin Midhir book—*To Drive Away the Northern Cold*.
Have you read it yet?"

"Uh . . ." Henk began.

"Well, it's not like her other stuff at all," she informed them.
"She's having fun here, with the way we see things in the here
and now, you know? But it's still got that magicky feel that—"

"Excuse me," Johnny broke in, "but would you mind
knocking on her door to see if she's in?"

The woman blinked, then frowned.

"Room eleven," she said. "Go knock yourself."

The she turned and went back down the hall.

"What floor?" Johnny called after her.

"Second. Turn right at the top of the stairs."

"Thanks."

There was no reply.

Johnny and Henk looked at each other, then shrugged.
Johnny took the lead up the stairs. Room 11 was at the far end
of the hall. The door had an All Kindly Toes poster on it,
dating back to a gig at the Rainbow earlier in the summer.
Johnny knocked briskly, knocked again after a few moments
when there was no answer.

"Well, that's that," he said, turning away from the door after
a third knock had the same lack of success.

Henk bent over the lock. "I can get us in."

"We can't do that, Henk. It's not right."

"Maybe your fiddle's just sitting in there, Johnny. Besides,
she gave you a runaround last night, didn't she?"

"Yeah, but—"

"It'll just take me a couple of secs."

"That woman downstairs knows we're up here," Johnny said as Henk took his wallet out. "She's probably listening for us right now."

"Let her listen."

Henk took out a credit card and wedged it behind the door's casing trim. The trim was loose—obviously somebody had used this way of getting in before.

"What are you doing with a credit card?" Johnny asked.

"I just use it for ID when I'm writing a cheque. Hang on now."

He slipped the card down behind the angled latch bolt, turned the door handle, and pushed. The door swung open.

"See?" he said. "Nothing to it."

Johnny looked nervously back to the head of the stairs.

"Come *on*," Henk said, and pulled him inside, shutting the door behind them.

Now that they were inside, Johnny looked curiously around. At first glance there was no sign of either his fiddle or Jemi's tenor saxophone case. Instead there was a double bed that took up about a quarter of the room, a closet, a dresser, a bay window with an easy chair and a reading lamp beside it, and a small bookcase near the bed, the top of which was obviously being used as a night table.

The two men moved quickly through the room.

Under the bed were dozens of pairs of shoes and boots. The closet was full of clothes, mostly brightly-coloured and dating from the forties and fifties, though there were some T-shirts and jeans. A sopranino sax sat in its case on the windowsill with a handful of tin whistles, all in different keys. The bookcase held mysteries and best-sellers. The dresser was a clutter of makeup and costume jewelry. Necklaces hung from a small knob on the side of the dresser's mirror—rhinestones and fake pearls, beads and coloured glass.

"Look at this," Henk said.

Johnny came over to the dresser and saw what Henk was pulling free from the other necklaces. It was a carving of a little bone flute that was hanging from a leather thong. Johnny took his own bone carving from his pocket.

"They're like a matched set," he said.

Henk nodded. "Well, they *were* sisters, you said."

Johnny frowned, remembering Jemi's anguished features.

"Let's get out of here," he said.

"You should take this," Henk said, holding out the bone flute. "Trade it to her for your fiddle."

"It's just a pendant."

"Yeah. But I don't know. I've got a feeling it means something important."

Johnny did too, more so than Henk perhaps. He'd felt a tingle touching it, and for some reason envisioned the two carvings pulling at each other like the opposite ends of a pair of magnets.

He took the pendant from Henk's hand and rehung it with the other necklaces.

"I'm not taking anything," he said. "Now, let's go."

He opened the door and peered nervously out, but the hallway was empty. Motioning to Henk, he stepped out into the hall. Henk joined him, shutting the door, and they made for the stairs.

Johnny felt terrible. He was missing his fiddle and last night was still a weird collage of disjointed images in his head, but it wasn't right to go poking through somebody else's personal things. It was too much an invasion of their privacy.

They made it downstairs and outside without meeting anyone. It wasn't until they were a few blocks away that Johnny began to breathe easier.

"Listen," Henk said. "I've got to get to work. Are you going to be okay?"

Henk worked afternoons in a record store called Record Runner on Rideau Street.

"Yeah," Johnny said. "I'll be fine."

"What're you going to do about your fiddle?"

"Drop in on the AKT rehearsal, I guess."

"Okay. Talk to you tonight—and watch it around those pink-haired ladies."

A faint smile touched Johnny's lips—gone almost before it was there.

"Sure," he said. "Thanks again, Henk."

Henk lifted a hand in farewell and set off, leaving Johnny at the corner of Laurier and King Edward. Johnny decided to walk home by way of the bike path along the canal, taking his time. When he finally got back to his apartment, he was feeling a little more clear-headed, if no closer to understanding anything. He had some lunch, then phoned Greg's place. Greg's wife, Janet, gave him Trudy MacDonald's number where the band was rehearsing. When he called there and got Greg on the line, Greg told him that Jemi hadn't showed up yet.

"Don't know what happened to her, man. She's usually pretty good about rehearsals—she just likes to play, you know?"

"Sure. If she shows up, will you have her call me?"

He gave Greg his number.

"No problem," Greg said. "And if you see her, tell her to shake her ass down here, okay?"

"Sure."

Johnny hung up and stared at the phone. When he thought of Jemi, the way she'd looked the last time he'd seen her, head tilted back, screaming at the sky . . .

If that was a true memory, he supposed he wasn't all that surprised that she hadn't shown up for the AKT rehearsal. But where did that leave him? He had a gig himself on the weekend—two nights at the Earl of Sussex—and while he had a spare fiddle, there was no way he was going to give up the one he'd lost. Tom had given it to him. Just one day, out of the blue. He'd handed Johnny the fiddle, saying, "I think you're ready for this one now."

Johnny had never played a fiddle that sounded so sweet. The bass strings woke a low grumble, the high strings just sang. Everything sounded good on it—though by the time he first played that instrument, he'd been studying with Tom for twelve years. If Tom hadn't taught him everything that Tom himself knew, Johnny couldn't imagine what it could be.

He got up and stared out the front window, hands in his pockets. He felt the bone carving, remembered the bone flute in Jemi's apartment, remembered a hollowed hill. . . .

He stood there for a few moments longer, just staring, then got his bike and pedaled down to Vincent Massey Park.

Puxill, he thought. I'm going to look for the Pook of Puxill.

He said the words aloud, then smiled, seeing the play of words on the title of the Kipling book.

He wondered which had come first.

* * *

Dunrobin Finn had a small underground home under the grassy verge between Rideau River Drive and the river itself. Fifteen years or so ago, the spot was a public beach. Now all that remained of its former use was a low stone wall near the river. The sandy beach had been taken over by reeds and rushes. Swans and ducks floated nearby in summer. In winter, the north winds blew down the frozen expanse of the river. But Finn's home was cool in summer, and snug in winter.

Physically it stood in Faerie, so that its grassy door, or the smoke from his hearth, could only be seen by those few mortals who could see into the Middle Kingdom.

Inside, the hollow was one large, low-ceilinged room, with a small sleeping area curtained off on one side. The hearth was used for both warmth in winter and cooking. At the moment a pot of tea sat steeping on the warm stones in front of it, the fire already burning low. Woven reed carpets covered the floor, except for near the old sofa and reading chair where a worn Oriental carpet that Jacky and Kate had given the hob lay. Like most faerie not directly connected to the Court, Finn preferred comfortable furnishings—old-fashioned stuffed sofas and Morris chairs with fat pillows.

Near the hearth was a tall pine kitchen hutch with an enamel counter where Finn did his preparations for cooking. A stool stood nearby that he used to reach the top shelves of the hutch, where he kept the herb simples and poultices that he used as a skillyman. The walls of the big room were covered with antique portraits. Finn collected sepia-toned photographs from bygone years—mostly portraits—and loved to hand-tint them on long winter nights. Each photo had its own wooden frame, ornately carved by the hob. Kate and Jacky each had a few of his portraits hanging in their bedrooms.

Kate and Finn were sitting by the hearth now, Finn in his chair, Kate stretched out on the sofa with Caraid on a cushion beside her. They sipped hot honeyed tea and were quiet now that Kate had finished telling the hob all of what she'd learned the previous night. She'd been nodding off when they first arrived, but the conversation and tea had quickly revived her.

"These droichan," Finn said finally. "They're quite rare now. So few mortals are prepared to accept that Faerie even exists, they don't much seek out its secret knowledge anymore."

"They don't sound much different from the Unseelie Court," Kate said.

"Oh, they're quite different. For all their enmity to us, the Host gets its luck the same as us—as a gift from the Moonmother Arn."

"But they're evil. . . ."

"Oh, they're bad all right, but not much different from our own Court, really. We're like two of your countries in a constant war, Kate. The folk of both countries need to eat the same food, need to sleep at night and relieve themselves. It's the same with faerie—only our ideologies are different. But droichan . . .

"They turn widdershins to Faerie. In the old days, they started out mostly as shargies—changelings that one or another of the Courts took in. Sometimes they'd just go bad, and no one knows why."

"Caraid says they could be giants or ogres, too, but that they're mostly gruagaghs."

Finn shrugged. "Don't know enough about it myself. But a droichan usually becomes a gruagagh in the end—there's no argument there." He looked at Caraid then. "Now, that book of yours—isn't it a skilly thing!"

Kate smiled. "I feel like I've had it all my life."

"That's a true gruagagh's use of magic, making that thing. I couldn't stitch a spell like that if my life depended on it."

"I just used a wally-stane."

"But there's a good and a bad way to use a wally-stane," Finn said. "As you well know from the first time you tried yourself."

He grinned suddenly. Mostly his eyes had a cunning, almost sly look to them, but when he was in a good humour, they sparkled with a light all their own and left others wondering how they could ever have seen him as other than a cheerful hob.

"And see," he added, "what you spelled just goes on. It's not a one-time thing—useful as that can be. This wee book of yours will give you knowledge, Kate. Maybe even turn you into a wisewife or gruagagh yourself. You've already got the name—the only Crackernut in Kinrowan, that's for sure, though once the name was a bit more common. You're clever enough, by far. All you need to do is learn a few tricks and a bit of magic, and away you'll go. I didn't know you were looking to learn, or I would've taught you some stitcheries myself. It's not too late to start now."

"There's the droichan to be dealt with first," Kate said.

"Oh, yes," Finn said grimly. "There's not a light in the sky that a cloud can't cover. Spike the damn hound for breathing."

"Finn. What are we going to do?"

"I don't know. Rescue Jacky. Look for help." He sighed, staring at the last embers of the fire. "What does your book say?"

"Just that we have to find the droichan's heart."

"And that won't be easy. Let's see that book a moment, Kate."

She passed Caraid over. Finn took the stub of a pencil from his pocket and opened the book to a blank page. He sucked on the end of the pencil, thinking, then wrote:

Where do we start?

Kate leaned forward to see what Caraid would answer, but the book made no reply. She had the sudden fear then that it would only work in the Tower, in the Gruagagh's study.

"Oh, Finn. Does this mean—"

"Only that you spelled it to listen to you," the hob said. "To you and no one else." He handed the book back to her. "You ask it."

"I wish I could just talk to it and it could talk back to me," Kate said. "Could that be done?"

"Well, now . . . I can't make it speak to you, but maybe I can let it hear you."

He got up and fetched a silver needle and a spool of red thread from the hutch. The spool for the thread was a thick chunk of a rowan branch. He took the book back from her and with quick deft movements, stitched an embroidered ear onto the front of the book.

"Ask it something," he said.

Kate started to reach for the book, but Finn shook his head.

"Just speak the question," he told her.

Kate cleared her throat. "I feel silly—talking to a book."

"There's sillier things. Try chasing a spunkie into a marsh

like some mortals do. The sluagh just grab them and that's not nice at all—at least not for the one that's caught."

"I suppose." She cleared her throat again, then gave it a try. "Uh . . . hello, Caraid. Can you hear me?"

Under the four words that Finn had written earlier, her question appeared, in her own handwriting.

Hello, Kate, the book replied.

"Can you just hear me, or can you hear everything that goes on around you?"

Everything. But I'll only answer to you. You're my only friend.

"That's the thing with names," Finn remarked.

"What should we do?" Kate asked the book. "Where do we start? The droichan's caught Jacky and I can't just leave her to him while I go off looking for his heart. I might never find it."

Her words appeared on the page as quickly as she spoke them. Kate watched them take form, fascinated.

"We need help, Caraid," she added.

Rowan will break the droichan's spell on the Jack—unless he has blooded her. But you must be careful. The white wood or the red berry are only effective against his spells. If he was to catch you, neither will help you then.

"What does 'blooding her' mean?" Kate asked.

It made her stomach feel a little queasy as her imagination brought up images of what she thought the phrase meant.

"Luck flows like blood," Finn answered. "To free the luck from a body, the droichan will have to cut it open."

"Oh, God!" Kate stood up quickly. "We've *got* to get back to the Tower."

"First we need a plan."

"A plan? Finn, this is Jacky we're talking about!"

"Yes. But if he catches us as well, then what hope does she have? And there's this to think about as well: A creature like a droichan will gather the mean-spirited and evil about, simply by his presence. Bogans and other Unseelie folk."

"But wouldn't he just feed on their luck as well?"

"Not if he has all of Kinrowan's luck at hand—and that's what the Tower gives him."

"But—"

"The Host *will* gather to him, Kate. They have no leader at the moment."

"Caraid," Kate said to the book. "Jacky's my best friend ever. I can't let her die!"

I will still be your friend, the book replied.

Finn caught Kate's arm before she could respond.

"Don't make it jealous," he mouthed silently.

Kate looked at him, bewildered.

"That's the danger of names," the hob added, still just moving his lips but uttering no sound. "A skilly-born thing like your book here can take what it hears too literally."

Then Kate understood. It wasn't as if she hadn't had forewarning about this kind of thing.

"My best friend next to you, of course," she told the book. "Won't you help me rescue her?"

I've told you all I know, Caraid replied.

"But there must be something else."

Find allies, the book told her after a few moments. *Others that the droichan has harmed. Perhaps, with their help, you can find his heart and free your next-best friend.*

"The fiaina sidhe," Finn said.

Kate looked at him. "Are they related to the Pook?"

"They are all kin of a sort. Perhaps they could help us."

"Perhaps! But that doesn't do anything for Jacky now."

"Kate, there's nothing else we can do."

"Oh, yes, there is. We can go back to the Tower with as much rowan as we can carry and get Jacky out of there."

Finn regarded her mournfully. His eyes plainly said, Why won't you listen?

"Kate," he began.

"If I can get to the wally-stanes, couldn't I just use one of them on him and turn him into a toad or something?"

Unlikely, Caraid replied. *Wally-stanes are a Jack magic. They wouldn't be strong enough for such a task. Especially not with the droichan fighting the spell.*

"Jack magics work subtly," Finn explained. "And remember how much you had to concentrate to make them work properly. Just imagine the droichan's will opposing you at the same time. You'd never have a chance to collect your thoughts."

Kate nodded. "Okay. But I'm still going. I have to, Finn."

"I know," he said. "But at least let us find what help we can close at hand. Crowdie Wort left Gwi Kayleigh in charge of his bally before he left. Why don't we at least find her first?"

Ottawa South was known as Crowdie Wort's Bally to the faerie of Kinrowan, Crowdie Wort being its Chief. Like most of the Court, he was in Ballymoresk for the Fair, and like the other Chiefs, he'd left a few foresters behind to keep watch over the acres under his care.

It's unlikely that a forester could stand up to the droichan, Caraid offered.

Kate ignored the book.

"Where can we find her?" she asked.

"She'll have left word at the bridge as to her whereabouts."

Kate closed Caraid and stuffed it in her pouch.

"Then let's go," she said.

Finn gave his comfortable home a longing look, then hurried after Kate, who was already outside and striding west to Billings Bridge.

Her predicament was the most terrifying thing that Jacky could imagine. She could hear and see and smell and feel and think, perfectly well. But she had no control over her body. Her lungs still worked, drawing in air, letting it out. The blood kept moving through her veins and arteries. All the automatic functions of the various systems that kept her alive still worked. But she couldn't get up out of the chair. She couldn't turn her head. She couldn't even blink.

The gruagagh had paralyzed her and she was as helpless as a newborn babe.

She heard footsteps. As she listened, she remembered Kate appearing in her range of vision earlier, moving a hand in front of her eyes. She hadn't been able to warn Kate. Hadn't been able to do a thing. But these footsteps weren't Kate's. They belonged to the gruagagh, who sat down across the table from her and regarded her with a smirking expression on his handsome face.

How could she have been so stupid as to have let him capture her? Kinrowan was her responsibility and she'd as good as handed it over to him. She thought of what Bhruic would say if he could see her now, what the Laird's Court would say when they returned from Ballymoresk, and hated Cumin of Lochbuie with a vengeance.

"There's a thing or two about this Tower," Cumin said, "that I don't understand. The smell of Bhruic Dearg's enchantments are very strong. I know the luck of Kinrowan is bound up in this place. But he's hidden the workings of the how of it from me. I think it's time we took a walk upstairs and you showed me the lay of things."

Dream on, Jacky thought.

Cumin smiled. "I know you're raging, locked in there behind those glazed eyes, but it makes no difference, Jacky Rowan. You're mine now. And you'll show me what I want—don't doubt it for an instant."

To Jacky's dismay, her body lurched to its feet and, whether she wanted to or not, the gruagagh set her to walking across the floor and up the stairs. She moved like a marionette in an amateur puppeteer's jerky hands, but she moved. And there was nothing she could do about it.

As they reached the top of the stairs, her gaze touched briefly on her room, before the gruagagh moved her on. There were a pair of bogans in there now, rooting through her belongings. Bogans in the Tower! There was a boggy smell in the air, too. The whispery sound of sluagh voices.

The gruagagh moved her up the next flight of stairs before she could see more, up to Bhruic's study, up to his books of lore and the window that looked out on Kinrowan and showed the criss-crossing network of the moonroads that gave the realm its luck.

Kinrowan was doomed, she knew. And it was all her fault.

"There's nothing so satisfying," the gruagagh said from behind her, "as learning new lessons, discovering how things work. Perhaps when you've shown me Bhruic Dearg's secrets, little Jacky, I'll take you apart and see how you work." He laughed. "Would you like that?"

I'll see you dead in hell first, Jacky thought, but how she was going to manage that, she didn't know. The way things were going, she'd be lucky to make it through the next half hour, little say take her vengeance on her captor.

The door to the third floor loomed before them. Her hand—directed by the gruagagh's will—moved to the knob, twisted it, and then she was leading the gruagagh into the heart of Kinrowan.

CHAPTER
10

Johnny couldn't find Puxill.

What he did find was Vincent Massey Park on a Wednesday afternoon, late in the summer. There were no sidhe, pink-haired or otherwise. No crowds of strange faerie creatures. Just the odd jogger—perfectly human—in jogging suit and running shoes. Once another cyclist passed him by, seriously bent over the handlebars of his ten-speed, stretchy black thigh-length shorts half-covering muscular legs, gaze fixed on the path ahead. Black squirrels were busy burying nuts. Sparrows and crows watched him from the trees.

But there were no magical beings.

No faerie.

He chained his bike to a tree by the railway bridge and hiked up to the spot where Jemi had led him into her hollowed hill. The glade lay still in the afternoon sun. He walked slowly up and down its length, trying to remember just how they had approached it, until he was sure he had the right stone. Kneeling beside it, he studied it carefully. After a few moments, he lifted his hand hesitantly, then knocked on it the way he remembered Jemi had done.

Two quick knocks, pause, another knock.

Nothing.

He lifted his hand to try again, then turned away. What was the use? He sat down on the grass beside the stone and stared out through the trees to what he could see of the university.

He had to be crazy to have taken any of last night seriously. Something had happened to him—he didn't doubt that—but it hadn't been real. Whatever her reasons, Jemi had slipped him something and then his own imagination had taken over, peopling the park with the weird beasties and beings from his grandfather's library.

They had appeared to be real—*very* real, oh, yes—but then hallucinations usually were.

Illusions. Delusions.

Why was she—Jemi, Jenna, whatever her name was—doing this to him?

He pulled the bone carving from his pocket and fingered its smooth surface. The bone gleamed in the sunlight. He remembered the bone flute carving in Jemi's room on Sweetland, the attraction he'd felt between the two artifacts. . . . He kept rubbing the little fiddle with his thumb, only now his thoughts turned to Tom.

It was hard to believe the old fellow was gone. That didn't seem real either—never mind his being so sick this past while. The world didn't seem the same anymore, knowing Tom wasn't in it.

Sitting there in the sunlight, this was the first time Johnny had thought of his grandfather without wanting to cry. The sadness was still there—the empty place inside him hadn't been filled, or gone away—but it was different now. He found himself remembering good times—long nights spent talking. Times when they played tunes, the two fiddles singing in unison until Tom suddenly went into the perfect harmony, underlying the original tune with a resonating depth that made it sound like far more than a simple two- or three-part fiddle tune. There were times when the music bridged something between them and some mystery that lay just beyond their reach.

Tom had talked about it a few times. Johnny wondered now if what his grandfather had been talking about was Faerie. Was that where he'd gone? Was Tom some ghostly fiddler in a fairy hill now? Johnny's fingers yearned for the instrument that wasn't in his hands. If he played a tune now, would it reach to Tom in that otherworld?

Johnny turned once more and, using the bone fiddle, rapped on the stone again.

Twice, pause, another rap.

Nothing.

"Goddamn you!" he cried. "Just give me back my fiddle! Give it back, or I swear I'll come back with a shovel and dig you out. . . ."

His voice trailed off as he sensed someone behind him. He looked up from the stone. In the meadow between the bike path and where he sat stood a skinny man in shorts, T-shirt, and running shoes, watching him. The curiosity in his eyes turned to guilt when he realized that Johnny had caught him staring. He began to back away, then simply vanished.

"Oh, Christ," Johnny muttered. "Let's not start this disappearing shit again."

"It's not him," a familiar voice said from higher up the slope. "It's you that's been moved into Faerie."

She was crouched above him, something feral in her stance and in the look in her eyes, her pink hair standing up at all angles from her head. She was wearing calf-length trousers and tunic-like shirt, both tattered and of an old-fashioned cut. Their greens and browns gave a first impression that she was wearing clothes made from twigs and leaves. Her face was washed out and pale without its makeup.

Beside her, its head on a level with hers as she crouched, was what Johnny first took to be a dog. Then he realized it was a small wolf.

"Listen," he began.

He wanted to just grab her and shake her, but he found his anger had just drained away again. Instead, he felt close to something rare, something wondrous, and he didn't want to lose it. He wanted to comfort the hurt he saw lying behind the fierce look in her eyes. He wanted to run away from her and never see her again.

"I know you mean well," Jemi said. "And we've given you nothing but grief."

"It's just . . . I don't . . . I'm not sure what's real."

Jemi moved suddenly, scuttling down the slope towards him. The dog, or wolf, turned and loped off into the trees. Johnny watched it go, then looked at Jemi. Her face was very close to his.

"Oh, we're very real," she said.

She lifted her hand to touch his cheek in that curious gesture that both she and her sister had.

"Your sister," Johnny said.

Her eyes went bleak.

"I just wanted to say I'm sorry about what happened to her. I know how you're feeling. . . ."

Jemi looked away, past his shoulder, into unseen distances.

"I won't let them get away with it," she said. "Whoever killed her—they'll pay." Her gaze went to him, the feral light fierce in her eyes. "Will you help me, Johnny Faw? I want to call the sidhe. I want to ride on Kinrowan. Something in Kinrowan killed my sister, and not just her alone. The Seelie Court *has* to pay for what they've done."

"What can I do?"

Here I go again, Johnny thought as he spoke. Believing it all again. But it was impossible not to—not with her sitting so close to him, radiating her otherworldiness.

"Be my strength," she said. "I've never called a rade— never led the fiaina. But I'm all that's left with Jenna gone. I'm the Pook now."

"But what would I do?"

"There's power in music, Johnny. We both know that. We've both made people smile, made them dance. Now we must gather my people from all their hidden places. Summon them with skilly tunes. Lead them against our foe."

She was using words that made no sense to Johnny. Rade and Kinrowan and skilly.

"How will you find this—foe?" he asked.

"We'll ride on Kinrowan, and if the Court don't deliver up the murderers, we'll take up our quarrel with them. Will you help me?"

"I . . ."

Johnny looked away from her. It was hard to think with her sitting so close. She smelled like apples and nuts, freshly harvested. She radiated heat, presence.

He didn't want to promise what he might not be able to deliver. He wanted to help her, wasn't sure he could, wanted her. . . .

And that was another part of the problem. He was drawn to her, as surely as the two bone carvings were drawn to each other, and he was afraid of that. He was also afraid of it all turning around on him again. Of accepting that this was real, then finding himself alone once more. In a glade. Or on a riverbank. Without her. Thinking he'd imagined it all again. Thinking he was crazy.

He caught hold of her hand.

"They say that faerie can enchant mortals," he said. "Is this . . . have you laid a"—he searched for the right word— "a glamour on me?"

Jemi shook her head. Her fingers tightened around his.

"I've felt it too," she said. "With you. I might ask you the same question. But I didn't spell you, Johnny. All I know is that together we can make a skilly music that'll set our world a-right again. Heal its hurts. That can't be wrong, can it?"

"No."

He turned to her, lost himself in her eyes again, and had to look away. He remembered her anguish last night. The dead face of her sister, so like her own. The dislocation from reality that he'd been feeling ever since he'd escaped the crowd of faerie creatures that had been pressing around him. . . .

"I'll help you," he said. "Or at least I'll try. Just don't disappear on me again."

For a long moment neither of them spoke. Then Jemi put a hand on either side of his face and turned his head until he was facing her once more. She rose slightly off her heels and kissed him once on each eye, her tongue licking the lids.

"Now I *have* enchanted you," she said. "But only so you can see into Faerie on your own."

She smiled. The sadness, the fierceness in her eyes, eased slightly. She kissed him on the lips, a brief, brushing contact, then rocked back onto her heels, hands on her knees.

"Just . . . just like that?" Johnny asked.

A simple nod was her only reply.

Johnny sighed. He wanted to reach for her.

Instead, he said, "I was in your room on Sweetland. I was looking for my fiddle."

"It was a bad night," Jemi said softly. "I'm sorry you were pushed from Faerie the way you were."

"That's okay. I just wanted to tell you. I wasn't snooping, you see, but . . ." He opened his hand. The bone fiddle lay in his palm. "I saw a flute pendant that looked—no, that's not right. It *felt* like a twin to this."

Jemi looked down at the carving.

"I'd forgotten about the flute," she said. "It was Jenna's, but she gave it to me a long time ago. The Bucca gave them both to her. I think he got them from my mother, but he might well have given them to her in the first place."

"Do they mean something?"

"I'm not sure. Maybe there is some glamour involved here after all, though it's neither mine nor yours."

"What do you mean?"

"We fiaina aren't like the Courts, Johnny. We don't get our luck in the same way they do. We need our rade. The Bucca led the rade until Jenna learned it well enough to take his place, and then he left. It's always been a Pook or a Bucca or someone like that who leads the rade, but old tales say that a mortal leads it best. Man or woman, it doesn't matter. It depends on the Pook at the time, I suppose."

"What's a Bucca?"

Jemi smiled. "An old and very wise being, Johnny. He's been gone for a long time now. We're a restless folk, we fiaina sidhe. Me, not so much—I think it's my human blood—but the others, oh, how they like to wander. . . ."

"And the two carvings?" Johnny asked. "Where do they fit in?"

"They shape a bond between mortal and sidhe."

"Is that why your sister gave it to me? So that I'd meet you? Not that I'm complaining or anything, but how could she know that we'd like each other?"

The sadness washed over Jemi again.

"I don't suppose we'll ever know," she said.

Johnny reached for her and held her head against his shoulder, but she didn't cry. She pressed against him, then slowly sat back.

"Evening will be coming on—sooner than we'd like," she said. "Let's go inside and see what skilly tune we both know that we can use to summon the sidhe."

She slipped past him, into the hollow hill. Johnny stood at its sod entrance. He looked around the glade once more, trying to figure out why this was all happening to him. Then he shrugged and followed her inside.

* * *

"I see bogans," Gwi said.

"And I smell sluagh," Finn added.

Kate nodded glumly, her gaze fixed on the Tower.

It was late afternoon now, the past hours spent in tracking down Gwi Kayleigh. The forester was a tall faerie, lean with angular features. There was troll blood in her, from a few generations back, Finn had explained to Kate before they found her, but before Kate asked how that had come about, they'd spied Gwi and the chance was gone. Gwi wore the mottled greens and browns preferred by most foresters, and carried a bow and quiver. Instead of a pony, she trusted her long legs to carry her through her patrol.

She had listened to Kate's tale, added a curse or two to Finn's, then returned with them to Learg Green, where they now spied on the Tower.

"A few bogans we can deal with," she said, after studying the lie of the land, "and the sluagh won't be a danger until nightfall."

"That leaves the droichan," Kate said,

Gwi looked at the small bundle of rowan twigs that Finn was carrying.

"Those won't be enough," she said. "Not if he's all that the old tales make droichan to be."

"I'm *not* leaving Jacky in there with him," Kate said firmly.

"No one's asking you to," Gwi replied. "We just need more of a plan than catch-as-catch-can."

Kate sighed. She didn't like to admit it, but the forester was right. What Kate wanted to do was just rush in and get Jacky out of the gruagagh's clutches. Never mind waiting and thinking and planning. Just get in and out with Jacky, and worry about the gruagagh later. But the gruagagh was the whole problem, as Finn had rightfully pointed out earlier, and if they just charged ahead, they'd all end up as his captives with no one left free to rescue any of them.

"What're we going to do?" she asked.

Gwi plucked a stem of grass and put it between her lips.

"What we need," she said, chewing thoughtfully, "is a skinwalker."

"A shapechanger," Finn explained at Kate's puzzled look.

"Like those with Lairdsblood who can take swan or seal shape."

"But the Laird and the whole Court's gone," Kate said.

The only other person with Lairdsblood that she knew was Jacky's sometimes beau, Eilian, the Laird of Dunlogan's son, but he was too far away to reach quickly, having gone back north to his father's Court at midsummer.

"There's others that know a trick or two about changing their skins," Gwi said.

"What good would a skinwalker even be?" Kate asked. "Just saying we could find one?"

"We need to get inside," the forester explained. "Without raising an alarm. And what better way to do so than disguised as one of their own? Then, with a bit of luck and surprise on our side, I'd hope we could snatch the Jack and win free with our hides all still in one piece. Now's not the time to confront the droichan. I'd rather wait until I have his hidden heart in my hand before I go face to face with him."

"And with Jacky free," Finn said, "we'll be able to concentrate on finding that heart."

"So where do we find a skinwalker?" Kate asked.

"In the borderlands," Gwi said. "I know a sidhe or two that have the knack and might be persuaded to help."

Finn shook his head. "No need to go that far." Before either of the women could ask him what he meant, he took out a needle and a spool of thread. "I can stitch us the illusion of being a bogan or whatever you wish."

"Oh, I don't know," Gwi said. She pulled the grass stem from her mouth and pointed it at the hob. "How well would it hold?"

"Well enough for what you want. If we're subjected to close scrutiny . . ." He shrugged. "But for something like this, it'll do."

"All right," Gwi said. "I'm game. Kate?"

Kate blinked. She looked from the forester to the Tower, then back again. She wished she felt a little braver, or at least more competent. But there was Jacky to think of.

"I guess so," she said.

Finn rubbed his palms together.

"Fine," he said. "I'll use buttons to start the spell. Strips of cloth for headbands to keep it firm. . . ."

He began to pull pieces of cloth from the small bag that held his bundle of rowan twigs and set to work.

"There's nothing like stitcheries to enthuse a hob," Gwi remarked dryly.

Finn didn't look up, but he grinned.

Kate nodded and went back to studying the Tower. From time to time she'd see a bogan move across a window, or in the backyard.

We're on our way, Jacky, she thought, wishing she could feel as enthused about bearding the gruagagh in the Tower as Finn was about stitching his spells.

What if Jacky wasn't even alive anymore?

She remembered what Caraid had said earlier. That Jacky would be fine—

Unless he had blooded her. . . .

"Don't worry," Gwi said. "We'll get the Jack free."

Oh, I hope so, Kate thought.

She gave the forester a quick smile, but returned to her worrying all the same.

Both Kate and Gwi eyed the result of Finn's handiwork with a certain dubious concern. Lying on the grass between them were three headbands. Each was made of strips of cloth, woven and stitched together, from which hung a number of long loose pieces like the ribbons of a May tree. To each of their jackets he had sewn a small wooden button.

"I know what you're thinking," the hob said with a grin, "but watch first before you decide."

He put on one of the headbands, adjusting it so that the ribbon-like streamers hung at his sides and back. It gave him a curiously festive air. Before either of the women could comment on the silliness of it, he attached the foremost ribbon on his left side to the button on his jacket. Kate blinked as he wavered for a moment, then blinked again and edged away from the hob as the bulk of a small bogan appeared where he'd been sitting. The bogan had a foolish look on his face.

"Not bad," Gwi said, reaching for one of the headbands. "Not bad at all. A little fuzzy about the edges, and it wouldn't stand up to a scrutiny by the beastie's mother—just saying such creatures are born and not hatched from refuse—but it'll do."

A moment later, Kate was sitting with two bogans.

"We'll have to growl a bit when we talk," Finn said. "I've disguised our looks and our scents, but I can't touch voices."

Kate nodded and grabbed the last of the headbands. She put it on, slipped the button on her jacket through the buttonhole that Finn had provided in the appropriate ribbon, and then there were three of the Unseelie creatures sitting on the riverbank in Windsor Park. The Finn bogan studied each of his companions critically, then nodded to himself and undid the button from his own ribbon.

"We'll wait a bit," he said as Kate and Gwi followed suit. "The day'll be gone soon and the twilight's the best time for this sort of work."

"What about the rowan twigs?" Kate asked.

"I'll stitch one in Gwi's jacket and one in my own," Finn said. "The rest we can each carry in our pockets. But don't forget, Kate. They might work well enough to shield us from the droichan's spells, but a bogan can still spike us, quicker than you'd like, and the rowan won't work if the droichan should lay his hands physically upon us."

"I don't like waiting," Gwi said. "We'll have the sluagh to deal with then, as well as the droichan and his bogans."

Not to mention, Kate thought, that the longer they waited, the less chance there was of Jacky still being all in one piece.

"Twilight's best for this sort of work," Finn insisted.

"Oh, I know that," Gwi said. "I just don't like it."

The forester found herself a new long stem of grass to chew on and settled down against the bole of a fat oak to wait, her gaze fixed on the Tower across the park. She had a hunter's patience—an attribute that neither of her companions seemed to share, for they fidgeted and were continually adjusting this and that, shifting their weight from one side to another, and generally feeling uncomfortable. It seemed to take forever before Gwi sat up, head cocked and nostrils widening.

"It's time," she said. "I can smell the nightfall on the wind."

"A bare room," the gruagagh said, "yet it stinks of magic." He stepped past Jacky and walked into the center of the room. "Having spent the better part of the day attempting to discover the secrets of Bhruic's Tower, I think it's time now for you to show me what has been hidden so well from me."

Jacky looked at him as though he were crazy. A bare room?

The third-floor study looked no different than ever, except that there was an unruly pile of books around Kate's reading chair. Was Cumin blind?

He walked out of her range of sight once more and she heard the door close.

"I'm guarding the door," he said, "and the window lets out on a three-story drop. I trust you'll agree that escape is futile. Turn and look at me."

Her body obediently turned her around so that she was facing the gruagagh. He lifted his left hand and made a brief pass in the air between them, fingers moving in a quick, controlled pattern. As his hand dropped to his side, she regained control of her body, only to have it crumple to the floor.

Every limb was numb. Pin pricklings went through her as circulation was restored. She remembered what he'd said about having spent the better part of the day searching the Tower. A quick glance at the window showed that it was indeed late in the afternoon. Almost night. No wonder she had this numb, swollen feeling in every part of her body. She'd spent the same better part of the day, and some of the night too, sitting on a hard kitchen chair.

The gruagagh watched her patiently as she got the lumps that were her legs under her and pushed herself up, first to a crouching position, then finally to her feet. She swayed there, lifting and putting down her feet, shaking her arms, trying to get the numbness out of them.

"Show me the key," Cumin said.

"Can't you see it?" Jacky asked.

A frown moved fox-quick across the gruagagh's face.

"Would you like me to have your body throw itself out that window?" he asked.

"But then you'd never find out, would you?" Jacky replied sweetly.

She was acting far bolder than she felt, but knew she had to put up a good front.

"You are trying my patience, you little fraud of a Jack."

"Why don't you just read my mind?" Jacky asked. "Why don't you have my hand write it all out for you? Or are those tricks beyond *your* capabilities?"

Something flickered in the gruagagh's eyes. Before he could do anything, Jacky shrugged.

"But I'll show you what you want," she said. "Why should I care? I'm tried of this Tower, tired of its responsibilities. Everyone wants me to be a gruagagh—to replace Bhruic—but I'm sick to death of being compared to him. Let them see how much they like having a gruagagh back in charge when it's you."

Jacky knew that there was enough of her real frustration in what she said to make her words ring true to the gruagagh. She looked around the room, still surprised at how it seemed empty to him, while its clutter and furnishing were very physically present to her—from a pair of teacups that hadn't been taken downstairs last night, to the books around Kate's chair, to the mess Kate must have made last night on the worktable where a scatter of twigs lay on top of a mess made up of a sheaf of papers, one of Bhruic's journals, a rolled-up map, an empty porcelain jar, a knife. . . .

Jacky wandered over to the table and stood near the weapon.

"I guess Bhruic was paranoid about what someone like you would do with this place," she said, "so he put some spell on it to keep it invisible from you." She turned, her back to the worktable. "The trouble is, I don't know how to make you see what's here. What if it's keyed to one's purpose? What if when someone comes in with all kinds of bad intentions, everything just shuts down? What can we do about that? Do you know a spell to hide your intent?"

Cumin regarded her through narrowed eyes and Jacky knew just what he must be thinking. He had to be reconsidering his earlier impression of her. Last night she'd been childishly easy to put under his control—but then he'd taken her by surprise. But if Bhruic had left her in charge of his Tower, if Kinrowan's Laird had agreed and not replaced her with someone else for as long as the year since Bhruic was gone, then there must be more to her than what he could see. Right now her assessment of why the key to the Tower remained locked away from him had to be making sense because, as anyone who knew, or had even heard about Bhruic knew, it was just the sort of thing that Kinrowan's Gruagagh—with his old-fashioned desire "to do things right"—would lay upon the place.

"I know such a spell," he conceded, "but it is based upon

hiding one's intent from a living creature . . . not a wizard's Tower."

Jacky shrugged and leaned back against the worktable.

"That's too bad," she said. "This is a table I'm leaning against right now. A worktable. Should I try to hand things that are on it to you? Maybe one of Bhruic's journals? Tell me what you want me to do. I'm not a gruagagh. I can't wave my hand and make everything visible to you."

"His journals are there?" Cumin asked.

"One is," Jacky replied.

She lifted it from the table, noted that Cumin could see it while it was in her hand, then set it down again.

"There's more of them over there," she added, waving to the bookshelves on another wall.

"Give me that one," Cumin said, pointing to the invisible spot where she'd set the journal down.

"Sure."

Jacky swallowed dryly as the gruagagh moved towards her to take the book. The knife was lying there, waiting for her hand, but she didn't know if she could use it. It was for the good of Kinrowan—which was under her protection. It was to save her own skin. But it was one thing to knock a giant down a flight of stairs and kill him in the heat of the moment, and quite another to deliberately stab a human being—even one so evil as this gruagagh.

"The book," Cumin demanded, looming over her.

"What . . . what do you think these are good for?" she mumbled, trying to buy time.

In her left hand she held up a handful of rowan twigs, plucked from the table.

The gruagagh bared his teeth, like a dog snarling, and swung a fist at her, but she ducked. And grabbed the knife. She saw him step into the same space that the table occupied, still unaware of its presence, except intellectually because she had told him it was there. On a physical level, it didn't exist for him.

He stopped when he saw the knife in her hand.

"You pitiful thing," he said. "What do you mean to do with that?"

Jacky's anger returned in a rush. She stepped in close, stabbing him in the chest. He staggered slightly under the blow, but remained standing, a faint smile touching his lips. Jacky stumbled back. Before her horrified gaze, he reached up and plucked the knife from his breast, tossing it to the floor.

"You can't kill what has no heart," the gruagagh said.

It was too much for Jacky. Seeing him standing there in the middle of a table which didn't exist for him . . . plucking the knife from his chest . . . and there was no wound, no blood, nothing. . . .

She backed steadily away from him until she bumped against the sill of the window and could go no further. She lifted her hands to ward off the approaching gruagagh, and didn't know why she bothered. There was a shadow around him now, a black aura that clung to him, and it seemed that he wore the head of a black hound superimposed over his own features.

Desperately, she flung the handful of rowan at him. The gruagagh threw back his head and laughed.

"Was that your best?" he asked. "A knife and a handful of rowan twigs? You're mine, child, and I will have the secrets of this Tower from you. I will tear them from you as my bogans chew your flesh. You'll die—eventually—but in such pain . . ."

Jacky glanced behind her. The gruagagh saw a three-story drop through the window, but she saw all of Kinrowan spread out before her.

"Oh, no, you don't!" the gruagagh cried.

He lunged for her, but he was too late.

Jacky's gaze, drawn by the flash of a hob's red cap and a familiar head of tousled curls, latched onto Kate, Finn, and a tall woman who were crouching together by the riverbanks on the other side of the park. Before the gruagagh could reach her, she threw herself out the window, screaming Kate's name.

Behind her, she heard the gruagagh howl in rage. He grabbed for her leg, but caught only a handful of air. He was either not brave enough or not foolish enough to follow her when she vanished from his sight.

Henk stopped off at Johnny's apartment after work, but there was no answer to his knock. He went around back, fetched the key from under its brick, and let himself in. A quick prowl-through told him that, while Johnny had been back since they'd gone up to Sandy Hill earlier this morning, he was gone now.

His bike was missing as well. It didn't take Henk long to work out where his friend had gone.

"Christ, Johnny," he muttered as he returned the key to its hiding place. "You've got to give it up."

But he knew Johnny too well, knew that Johnny wasn't one to give up. Whatever Jemi Pook had done to him, Johnny would push through it until he'd worked it all out. Henk had seen it too often before.

So where did that leave Henk himself? There was really no question about it, he realized. He wasn't exactly happy to have to be doing it, but he wasn't going to leave Johnny on his own to wander around Vincent Massey Park, knocking on rocks until God knew what kind of trouble he might get into.

Giving the empty apartment a last look, Henk set off for Bank Street, where he could catch a #1 to take him down as far as Billings Bridge. It was a relatively short walk from there to the park.

CHAPTER
11

Jenna's cairn was smaller than Johnny had imagined it would be. He'd been thinking in terms of the stoneworks in the British Isles and Brittany, in larger-than-life terms, but the cairn was just a small mound of rocks at the top of the hollowed hill above the entrance, not even visible from outside of Faerie.

With his fiddle case in one hand, Johnny took Jemi's hand in his other and gave it a squeeze. She turned to him, grateful, then looked back at the cairn, eyes brimming with unshed tears. The small wolfish dog had been waiting for them by the mound of stones. It gave Johnny the impression that it had been guarding the cairn.

"Is that your pet?" Johnny asked.

Jemi shook her head. "No. That's Mactire."

At the sound of its name, the animal wavered in Johnny's sight. It stretched, lost hair, gained stature, took on recognizably human-like figures. . . . In the next moment, a small feral boy crouched by the stones. He appeared to be about twelve years old—but only until Johnny looked into his eyes. He was naked, except for a soft covering of light downy hair that was the same grey colour that his wolfish fur had been, only not so thick. A mane of longer, coarser hair tumbled down his shoulders, matted with twigs, leaves, and dried mud.

"Ah . . ." Johnny mumbled.

He really wasn't ready for this kind of thing yet. Maybe he never would be. Jemi he could take, Faerie in small doses, but the rest of the denizens of the Middle Kingdom still left him with the feeling that he was tripping out.

"Mactire's a skinwalker," Jemi explained.

"Right."

"He's a friend, Johnny."

Johnny nodded. "How do you do?" he said lamely to the small wild boy.

"Not good," Mactire replied gruffly.

His voice was deeper than Johnny had expected it to be, coming as it did from that slender frame. The wild boy met Johnny's gaze steadily for a long heartbeat, then turned to Jemi.

"Are you calling up a rade?" he asked.

Jemi shook her head. "It's the wrong time of the Moon, Mac. I'm calling up an army."

The wild boy grinned, baring two rows of sharp, pointed wolf's teeth.

"Oh, that's good," he said. "It's time we showed the night that we can bite back."

Looking at those teeth, Johnny didn't have any doubt about that. The wolf boy looked at his fiddle case.

"Can you play that thing?" he asked.

Johnny nodded. That, at least, was something of which he was sure.

Mactire grinned again. "That's good," he said, looking at Jemi once more. "He's not a Fiddle Wit, but they'll follow him all the same."

"I know they will," Jemi replied. "Pipe and fiddle and Arn's own luck—they'll have to follow. And he might make a Wit yet."

"What are you talking about?" Johnny asked.

"Remember what I told you before?" Jemi asked. "That a mortal leads us best? Don't ask me why, but that's the way it is."

"A brief flicker in the night," Mactire said. "Gone quick, but oh, they burn so bright."

That was almost poetry, Johnny thought, giving Mactire a considering look.

"And what's this about a Fiddle Wit?" he asked.

"It's just a name," Mactire explained. "See, the thing that binds us is music—music and the rade when we catch our luck.

We can't have one without the other, and the luck's never so strong as when a tune calls it down. A Fiddle Wit is like a Jack—do you understand? Clever. A skilly sort of a person. Like our own Pook here, but all the way mortal. Not tied to any Court. No allegiances but to the Moonmother Arn, whatever shape she takes. It's a good name, Johnny Faw."

Johnny didn't even bother to ask how the wolf boy knew his name.

"It's time now," Jemi said, and then that unspoken question faded from Johnny's mind as well.

He cracked open his fiddle case and took his grandfather's gift from it. Plucking the strings, he found them still in tune. He put the fiddle under his chin, then reached into the case for his bow. Tightening the frog, he gave the bow a quick shake to loosen the hairs. When he was ready, he gave Jemi a nod.

She had taken a wooden flute-like instrument from her pocket and she was sitting by the stones, watching him. Her instrument had reeds at one end, finger holes along its length, and a bell shape at the other end. Resembling a bombard, it played more softly with a sweet tone that was like a cross between an oboe and a Northumbrian pipe chanter. When he nodded, she brought the reed end to her mouth and blew softly.

Watching her play, Johnny felt a closeness to her once more. She made such an incongruous picture with the mottled greens and browns of her shirt and tunic, her black piper's jacket with its tarnished brass buttons, and the pink hair standing straight up in a wild thatch. For a long moment he forgot to play, then he remembered why they were here and set his bow to the fiddle's strings.

The tune they played was "Brian Boru's March"—an old harp tune, supposedly composed in commemoration of the Battle of Clontarf, when the Irish under Brian Boru repelled an invasion of Vikings in 1014. But the tune was only a borrowed one, Jemi had told him that afternoon, and dated far earlier than that.

"It's the 'Bri' in Brian that's as close to the original title as your people can remember now," she had explained, "and that's an old word that the Gaels borrowed from the people of the hills. It means the female force, you see—the earth, the moon, growth and growing things. Like the luck we need to keep us hale. They found Brigit's name in that word, and many another word besides, but the old bri was more than just the Bride—it was every face that she ever wore. 'Briall Ort' is what we call this tune, and the closest I can tell you to what that means is 'cheer up.' Be happy. Persevere. Rise from your sorrow."

And it was that kind of tune, Johnny thought. It had always been one of his favorites. A tune that dripped age, was solemn as a saraband, yet sprightly too. Sadness and happiness mingled in its bittersweet turns, just as they did in one's life.

That evening, with the grey twilight creeping over the hills, Jemi's piping joining his fiddling as though they were meant only for each other, "Brian Boru's March" made a music that lifted his heart the way a hymn cheered a devout Christian, but it kept his foot tapping at the same time. There was mystery in it, and a magic, and a calling on, too. For he could see now, as the twilight deepened, that they were no longer alone by Jenna's cairn.

Like the previous night, the fiaina sidhe came by ones and twos. One moment there were just the three of them on the hilltop—piper, fiddler, and listening wolf boy—and in the next, a crowd of faerie had gathered. But tonight they were different.

Last night they had come as the moment had found them—drawn from whatever task they were about when they first heard the call.

Tonight they came riding for war.

Hobs on their shaggy ponies and a big troll with a shield the size of a small car and a club like a sawed-off lightpost. Skinwalkers in their beast shapes: foxes and wolves, bears and snarling bobcats. Three kelpies in horse shape, their black flanks shining in the dying light. Tiny creatures armed with little bows and arrows, spiked armour on their backs and arms, making them look like oversized hedgehogs riding small spotted brown dogs. Narrow faces, broad faces, painted for war, like ancient Celts or Native Americans. Stout dwarves with knobby walking sticks spiked with sharp silver tips, and wearing leather helmets.

By the time the twilight gave way to night, there were over two hundred of them gathered on the hill. A bearded hob on a small pony rode forwards as Jemi and he finally set their instruments aside. He nodded briefly to Johnny, then turned his attention to the new Pook.

"Jenna was wrong," Dohinney Tuir said, "and I was right, but I take no pleasure from it. She should have listened. She should never have gone. For now she's dead, and we still have war on our hands—a war we cannot hope to win. Kinrowan is not our enemy, Jemi."

"Jenna died in Kinrowan," Jemi replied.

"And curse the creature that slew her—but it was not a member of the Seelie Court."

A murmur rose from the gathered sidhe, but Johnny wasn't sure if it meant that they were agreeing with the hob or not.

"Our enemy is in Kinrowan," Jemi said. "They must deliver him to us."

A black horse stepped forwards, shifting its shape, and then a kelpie stood at Tuir's side.

"I want revenge as much as you do," Loireag said, "but Tuir has the right of that much of it. Do you have the name of our enemy for us, Jemi?"

The new Pook shook her head.

"We can't ride to war without a name," Loireag said.

This time the murmur of the sidhe was in agreement—even Johnny could hear that much.

"This murderer—" Jemi began.

"Must be punished!" Loireag broke in fiercely. "But our quarrel isn't with the Court in Kinrowan."

"So we're supposed to wait?" Jemi demanded. "Wait while more of us are slain or chased away? Wait without our rade until we're so diminished that we're not strong enough to even flee, little say fight? Look at us. We've lost a third of our number as it is. Kinrowan owes us the name of our enemy."

"And if they don't know it?" Tuir asked.

"They have troubles of their own," a new voice said.

Deep and grumbling, it issued from the troll who stepped closer, towering over them all.

"There are bogans loose in Kinrowan again," he went on, once he had their attention. "Bogans and sluagh and all the Host. The better part of the Court is gone south to the Harvest Fair and what's left is just beginning to discover the troubles that they have. They can't give us what they don't have, Jemi Pook."

"If we ride on Kinrowan with your demands," Tuir added, "we might well make an enemy of the Seelie Court as well. We're borderfolk, Jemi. We live at the sufferance of both Courts. Either of them could easily rise and finish us off—the Seelie Court, if we bring trouble to them, or the Host, if it can gather itself, for the sake of mischief alone. We can't fight them both and this new enemy besides."

Johnny could feel Jemi wilting at his side.

"Then what are we supposed to do?" he asked.

The weight of hundreds of sidhe gazes settled on him and he wished that he'd never spoken. There were feral lights in those eyes, and no love for humanity.

"Find the enemy's name," Tuir said wearily. "We will help. Each one of us will peep and pry, but until we know what we face, there must be no battle rade." He shook his head slowly. "That such a thing should *ever* be. I don't doubt that we could lose the Moon's luck for all time, whether we win or lose."

"But—" Johnny began.

"Watch where you step, tadpole," Loireag said. "Some might have use for your kind, but there's few of them among our number."

Jemi drew herself up at that.

"Do you forget it all so soon?" she asked. "Who can lead a rade better than a mortal?"

"It need a mortal with some wit," Loireag replied immediately. "And that tadpole has none. He might find it, given time, but time we do not have."

Jemi laid her pipe down by Johnny's knee and stood up to face them, arms akimbo.

"Fine," she told them. "Go! We'll seek out the enemy. And maybe we'll find him and be able to deal with him, and maybe we won't, but I'll tell you this—you, Loireag, and you, Tuir, and you, Garth." She held their gazes with her own, that of kelpie, hob, and troll, and other in that number. "When all's said and done, you'll not have a rade led by this Pook, nor by any mortal that I can put a name to. I'll do what needs doing for Jenna's sake, but after that you can lead your own rades."

"You know we can't," Tuir said. "We need—"

"Don't tell me what you need," Jemi said. "I've given you my need, and you've thrown it back at me. Don't you ever tell me what *you* need."

Loireag took a step towards her, but backed down from the fierce glare in the Pook's eyes.

"Jemi," she tried softly. "Listen to reason—"

"Go!"

The word hung in the still night air, for one long moment, for another, and then slowly they began to disperse. Once moving, they were quickly gone. Johnny watched them, but they faded too fast for him to make them all out in the dark.

The last to go were the kelpie and hob. Tuir looked as if he might speak again, but then he shook his head, turned his pony, and walked it slowly away into the trees. Loireag followed him a moment later. When Johnny turned to Jemi, they were all gone, even the wolf boy, Mactire.

"If the Bucca was here, they'd follow him," Jemi said. "If it was Jenna asking them, they'd follow her. But not me." Her gaze met Johnny's. "This is what I get for straying, Johnny. I've walked among men for so long that their blood must run stronger in me now than my Pook blood does."

Johnny shook his head.

"You chased them away," he said.

"Please. Don't you start."

"No. Listen to me. I don't know everything—about the Courts and where you people stand with them—but what your friends were saying made sense."

"They're not my friends."

"Whatever. But think about what they said. Why take it out on Kinrowan? You don't think that the Seelie Court is behind this, do you?"

Jemi didn't answer for a long time. She stared off into the distance, looking for something. When she returned her gaze to Johnny, he could see that, whatever she'd sought, she hadn't found it.

"No," she said softly. "I guess I don't really think they are. But surely they must know our enemy's name? How can such an evil thing live in their realm and they *not* know?"

"Maybe we should just go talk to them."

"I suppose."

Johnny put away his fiddle and bow, then picked up Jemi's pipe.

"Come on," he said. "Let's see what they have to say."

Jemi let herself be led along.

"It's just that they know it all," she said. "Do you know what I mean? Loireag and Tuir and the rest. Even when they don't know, they still act like they know it all. A show of force wouldn't hurt. It'd prove that we mean business. I wasn't trying to start a war."

"You came off sounding like you did."

"I just want Jenna's killer to pay for what he's done."

"We'll find him," Johnny said.

He just hoped that they'd be able to deal with him when they *did* find him. The sidhe had seemed like as tough a bunch as he'd ever want to run up against, but he'd sensed a genuine fear in them. And if *they* were scared . . .

He tried to put that out of his mind for the moment, concentrating instead on getting them both back to the entrance of Jemi's hollowed hill without either of them breaking their necks in the darkness. Jemi might be able to see like a cat in the dark, but she wasn't being much help right now, and whether he could see into Faerie or not, once they left the relative brightness of the hilltop, he was lost in the shadows.

"I shouldn't have gotten so mad," Jemi said. "That always happens to me with them. I always get mad. That's the real reason I don't live with them."

"Why do you get mad?" Johnny asked.

Jemi's shoulder moved up and down under his arm in an invisible shrug. "I don't know. I wish I could tell you, just so *I'd* know."

It was because she tried to be too hard around them, Johnny thought. Too tough. He'd seen her doing it when she was arguing with them, seen it while she was getting ready to call them up this afternoon, but he didn't think this was the time or place to bring it up.

"Let's get some tea," he said, "and then see what we can do about finding someone in Kinrowan who'll talk with us."

"I don't really know anyone there," Jemi said.

Which made two of them, Johnny thought. But he just gave her another hug.

"That's okay," he said. "We'll find someone. We'll just ask around. We can look in the phone book under 'Kinrowan faerie, information.'"

"If only it could be so easy," Jemi said.

They reached the entrance to the hill then. As they went

inside, Johnny wondered, not for the first time that day, just exactly what he'd gotten himself into. The only thing he really knew, when he thought it all through, was that so long as Jemi was here, he'd stick it out. Maybe they were enchanted by two little bone carvings, or maybe they weren't, but he couldn't deny that he wanted to be with her, no matter how weird it got.

Jacky pinwheeled through the air.

Arms outspread, she spun and whirled like a winged sycamore seed. She expected to hit the front lawn of the Tower, for all that the whole of Kinrowan was spread out from the study's window, but instead found herself in a sort of free-fall where time had stepped out for a moment, leaving her in an endless spiral, eyes shut tight and her own scream for Kate still ringing in her ears.

Kate.

She opened her eyes, blinked back a blur of tearing, and looked for the threesome she'd spotted by the riverbank.

Kinrowan was still spread out below her, the Tower now a part of that panorama. She was turning slowly, falling but getting nowhere, above it all, stalled like a bird riding an updraft. She found the Tower, Windsor Park, and then—her eyesight sharp as an eagle's—focused on Kate and Finn and the tall woman with them. She tried to angle herself towards them, gasped at the sudden rush as she dropped like a stone.

This, she realized belatedly, was probably the wrong way to go about it.

She tried to pull up from the fall, but the long moments of timeless floating had been swallowed by the inevitable march of microseconds into seconds, seconds into minutes. Time sped on again; accelerated. There was no stopping the momentum of her fall now that it had begun again. All she could do was angle herself towards the river beside her friends, but for all the panicked flapping of her arms, she fell straight and sure in the wrong direction.

She was going to miss the river. She was going to land directly on top of Kate and the others.

She cried Kate's name again, this time in warning, saw her friend look around herself puzzledly, and then it was too late for Jacky to do anything but close her eyes and tense herself against the coming impact.

She knew it was the wrong thing to do. She should be concentrating on relaxing her muscles, but they were bunched so tight she couldn't even breathe, little say let up the knots of her tension.

It was dark by the time Henk reached the beach of flat stones where he'd found Johnny the previous night.

It was still early in the evening and he could hear the traffic on the nearby thoroughfares, but here in the park he felt entirely cut off from the city that surrounded him. He started at little noises, and had the feeling that he was being watched from all sides. It was patently ridiculous, of course, but Johnny had filled his head with those stories about goblins in the park, and all grown up and matured as he was, Henk found himself returning to a childhood fear.

He'd always been terrified of the dark.

It was something he'd had to work hard at to get rid of—this uncontrollable fear that there were bogeymen out in the shadows, just waiting to tear him apart. He'd grown up outside the city, in a rural area where, when night fell, it came like a black curtain. He used to have fights with his father about it back then. One night in particular he could call up with disturbing clarity. He'd forgotten to put the garbage out by the road that afternoon and, because the garbage collectors came at dawn, he'd had to go put it out in the dark.

It had been his own fault. He should have remembered. But he hadn't, and he couldn't face the walk down the lane to the road. Even with the light on by the garage, it was too much. Its light only went so far. Shadows pooled beyond its reach, thick on the route he had to take, and he just couldn't do it.

He was twelve years old. At that age he knew how stupid it was to feel like that. But the unreasoning fear wouldn't go away and he'd wept as his father made him go out and do it. By the time he got to the road, loaded down with the unwieldly pair of aluminum cans, he was sobbing uncontrollably.

The bogeyman hadn't gotten him that night, but the darkness had lodged itself inside him even deeper than before, so that years later he might be walking down a street at night and suddenly be hit by that same blind panicking fear.

Last night he'd been fine. He'd been worried about Johnny, looking for him, finding him. No problem. He hadn't even thought about it. But tonight. It was just too quiet. Too dark. And Johnny had been too serious about the things he said he'd seen.

All bullshit, of course.

But what if? Just *what if?*

People did disappear—*snap!* Just like that. Going out for some milk to the corner store and never coming back. Ordinary people, with no problems, no reason to drop everything in their lives and just take off. Vanished. Into the night.

So maybe a supernatural answer was unfounded. Sure, it was all bullshit anyway—right? But what about your plain, everyday psycho? Some serial killer, hiding in the bushes. In the shadows.

Christ, why did the darkness seem to be watching him?

Henk knew he was cursed with an overactive imagination. He just wished he could figure out how it got turned on, what kicked it in. That way he might be able to shut it off.

He stared across the river to the lights of the university. Mist was rising from the water again tonight—another too-cool night following a warm day. That was all it was. Nothing mysterious about it. Just the natural order of things. Like the darkness. The sun was on the other side of the planet, that was all. Nothing creepy about that. Nothing hiding in the shadows, waiting for him. . . .

He froze, staring at a clump of trees by the bicycle path.

He'd heard something. He was sure he'd heard something. He took a step forwards, determined to walk right up to the trees and get rid of this bad case of the nerves that was giving him the heebie-jeebies.

"Johnny," he called softly. "Is that you, man? Jemi?"

He took another step forwards and that was when a tall shadow detached itself from the darker bulk of trees and moved towards him. Henk stared at the figure, not willing to accept what he was seeing. It was a tall black woman with a horsey face, entirely nude, nightmares burning in her eyes.

Henk wanted to bolt, but he just couldn't move. He remembered Johnny describing this woman to him. She'd been with the crowd of faerie that had encircled Johnny last night. Right here. On this beach.

He shot terrified glances from the corners of his eyes,

looking for more of the creatures, but he and the woman were alone.

"I am weary to death of your kind," the woman said.

And then she changed.

There was a moment when her features seemed to melt into each other, when she became a swirl of shadow. The spin of the air made Henk dizzy and he stumbled back, slipped on a stone, and tumbled to the ground. When he looked up again, the woman was gone and a huge black horse was in her place.

It snorted, breath wreathing from its nostrils in the cooling air. Prancing in place, its hooves made a clatter against the stones. And then it reared up above him, forelegs cutting the air.

Henk scuttled out of the way of the dropping hooves, too panicked to even try to get to his feet. He just churned his arms and legs and moved like a crab across the stones.

The horse reared again.

All Henk could see was its eyes. That's what scared him the most. The horse's eyes were the same as the woman's had been. They were *her* eyes.

He didn't want to think about what that meant. But the part of him that had always succumbed to his childhood fears was chanting, *It's real, it's real, it's real. . . .*

The bogeyman had turned out to be a woman and she'd finally come to get him.

With the coming of twilight, Kate and the others buttoned the appropriate ribbons to their jackets and made ready to cross Windsor Park. She felt weird looking at her companions, knowing that she looked the same as they did.

Bogans were an unpleasant sort, and all of a kind. They had dark oily skin, wrinkled like old leather, and greasy yellow hair. Broad and squat, their wide heads sat on their shoulders without the benefit of necks. Their eyes were narrow, noses flat, and for clothing all they wore were animal skins tied around their waists. And they stank.

Kate wrinkled her nose at the smell that was a part of Finn's enchantment.

"Are we all ready?" Gwi asked.

Kate started to nod, but then she heard it.

At first it didn't register. When she realized it was her own name being called, she looked around, trying to find out where the sound was coming from—for it was Jacky's voice that she heard. And it wasn't coming from very far away.

"That's—" she began.

Before she could finish, there came a loud *fwhuft* of displacd air and a small familiar figure appeared in the middle of where they stood, tottered for a moment, then collapsed in a heap on the ground.

"It's Jacky!" Kate cried.

Jacky looked up at the sound of her name, but then she frantically began to sidle away from the trio.

"Gagh!" she mumbled. "Bogans."

Kate ran over to her, which only made Jacky increase her attempts to get away.

"It's okay, Jacky," Kate said. "It's us. We're just disguised."

Jacky studied her nervously, obviously puzzled by the sound of Kate's voice coming from the ugly mouth of a bogan. Then another sound came, this time from the direction of the Tower, and they all froze. It was an outraged roar—a howl that sent a shiver up their spines. Looking towards the Tower, they could see bogans and sluagh streaming out into the park.

"Quick!" Gwi cried. "Finn, get a button on the Jack's coat and give her your headband."

The forester had a voice that was obviously used to commanding—and to being obeyed. Before Finn could even question her orders, he found himself doing as she'd asked. He tore the button off his jacket and immediately began stitching it to Jacky's shirt. Gwi took off Finn's headband and fitted it to Jacky's head.

"No one speaks but me," she said.

"This won't work," Kate protested. "Finn won't be disguised."

"All Finn has to do is pretend he's frightened. We're three bogans and we've caught him for our supper."

"I won't have to pretend," Finn muttered as he tied off his thread. "It's good to see you, Jacky," he added as he attached the ribbon from her headband to the newly-attached button.

Her form wavered and a bogan's shape took its place. They were not a moment too soon. The nearest bogans had almost reached the lip of the riverbank where they were hiding.

"Oh, no, you don't!" Gwi cried.

Her voice was deep and very bogan-like—so much so that when she grabbed Finn, he struggled against her in earnest.

"You'll not get away from us so quick," Gwi went on. "Hot damn!"

Kate and Jacky exchanged glances, remembering the times they'd been in the clutches of bogans and it hadn't been "let's pretend."

Before either of them could speak, real bogans appeared at the top of the riverbank.

"Whatcha got there?" the foremost one demanded.

"Supper, arse-breath," Gwi replied. "Are you blind?"

"Give us a leg."

"Get spiked."

The bogan growled and was about to start down towards them when his companion grabbed his arm.

"The Jack's escaped," he told Gwi.

He glanced at Kate and Jacky. Kate put a fierce look on her face and almost grinned when the bogan took a half-step back. Now that Jacky was safe, so to speak, she thought, this could almost be fun.

"The boss won't like you snacking when there's work to be done," the second bogan added. "Put you in his bad books, he will."

"I can't read, so what do I care?" Gwi replied.

"Haw! That's rich. Can't read."

The bogan nudged his companion, but the first of the pair was still scowling and looking hungrily at Finn.

Gwi dragged Finn protectively closer. Pushing him to the ground, she put her foot on the hob's neck and glared at the bogans.

"Whatcha staring at, shithead?" she demanded.

Kate made a snorting sound and stepped nearer to Gwi.

The two bogans retreated. Among their kind, bravado ruled.

"Save us a bite," the first bogan said, trying to save some face.

"I'll save you his arse," Gwi told him.

"Haw!" The second bogan was having a good time. "That's richer. They'll save his arse for you, Groot."

Groot snarled. "Get your own arse in gear, Lunt. There's

work to do—the boss is waiting and you don't want that, hot damn."

They retreated from the lip of the rise and fared on. Kate was ready to collapse with laughter.

"We did it!" she cried. "Did you see their faces? I thought—"

"Whisht," Gwi said. "We must be gone and quick. Those bogans won't be gone long. They'll search awhile, but their stomachs will soon send them back here to see if they can't beg a piece of the hob from us. We've got to be gone by then."

"Where will we go?" Kate asked.

"My hollow's close," Finn offered.

Gwi considered that. "Too close."

"The Court?" Kate tried.

"That's no good either. We'll want to be free to move and they'll be watching the Court now. We might get in, but we'd never get out again unseen."

"*What* is going on?" Jacky asked. "Has everyone gone mad?"

"It's too long to tell you it all," Kate said. "But your gruagagh's not what you think he—"

"I know just the place!" Finn broke in.

"Where?" Gwi asked.

"Never you mind. What isn't spoken can't be overheard. Just follow me."

Gwi regarded him for a moment, then shrugged. "All right. But you two," she added to Kate and Jacky. "You keep those bogan shapes on until we're somewhere safe. That droichan will have your scents and it won't be more than a moment's work to track you down if you take off your disguises."

"Droichan?" Jacky asked.

"I'll explain it all to you later," Kate said.

"I feel like I've come in at the middle of a movie."

"You're not far off."

Finn had already set off and they all hurried along behind him—three bogans chasing a hob.

"I'm glad you're safe," Kate told Jacky between breaths. "We were just about to storm the Tower, looking for you. That's why we're wearing these disguises."

Jacky wrinkled her nose. "I hope Finn can stitch us something not so smelly when he's got a chance."

"There's gratitude."

"Thank you, thank you," Jacky replied. "Don't mind me—I'm just a little stunned from it all."

Kate glanced at her. "How *did* you pop in out of nowhere like that?"

"That's *my* long story that I'll tell you later."

They conserved their breath then to keep up with Finn and the forester. As she trotted along, Jacky went back over the last few moments after she'd jumped out of the window. It seemed that the gruagagh had inadvertently showed her yet another of the Tower's magics—one that made sense, too. If all of Kinrowan was in one's responsibility, one would want to be able to reach any part of it as quickly as possible in case of an emergency. By that reckoning, she wondered, there should also be a quick way back. So how did that work?

"Beam me up, Scotty," she muttered.

"What?" Kate asked.

Jacky shook her head. "I'm just thinking about teleportation," she said.

"Oh, is that all? I thought it was something more humdrum, like reliving old episodes of *Star Trek* in a moment of danger."

Jacky grinned. "It's good to see you again, too, Kate."

They slowed down once they were out of the park and a few blocks north of the Tower, but Gwi would let no one remove their disguise. She kept her own on as well.

"He'll be looking for you, too," Gwi said when Kate complained. "And besides, we don't have it so bad as Finn. He's got to both smell and look at us."

It was an hour or so later that Finn brought their roundabout journey to a halt in the shadows under the MacKenzie King Bridge. He knocked on the stone wall, a sharp *rap, rap, rap*.

"Who lives here?" Jacky asked.

"My friend Gump," Finn said.

As he spoke, Gump's bulk stepped out of the stones and peered down at them. Jacky and Kate took quick steps back until they were up against the railing by the canal.

"He's a trow," Finn added unnecessarily.

"Now, here's a strange sight," Gump boomed. "Dunrobin Finn in the company of three bogans."

"They're not what they seem," Finn said.

The trow nodded. "Nothing ever is." He waved to the

stones. "Come along inside. I know there's a tale behind what I see here, and I'd rather hear it in comfort than stand out here with the mist curling up at my toes."

Jacky and Kate regarded the stone wall with misgivings, but Finn waved them through. To their surprise, they didn't run smack up against the stones, but passed right through them. Finn and Gwi followed—Gwi removing her disguise—and Gump brought up the rear.

"I hope I can get the bogan smell out again," the trow muttered to himself.

Then he remembered that he was playing host. He put a smile on his face and led the way down the tunnel to the big hollowed-out room that was his home. Everything was oversized—the chairs around the big table, the hearth with its cookware hanging from its stone mantel, the worktable along one wall where Gump pursued his hobby of making mechanical birds, the bookcases which held hundreds of his creations as well as a small library of bird books, and his big four-poster bed.

"Who'd like tea?" he asked.

A chorus of yesses sent him to the water barrel. He lifted its lid, dipped in a kettle, and set it hanging above the coals in the hearth. Drops of water hissed and spat as they fell from the kettle. Kate and Jacky seated themselves on the edge of his bed. Gwi climbed onto a chair. Finn remained standing, looking up at his friend.

"This is very kind of you," Kate said.

"Mmmm," Gump replied.

He studied the pair of them on his bed and wrinkled his nose.

"If you're wearing those shapes as a means of disguising your essence as well as your looks," he said, "there's no need in here. A trow's home is always shielded against magic."

Kate undid her button and showed Jacky how to undo hers. Then she hopped off the bed and studied her face in the bottom of one of the trow's shiny pots.

"Thank God for that," she said. "I was beginning to feel the way I smelled."

"A marked improvement now," Gwi said with a smile.

"So what's the to-do?" Gump asked.

He looked at Finn, but the hob shrugged.

"There's more than one tale to tell before it's all untangled,"

Finn said. "I think Kate should start off, since she knows the most."

Oh, no, Kate thought.

She shot Jacky a quick glance. Now she'd have to tell Jacky about using the wally-stane. She touched Caraid in its bag at her side, gave Finn a withering look which he ignored, then started to tell what she knew.

Three times Henk managed to evade the kelpie's flashing hooves. He scuttled backwards over the stones, scraping his fingers, not caring, just trying to get out of the way. But now the river was at his back and there was no place left to go.

The mist wreathed around his legs as he slowly rose into a kneeling position. The kelpie moved towards him, hooves clacking on the stones. Henk could smell the sweat of his own fear, clinging to him. He'd gone all the way through and past his terror into a place where only resignation was left.

The kelpie rose on her hind legs.

This was it, Henk realized. There was no escape, not with the river at his back, the kelpie in front of him. He was too tired to even stand—adrenaline having stolen all his strength in his earlier moments of panic.

But before the hooves could strike, a voice called out.

The kelpie hesitated, forelegs slashing the air close enough to Henk's face that he could feel the air of their passing. She backed away, came down on all fours, then turned her head in the direction of the interruption, regaining human form as she did.

Henk stared numbly at the little man on his shaggy pony and couldn't feel a thing.

I don't want to be here, he thought, but he still couldn't move to take advantage of the distraction and escape.

"Why do you deny me his life?" the kelpie asked Henk's saviour.

Dohinney Tuir sighed. "Because it's not yours to take, Loireag. He's an innocent."

"He's a man," Loireag replied. "That used to be reason enough. And he's no innocent. He called the Pook's name—and that of her consort as well."

"You turned Jemi away from Kinrowan. If you killed this

man, you would do as great an injustice as the Pook would have done had she led us against the Court."

Loireag grimaced.

"I have to do something," she said finally. "Jenna's dead, Tuir. I can't just leave it at that."

"Now you know how Jemi feels—why she called the rade to go against the Court. Neither of you has the right of it."

"The man is on my shore," Loireag said. "He's prying about my haunts. It's my right to take him if I so choose."

"When your anger is directed against another—not him?"

"Don't, Tuir. Don't confuse me."

Henk listened and watched, still not moving. The woman was silent for a while now and the little man on the pony turned to him.

"This is a bad place for such as you," Tuir told him. "On a night like this—and for many a night to come, I'll warrant. Go. Now."

As though the hob's words were the catalyst to free him, Henk stumbled to his feet. He stared at the two figures, then, from his new vantage point, caught a metallic gleam by a tree nearby and knew it to be Johnny's bike. As he thought of his friend, his mind began to work once more.

"Johnny," he said. "Give me back my friend."

I don't believe I'm doing this, he thought. I'm talking to fairies in Vincent Massey Park, for Christ's sake. I'm going as bonkers as Johnny.

Except it was all real.

"We don't have him," the hob said.

"And we don't want him," Loireag added.

"But—"

"Go!" Tuir cried. "This is not your place, man. Tonight it belongs to us."

Henk fought down the impulse to argue any further. He edged his way around them to where Johnny's bike was chained to the tree. With fumbling fingers, he worked over the combination lock, loosened the chain, and wound it around the bike's seat post. The two faerie watched him, eyes not blinking, silent as statues.

Shivering, Henk got on the bike and turned it away from them. Fear cat-pawed up his spine as he turned his back on them. He aimed the bike in the direction of Billings Bridge and set off down the bike path. When he dared a quick glance back, the stony beach was empty.

He tried to fight down his fear, but it built up in him again and he pedaled for all he was worth until he reached the shopping mall near the bridge. Gasping with relief and lack of breath, he steered the bike into its lit parking lot. He was shaking as he chained the bike up to a lightpost and stuck his hands in his pockets as he entered the twenty-four-hour donut shop standing by itself across the parking lot from the plaza.

He ordered coffee and managed to take it to a stool by the window without spilling it. As he sipped, his nerves slowly grew less jangled. He stared out the window then, into the almost empty parking lot.

It was a Wednesday night. Sensible people were at home, watching TV, maybe reading a book, doing normal things— not tripping through a park looking for a friend who'd gotten himself kidnaped by goblins.

Faerie.

We don't have him, the little man had said.

Then who did?

And we don't want him, his nightmare had added.

But I still want him, Henk thought. Only I don't know how to get to him.

The kelpie had called Johnny the Pook's consort and what the hell did that mean? He took another sip of his coffee and continued to study the parking lot. He wanted to do something, but didn't know what. In the end, he just sat there, trying to convince himself that none of it had really happened, knowing all the while that it had.

After a while, he got a second cup of coffee, then a third, but by the time he'd finished them as well as some donuts, he was still no closer to an answer. At length he returned to the bike and started to pedal back to Johnny's apartment.

CHAPTER
12

His true name was Colorc Angadal and though he'd passed through Lochbuie once, it was not a place that he could call home.

There was no place he called home. A droichan could have no home. They stole their sustenance from the Moon and, sooner or later, if they remained in one place too long, the Moon would see that a price was paid. So the droichan took what they wanted, from here, from there, moving on before the local faerie grew aware of what it was that threatened them and banded against the enemy, or the Moon found some other method of payment.

It was heroes, usually, that the Moon called up. Sometimes skillyfolk, like a Pook. Sometimes it was a combination of the two and Colorc hated them the most: the Jacks. Too clever. Too brave. The Moon sained them too well, and filled them with luck in the bargain.

When Kinrowan's Jack disappeared through the third-floor window of her Tower, his anger at her kind burst forth in a long shrieking wail of rage. Then he regained control of himself, went downstairs, and sent them out—those of the Host who'd come under his banner in their twos and threes, eager to feed on the luck he gave them and always eager to bring chaos to Seelie folk. He sent them out to hunt that Jack—bogans and sluagh, little twig-thin gullywudes and toothy hags, trolls, and other Unseelie creatures. He sent as well the shadow from his own back that could take the dark shape of a kelpie and the winged shape of a crow, but mostly ran free as a black hound.

They would find her and bring her back. If not the Host, then surely his shadow, for his shadow had her scent.

He watched them go, then returned to that room on the third floor that stank of Bhruic Dearg's magic. The Jack had played him for a fool, but she'd had it right. The Gruagagh of Kinrowan had left a strong spell to protect his Tower and especially its heart—this room. He'd tied it to intent, no doubt of that, and there was no way that Colorc could hide his intent from its spell.

He frowned, walking about the room. He stood where the Jack had lifted a book from a worktable, but there was nothing for him to feel there. He looked out the window and saw only the street outside, not what the Jack had seen. Not what she had escaped to.

"Too clever by far," he muttered.

Both the Jack and he himself had been too clever, but she'd won out while he was left with only the ashes of her trick tasting dry in his mouth.

He had heard of Kinrowan, of its troubles and how this Jack had put an end to them. By luck, the tale went as it journeyed through the Middle Kingdom. Shining with luck was Kinrowan's Jack. And then he heard the rumour that Bhruic was gone, leaving this new Jack—lucky, yes, but largely untried—in his stead.

Colorc hated Bhruic. Colorc had known the Gruagagh before becoming a droichan; more than once in those early years Bhruic had stood against him. It was Bhruic that convinced Yaarn not to take him on as an apprentice. Bhruic who had kept him from the sea wisdoms that the merfolk had been willing to teach him. Bhruic who spoke against him in the owl's parliament.

"He has no compassion,'" was the Gruagagh's explanation for his persecution. "He has no heart."

No heart? If that was what they thought, then let it be true. And he turned to the forbidden knowledges of the droichan.

He kept a wide berth of Kinrowan, for he was unwilling to confront Bhruic Dearg until he was sure of his victory. But he'd kept an eye on the realm. And when he learned of

Bhruic's departure . . . It seemed befitting that he choose the faerie of Kinrowan as his next prey.

The risk to himself appeared minimal. Kinrowan no longer had a gruagagh. Its Court was small. Its Unseelie neighbors were recently defeated and in need of a leader. Its fiaina sidhe few in number. It had seemed perfect.

And at first, it had been so.

Colorc had begun—as he always did—by stealing the luck of the sidhe. The solitary faerie rarely banded together for anything but their rade so it was unlikely that they would rise against him in a group. All went well, until their Pook went in search of help. That he couldn't allow. He'd meant to play her out for as long as he could—the taste of her luck, even diminished from lack of a rade, was so tenderly sweet—but he had no wish for a Bucca in Kinrowan. A Bucca was worse than a Jack. And almost as bad as a gruagagh.

With the Pook dead, he'd meant to continue his slow assimilation of Kinrowan, but that was before luck—ill luck, he saw now, the Moon's sainly curse on him—had delivered the Jack and her friend into his hands. It had seemed so clever to threaten them with his shadow, and then "rescue" them. Oh, yes. The Moon had made that seem so simple. And then the Jack's own naive simplicity had let her invite him into her Tower.

But he'd been—

"Too clever by far," he repeated bitterly.

And too greedy.

It was greed that made it all go wrong. For first the Jack's companion escaped. Then the Jack herself. All because he'd reached for too much, all at once.

He tasted the ash of his defeat again. He had to be careful. The Moon's influence was strong in Kinrowan. With the widdershinning of his plans, he could well lose it all. His heart. Safely hidden, yes, but with the Jack loose . . .

He turned away from the window, shaking his head. No, that must never be. Better he cut his losses than risk that. If they found his heart . . . A droichan who died, died forever. There were no further turns on the wheel of life for them. No final rest in the Region of the Summer Stars.

He would give it a day, he decided. No more than two. If the Jack wasn't in his power again by then, he would move on.

There were other realms. Not so sweet as Kinrowan, perhaps.
Without such a perfect mix of the Courts and sainly borderfolk.
But they would do.

Power was sweet, but life was sweeter.

Closing the door to the third-floor study, he made his way
back downstairs to wait for word. From the Host, perhaps,
though it was more likely that his shadow would bring her
back.

Without fire, there was no light, the old saying went. But the
fire could leave ashes, too—a good thing to keep in mind, for
a Jack's luck burned like fire. It was good to remember the
ashes.

Dark-eyed, Colorc stared out into the night beyond the
kitchen windows and waited for his shadow to return. But
when it finally did return, it was to bring him word that the
Pook was abroad in Kinrowan once more.

Colorc ran his fingers through his hair and frowned. That
could not be. He had stood over his body herself, drunk the
final flicker of her fire from her death. But the image that his
shadow gave him was of the Pook's face, dark with sorrow and
anger, walking the streets of Kinrowan.

For a long moment the droichan stared out into the night
beyond the kitchen's windows. Then he arose and, drawing his
shadow close to him like a cloak, he went out into the night
himself.

CHAPTER
13

Jemi Pook, Johnny discovered, was very easy to argue with. She insisted on going alone into Kinrowan, arguing that what she was looking for would be easier to find by herself. She had sidhe blood, after all; he didn't. She knew Kinrowan and its faerie, by sight at least, if not to speak to; he didn't. It was her sister who had died; not his. It was her responsibility; not his.

"I just want to help," Johnny said.

"I know. And you can help right now by letting me do this on my own. I'm not helpless, Johnny." Her expression softened. "It's better this way," she added. "I can go places that you can't. The faerie will at least talk to me. If they see you with me, they'll only hide. You see that, don't you?"

"All I can see is that something out there killed your sister and if you go chasing after it, it'll probably get you as well."

"I'll be careful."

Like Jenna was careful? Johnny wanted to say, but it was unnecessary. The question hung between them, unspoken.

"I'll go as far as your apartment with you," Jemi said. "Will you wait for me there?"

"It'll be hard—just waiting."

"I know. But I will need your help later, Johnny. Once I have a name. I'm not trying to shut you out of my life. We've only just met and I want to know you better. I want to see if the Bucca's bone carvings know what they're doing."

The look she gave him was pure warmth. It melted away

Johnny's reservations. The thought of enchantment, of being ensnared in a glamour, crossed his mind, then dissolved and was gone. He didn't care if it was magic that had brought them together. This Bucca, whoever he was, could work all the magics he wanted. What Johnny wanted to do was follow through on the promise he saw in Jemi's eyes, because he'd never before experienced anything like what he was feeling now.

"I'll wait for you," he said.

"I wasn't sure you would," Jemi said, "but I'm glad you will. Things have got to get better."

But the warmth was fading from her eyes and the pain was back again. She touched his cheek with the back of her hand, then stood. Johnny fetched his fiddle case and they went out into the night.

They didn't speak much on the walk up to Johnny's apartment. At the corner of Bank and Third Avenue, they paused.

"Wish me luck," Jemi said.

Her voice was small, almost plaintive, but Johnny didn't start the argument up again.

"Luck," he said.

A quick fierce grin came and went across her features. Johnny could see the strain of her sorrow, the dark feral light of her anger in her eyes.

It had to be her sidhe blood, he thought. That was what made her so mercurial.

She leaned close for a moment and tilted her head. When Johnny kissed her, she nipped his lower lip, then stepped quickly back. Without another word, she turned and headed up Bank Street.

Johnny rubbed his lip and watched her go until she reached Second Avenue. Sighing then, he turned down his own street. He didn't see the light on in his apartment until he was right on the porch.

As Jemi walked on alone, it all came back to her. She saw the Bucca's face—broad and dirt-brown, lined like the patterning luck of moonroads; the dark curly hair; the small eyes, darker still, but golden like honey as well.

Salamon Brien.

He was a fat-cheeked, stout old man no taller than her own shoulder, always dressed in a motley array of Gypsy colours, with a rattling necklace of bone ornaments around his neck, and in each earlobe a gold ring—the gold so pure it looked brassy. He'd left the borderlands near Kinrowan years ago. And Jenna had gone looking for him. To renew the rade.

She thought of the rade, of all those times—late afternoons crisp with autumn, nights dark with summer's mystery—listening to the Bucca talk of the moonroads and the rade, of the patterns in both and the luck they gave to the fiaina sidhe. He was teaching Jenna, but Jemi had listened to it all, feigning indifference, far more interested in the speckles on this mushroom than in what he said. Pretending to watch that bat flit, but her head was cocked near to hear it all.

The pattern of the rade rose in her mind's eye. She saw Salamon walking it, a crow with white-speckled wings perched on his shoulder, Jenna pacing at his side, silently mouthing what the Bucca told her so that she'd remember, and then there was her own younger self, straggling along behind them, hair as pink then as it was today. What Jenna studiously repeated to remember, Jemi could repeat word for word without needing to think about it. But Jenna was the elder and she had no mortal blood, and Jemi wasn't interested in any of it anyway. But now . . .

Now it was all in her lap.

The memories washed through her, impossible to avoid. Her eyes misted with tears. The Bucca long gone. Jenna dead.

She steered her steps away from the Court of Kinrowan where she had been going and turned instead towards her own apartment in Sandy Hill.

Click, clack.

She could recall the rattle of the Bucca's necklace so well.

Click, clack.

Little bone ornaments carved into the shapes of instruments and animals and trees, buildings and faerie and even mortals. He told stories about them. A gnarled brown hand would reach up to stroke a tiny badger and he would tell a tale of mischief and tricks that made everyone laugh until their stomachs ached.

Click, clack.

"A tale in each one," he'd said once. "And more tales when one touches another. And more again. And still more."

He stroked one perfectly carved ornament after the other, the creamy bone gleaming under the touch of his fingers. He would never say who made them or where he'd gotten them, only that there were tales in them. Tales of times past. Tales of days to come. Every kind of story.

Jenna wished he was here now. She wished that he would touch a carving and turn back the Moon until Jenna arose from under her cairn and was back in the world to argue with her again.

How often had they argued? A dozen times a day? A hundred? They couldn't agree about one thing, except they never fought. They weren't that sort of arguments.

"You're too much the same," Salamon told them once. "You argue with yourself."

But they weren't the same. Not anymore.

Jenna was dead.

Jemi had reached the front walk of her building. She wiped her eyes on the sleeve of her piper's jacket, wished for a Kleenex, but didn't have one. Sniffling, she dug about in her pocket for her key and went inside, up the stairs. She opened the door to her room and the air seemed stale inside. Dry. Like a crypt. A room where no one had been for decades.

But Johnny had been here.

She crossed to her dresser and lifted her little bone flute from where it hung.

Click, clack.

It had rattled against the Bucca's other ornaments once. She slipped it around her neck and tucked it under her shirt, then she stared at her reflection in the mirror.

They'd been too much the same, the Bucca said.

Jenna had talked to Jemi about her worries, about how the rade was disturbed time and again. But she hadn't spoken of any danger. She hadn't said she was going to look for Salamon. Where would she even begin to look? Had she known all along where he'd wandered off to?

Too much the same, and not the same at all.

She heard the floor creak in the hallway and turned quickly, adrenaline pumping through her, but it was only her next-door neighbour, Annie Hamilton. She tried to still the frenzied beating of her heart.

"Hi," Annie said. "There were a couple of guys here

looking for you today. I think maybe they broke into your room. Is there anything missing?"

"No."

Jenna's features flashed through her mind and she bit at her lip.

"It . . . it's okay," she told her neighbour. "They were friends."

Annie shifted her bulk and the floorboards creaked again.

"You don't look so good," she said. "Are you sure you're okay?"

Jemi nodded.

"Greg was by as well—around suppertime. He wants you to call him."

Greg. AKT.

Jemi remembered that there had been a rehearsal this afternoon. The memory came to her as though it belonged to someone else. It came from an entirely different world.

"I have to go," she said suddenly.

She flicked off the light in her room and shut the door. Annie looked at her with a worried expression, but there was nothing Jemi could say to her. They weren't really friends. A talk or two on the porch, or late at night in the kitchen after a gig. That was about it.

"Jemi . . ."

Before Annie could finish, Jemi bolted for the stairs. She ignored Annie's voice, calling her name after her, just took the stairs three at a time and ran outside, up the street, ran until she reached the brighter lights on Rideau Street, then leaned against a building to catch her breath. Her hand went to touch her flute pendant through the fabric of her shirt.

What's wrong with me? she asked herself.

But all it took was Jenna's face to rise up in her mind, and she knew. It was the pattern of the rade, incomplete. It was the luck lying broken on a moonroad, looking like a scatter of bone ornaments, a broken necklace, or like a stout, brown-skinned Bucca sprawled there in the dirt—

No!

She looked around herself, really frightened now.

All this time, she thought, and I never offered to help. Jenna's problems, the rade . . . Why didn't I do something?

Why wasn't I there? Jenna wouldn't have had to go looking for Salamon. She wouldn't have had to die.

The bright lights hurt her eyes, which were misty with tears again. She turned away from Rideau, back to the darker streets of Sandy Hill, trying to keep to the shadows, but the streetlights, though not so numerous as those she'd left behind, were still bright. Her eyes stung now, the tears fell freely. Her head was awash with memories that were all tied together with a moon-bright ribbon that was the pattern of the rade.

And something else. A presence that spoke to her from the shadows. A whispering sound. Beckoning, calling to her. . . .

She'd always preferred the loud sounds, music in bars, the bright lights, friends laughing, dancing, blowing her sax, and now she wanted only darkness and quiet. But it wasn't to be found. The city surrounded her. The lit windows of the houses were like eyes peering into her soul. The whole night seemed to be watching her. She sensed a malevolence loose in the darkness, and once again she started to run.

When she finally stopped, she was in amongst the buildings of Ottawa University. It wasn't so bright here, though her sidhe sight pierced the darkness as though it were merely twilight. It was quieter as well, but her head rang with an odd warning buzz. And then she realized what it was that she felt, what it was that was out in the night, loose and haunting—hunting—her.

It was the very thing she'd sought.

She turned slowly, pin prickles starting at the nape of her neck and scraping down her spine. The black dog regarded her from across an empty expanse of lawn. It was half-hidden in the shadows of a building, but she could see its gleaming eyes and black shiny fur, smell its strong odour, hear the rasp of its breathing. Behind it stood a silent figure in a brown cloak, its features hidden in the fall of its hood.

Now she knew why she'd really gone on alone. She couldn't have been brave enough for both Johnny and herself. She wasn't even brave enough for herself.

"The same," the figure in brown said softly, echoing her own earlier thoughts, "yet not. Who would have thought that there would be two of you?"

She wanted to throw herself at him, claw at his eyes, tear out the throat that voiced those words so calmly, but for once common sense got the better of her temper. As the dog rose from its haunches, she turned and, with fiaina skill, began to scale the side of the building, her small hands finding finger-holds in the stonework where a mortal would never even look. She could sense the dog coming for her—as it had come for her sister—but she didn't look down, not until she reached the roof.

The man in his brown cloak stood below, looking up. His dog—which seemed to be more ape-like now than canine—was climbing after her.

Now she knew what she faced.

The man was a gruagagh and the thing he had sent after her was his shadow. She couldn't match that kind of magic. She was just a Pook, a halfling at that.

She stared down at the creature, searching through the wash of her memories for something that the Bucca might have said about dealing with this kind of a creature, but her mind just went blank.

"You're not mad, are you?" Kate asked.

Jacky tried to put what she called her "Squint Eastwood tough gal" look on her face, but all it did was squinch up her features and make her look silly, so she gave it up. And looking at Kate sitting beside her on Gump's bed, the leather-bound Caraid on her lap and the worried look in her eyes, Jacky didn't have the heart to tease her.

"No," she said. "It's something we should have done a long time ago. But you know me—I'm such a pack rat. I always want to hoard everything for that someday when it's going to be needed, but in the end, nothing ever gets used at all." She put out a hand to touch the book. "It really makes you stop and think, doesn't it? All this magic. I wonder what makes it work."

"There's a piece of Bhruic in those pages," Finn remarked from beside the hearth.

He and Gwi were sharing cushions there, while the big trow sat in his chair. He was the only one who fit the furniture.

"The books replies as Bhruic spoke," Finn added.

A wistful look came into Jacky's eyes. "I wonder where he is now."

"With the Summer Stars," Finn said. "Or maybe not. He's traveling with Kerevan, after all. They could be anywhere— walking on the Moon, or deep in an Otherworld of the manitou."

"I'd like to go to one of them someday," Jacky said. "I'd like to meet the native spirits—the ones that were here before any of us came."

"They're skinwalkers, most of them," the hob said. "And Arn's luck touches them in other ways than it does us. She takes shapes for them and walks the world in different guises to teach and talk with them."

"Totems," Kate said. "That's what you're talking about. But I don't see Bhruic needing a totem."

Finn smiled. "I suppose not. But I don't doubt he'd like to talk to them all the same."

"I'd like to see *him* again," Jacky said.

Gump cleared his throat. "Better you were worrying about the gruagagh that's here—not the one that's gone. Time enough for Bhruic after. If there is an after."

Jacky's warm, thoughtful mood slipped away at the trow's words.

"How can we do *anything* about him?" she asked. "He could have hidden his heart anywhere. There's no way we can find it."

Gwi stirred beside Finn. "We don't even know his name," she added. "We can't kill him with weapons, and we can't kill him with spells."

Jacky nodded, remembering her knife sticking from the droichan's chest and the way he had just plucked it out again. There was nothing inside him, she decided. Just shadows, like the bit of himself that he let loose to do his killing for him.

"Maybe we're going about it all wrong," Kate said. "Caraid told us that we have to know him before we'll find the heart. What we should be doing is backtracking him—find out where he came from, that sort of thing."

"A good point," Gump said, "but we don't have his name, so how could we do that?"

"I don't know."

Kate frowned, idly flipping Caraid's pages. She looked up suddenly.

"He can't have come from nowhere," she said. "And

wherever he's been before—he'd have done the same thing there, wouldn't he? Can't we contact other Courts and find out if they've had this kind of trouble?"

"There would be nothing left of a Court for us to contact," Gwi said. "Not if he'd been there first."

"But what about their neighbours? Wouldn't they know something?"

"The idea has merit," Gump said. "We could put out the word, through all of Faerie. Someone will have to remember hearing of a similar situation in the past year or so. A Court suddenly barren of its folk, perhaps. A cairn emptied of its luck. A crossing of moonroads no longer so hale. . . ."

"It will take time," Gwi said. "Time that we don't have."

"But most of the Courts are in Ballymoresk," Finn said. "For the Fair."

Gump grinned. "Then what better place to ask? Who will go?"

"Wait a minute," Kate said. "You said something about a place where moonroads cross each other not being so healthy anymore?" When Gump nodded, Kate turned to Jacky. "Remember the night Mull came to the Tower to get us?"

"We were looking at that house!" Jacky cried.

"That's where he was," Kate said.

At their companions' blank looks, Kate explained what they'd seen.

"That also bears looking into," Gump said.

"But we can't ignore asking the other Courts," Gwi said. "I'll go to the Fair and get Deegan to ask the other Lairds and Ladies, but I'll need a swift mount for the ride."

Deegan was the Laird of Kinrowan.

"Hay will lend you one of the Laird's own mounts," Finn said. "I'll speak to him myself. You'll ride down in style, Gwi, and have the sons of Lairds falling over themselves to get to know you."

The forester harumphed. "Not with my blood," she said, but she smiled.

"And I'll go spy out this house," Gump said.

"You'll need someone to guide you," Jacky said.

Gump nodded. "That's true—but it can't be you. I can still hear the cries of Cumin's folk hunting you beyond the safety of these walls."

"I'll show you where it is," Kate said.

"That will be good. It's always better to have a skillywoman at your side when you go to spy on a gruagagh."

Kate laughed uneasily.

"I wouldn't put too much stock in any magics you think I've got," she said. "About as magic as I get is making tea without burning the water."

The trow hooted—a big, booming sound. "Oh, that's rich! Well, I'll take the chance. If you can't spell him, Kate, perhaps you can quip the information from him. Now, come on. We don't have much time. My sort of folk don't take to the sun, and the dawn's far closer than I'd like."

Jacky looked uncertainly about herself as there was a sudden rush of everyone getting ready to go.

"I won't be long," Finn told her. "Just up to the Court to get a mount for Gwi, then I'll be back."

Kate gave her a big hug.

"Don't do anything silly like stepping outside for some fresh air," she said. "I couldn't bear for the droichan to get his claws on you again."

"Not to mention that he might find some way to force you to break Bhruic's enchantment on the Tower," Gwi added.

"I'll be fine," Jacky said. "You're the guys who are going out there, not me."

There was some more bustling about, then a few moments later they were all gone. Jacky closed the door to the trow's home and walked slowly back to the bed. She poked at the side of it a few times, then wandered over to the hearth, where she slumped down on a pillow.

"Great," she muttered. "This is just great. Some Jack I've turned out to be. The first time something goes wrong and the most I can do about it is to hole up in some trow's place and let everyone else do my job for me. Lovely. Wouldn't Bhruic be proud of me now?"

The worst thing was that it was all her fault. She'd invited Cumin into the Tower in the first place. A real Jack would have sniffed him out for what he was right away. Bhruic would have sent him packing, quick as a blink. But *she'd* asked him home for tea.

She caught her own reflection in the shiny bottom of one of Gump's pots hanging from the hearth above her and frowned at it. Getting up, she trailed about the big room, not really looking at anything, just berating herself.

She should have sent Cumin packing. But he'd seemed important and she'd been flattered that he paid attention to her. And that was the problem—part of a bigger problem that kept screwing up her life. After years of being a relative nobody, becoming a Jack had finally put her in a position where she was somebody, never mind that it was all irrelevant, that in her heart she truly believed that people were important for who they were, how they acted, not for their position in life. Wasn't that what kept getting in the way of her relationship with Eilian? Did she care about him because of who he was, or because he was a Laird's son who happened to love her?

It was all so confusing. Things had to change. It was high time she got it all straightened out in her mind. She was going to have to do something better with her life. Buckle down with Kate and learn everything there was to learn in Bhruic's study, make her own Caraid, find an honest gruagagh to teach her more, or maybe go to a Billy Blind like the one in Eilian's Court.

Eilian.

She had to work out what they were going to do with their relationship.

Oh, yes. Things were going to be different. She was going to become responsible if it killed her.

She paused by the bed—having paced by it at least twenty times already—and picked up the curiously ribboned headgear that Finn had given her. She'd get Finn to teach her his skilly stitcheries as well, to learn how to make disguises like this where no one could recognize you. . . .

Her train of thought trailed off as she lifted the headband from the bed. Of course. With this, Cumin wouldn't be able to spot her. And neither would any of the Unseelie Court that had rallied around the droichan. She could just waltz into the Tower wearing it, grab the wally-stanes, and be useful for a change. Maybe she could wish up a magic mirror or something that would show them where the droichan's heart was hidden.

She put the headgear on, buttoned the appropriate ribbon to her shirt, then studied herself in another of Gump's pans. She didn't make a very fierce-looking bogan, but that didn't matter. She still looked like a bogan and *that* was what mattered.

Don't do this.

A voice of reason spoke up in the back of her head.

Be sensible for once.

She shook her head. I'm being *responsible* for once, she told it. I'm cleaning up my own mess.

But the voice inside her continued to argue. It told her that she was safe here. That she'd promised the others she'd stay. That even with her disguise, she wouldn't necessarily be hidden from the droichan. Not when he had her scent.

Except he's looking for Kate, too, she argued back, and Kate's disguise isn't any different from mine. If it's safe for her, then it'll be safe for me.

The voice seemed to have run out of arguments, because it stayed silent now.

I *won't* screw up this time, Jacky promised.

Finding some paper and a stub of a pencil, she left a quick note for Kate and the others. She didn't say anything in it about trying to regain some pride in herself, about wanting to fulfill responsibilities that were hers and alleviating the feeling that she was a half-wit for fouling everything up in the first place. It simply said:

Dear Kate,

I can't sit around doing nothing, so I'm going back to the Tower to get the wally-stanes. Don't worry. I'm being smart this time and wearing the bogan disguise that Finn gave me. No one'll even know me. I'll be a walking, talking "purloined letter" and very, very careful.

Love, J.

She put it on the table where it was sure to be noticed and left the room through the trow's tunnel.

Getting into the Tower was going to be the only problem, she decided as she followed the canal south to where it stood. Once she was in the study, it would just be a moment's work to grab the wally-stanes and jump through the window, landing right on Gump's front porch, as it were. But the getting in . . .

Worry about that when you get there, she told herself.

* * *

It just never stops, Johnny thought. As he sat listening to what had happened to Henk earlier tonight, he wasn't sure if he was glad that somebody else—somebody normal—was experiencing the same strangeness that he was, or if it just made things worse.

"I was never so scared in all my life," Henk finished. "Johnny, just what the hell's going on?"

Johnny didn't know what to say.

"I was sitting there in the donut shop," Henk went on, "and I just couldn't leave. I must've been there for over an hour, Johnny, just staring out at the parking lot, waiting to see more of them. To see if they were still out there. Waiting for me."

"But you made it back," Johnny said.

Henk nodded. "Yeah. I was on my third coffee, I guess, when it all just went away. Like someone had turned off a switch in my head. I got on your bike—"

"My bike. I'd forgotten about it."

"Well, it's back here, safe and sound. Just like us. Except I got the shakes again, waiting for you. . . ."

Henk took a sip from his coffee. His hand shook and the cup rattled on the table, slopping coffee over the side.

"Christ," he said. "Look at me. I'm a wreck. You know what's doing this to me—what's *really* doing it to me?"

Johnny shook his head.

"Knowing that all that stuff I was scared of when I was a kid—all those bogeymen—they're all real. I don't want to sound like a pussie, Johnny, but I had a rough time with that kind of a thing when I was a kid. It took me a long time to convince myself that that kind of thing just couldn't be real. And now look what happens."

Neither spoke for a while. Johnny got up and poured them both another coffee and then told Henk about his own night. He spoke in a quiet voice and, for all that what he was saying was only more fuel for Henk's fears, by the time Johnny got to the end of his story, Henk was more like his old self again.

"I just can't figure out why Loireag attacked you," Johnny said.

"She was pissed, Johnny. And with what you've told me, now I know why."

"I suppose."

"You'd better watch out with Jemi," Henk warned. "That's all I can say. She may look human—a lot of them do, if you believe all the stories—but they're still not like us. They're volatile. Christ, they're just plain dangerous."

"I don't know," Johnny said. "There's something special about her—not because she's what she is, either. I mean, not because it's like she stepped out of some storybook. There's just something that sparks inside me every time I'm with her—that kind of special. Like we were meant for each other. Something binds us together."

"Right. Two bone carvings from some other weirdo's necklace. Come on, Johnny. It's not right."

"You don't know—"

"You're right. I don't. But just tell me this: What does Jemi turn into? Can you tell me that? What kind of thing does she become? Another horse? A wolf, maybe? Some kind of slime monster out of a B-movie?" Henk shook his head. "Jesus. Maybe it's better that we don't know. . . ."

Johnny stared at him. There was nothing he could say. He didn't know either. He just knew the bond was there and, enchantment or not, he wanted it to be there.

"Do you mind if I crash here again?" Henk asked. "I don't think I can get it together to, you know . . . get myself home."

"No problem," Johnny said. "You can take . . ." He swallowed hard. "You can take Tom's old room."

He waited until Henk had left the room, then slowly got up and walked out onto his porch.

Tom. That's where it had all started. With Tom's bone carving and that talk about "The King of the Faeries" and where to play it. But with all that had happened, his grandfather had been pushed out of his mind, only returning now on the heels of that simple phrase. And with it, the sorrow returned as well.

Johnny sat down on the steps. His eyes were dry, but tears welled up behind them. His chest was tight.

Why did you leave me, Tom? he asked the night.

The street was still. Above the haze cast by the streetlights, he could see a speckle of stars, not nearly so bright and close as they were in Puxill. He wondered where his grandfather was—if faerie were real, then what about God and angels, heaven and hell? Or maybe, because of his music, he was hanging out in some Celtic afterworld, putting back a pint with Yeats and the lads, playing his fiddle.

And what part had Tom played in all of this? Had Jenna wanted Tom to lead the rade, so long ago, and Tom had turned her down? Had the needed spark between them just not been here, or was it all really enchantment and Tom had just been stronger than Johnny knew himself to be? Because whatever Tom had done, Johnny knew he couldn't resist the spell himself.

He wished Tom was here to talk to him now. They'd always talked things out, problems either of them had, problems they saw around them, just talking sometimes, sometimes not saying anything at all and communicating more in those silences than in all the words that had ever existed.

It wasn't what Tom had left him that was so important, as why he'd left him. Why did he have to be taken away? Why did he have to die?

The tears welled up in earnest now and filled his eyes. Then he looked out at the street and saw it all through a shiny sheen. He should never have let Tom talk him into letting him go into the old folks' place. He should just have kept Tom here, at home, where he belonged. Not in the hands of strangers, no matter how better qualified they were. Maybe if Tom had stayed here he wouldn't have died. Maybe. . . .

Johnny pressed his face against his knees and his tears wet his jeans. He never heard the scuffle of bare feet on the pavement, not the sound of breathing close by his ear. He started violently when a small hand touched his arm and a raspy voice broke the stillness.

"Why are you so sad?"

He was half off the porch and stumbling onto the lawn before he realized that it was Jemi's little wolfish friend who was crouched furry and naked on his porch. Mactire regarded him worriedly, Jemi's name forming on his lips, but no sound issuing forth.

Johnny took a deep steadying breath.

"No," he said. "She's all right. At least I think she is. She went off to talk to Kinrowan's faerie, but I don't know where she'd be looking for them."

Mactire frowned. "Its a bad night for faerie—Court folk and

sidhe alike. There's a darkness riding the wind that has nothing to do with a lack of light."

"Yeah," Johnny said. "I know."

He returned to sit on the steps, wiping at his eyes with the sleeve of his shirt.

"Why are you here?" he asked Mactire.

The wild boy shrugged. "I felt . . . bad. Running away with the others, instead of staying with you and Jemi. I was going to where she lives in the city, but remembered that this place was closer. I thought she might be here with you. I suppose I'll go look for her at her own home now."

"She won't be there," Johnny said. "She's gone off to do what everybody wanted her to do: find the name of whatever it was that killed her sister."

"It's not just her sister," Mactire said. "It's the rade, too. The luck's all gone."

"I know," Johnny said. "But it's because of her sister that Jemi's gone. It . . . it's not easy losing someone you love."

Mactire nodded. "He was a good man, Tom. We all knew him, you know."

"What did he do with you people? How did he get involved?"

"He played tunes for us. Not rade tunes, not luck music, but skilly tunes all the same. We'd dance to his fiddling, Johnny Faw."

"And Jenna?"

"There wasn't the light in her eyes when she looked at him as there is in Jemi's when she looks at you. But Tom—a long time ago, he led the rade. It was only once or twice, and as good a Fiddle Wit you'd be hard put to find, but it wasn't for him. He went away for a while, and when he came back, he'd only play for fun, not for the luck."

Johnny sighed. "I still miss him."

"He's not gone until you forget him," Mactire said. "So long as you remember him and love those memories, a part of him will still be alive."

"Words," Johnny muttered. "That's just words. Something you say to make someone feel better. But it doesn't fill the emptiness inside."

"Maybe you just need to catch hold of some more memories until you do fill that empty place."

"I suppose." Johnny glanced at the wolf boy. "Do you want a drink or something to eat?"

Mactire shook his head. "But a tune would be good. One of Tom's. Do you know the one he called 'The Month of May'?"

"Sure."

They went inside and after some hesitating stops and starts, Johnny played a few tunes for his sidhe guest. It did help to ease the emptiness a bit, but then he just found himself worrying about Jemi instead. It was getting so late. Where could she be, was she all right, would she come back?

It never stops, he thought for the second time that night. Tom was gone, his own life all changed, and Jemi . . .

Looking into Mactire's eyes, he saw the same question there that worried at his own mind.

Jemi.

Out there in the night.

Alone.

As her sister had been.

He set fiddle and bow aside and the two of them sat in the ensuing quiet, wondering where she could be.

CHAPTER
14

Jemi Pook was in the Ottawa University campus, on the roof of Tabaret Hall, standing near its domed skylight. She watched the black dog shape of the gruagagh's shadow approach her. The university was quiet all around her.

North stood Academic Hall, dark and still. Behind her, to the west, were red-bricked buildings, and then Nicholas Street, not one car moving on any of its lanes. South were the two grey-bricked buildings that housed the Linguistics Department. East was the broad lawn of the Hall, dotted with red-leafed maples. The gruagagh was down there, out of sight now as he'd moved from the lawn to stand by the fat round pillars at the front of the Hall. She couldn't see him, but he watched her through the dark eyes of his shadow.

The dog, now that it had her trapped, didn't appear too eager to attack her. Maybe the gruagagh was just being cautious, maybe he thought she was just like Jenna. How could he know that with her half-blood, she had only half her sister's strengths? She was fast, but not quicksilver as Jenna had been. Strong, but not as strong either. She knew a few spells, but nothing like those Jenna had known. The beast would have had to take her unawares, or Jenna would have escaped it.

Or maybe the gruagagh wanted to know where Jemi fit in. Knowledge was a powerful weapon. He'd been surprised by her existence. Perhaps he hoped to ransack her mind and spare himself more surprises.

The initial numbness clouding her mind had worn away, but she still couldn't think of what to do. She had nothing with her that she could use for a spell—only the Bucca's flute carving, and that was a different sort of charm. The small bag holding her pipe hung from one shoulder, but this wasn't a moment for skilly music. If she played the right tune, she might be able to call up some luck, or sidhe, but she doubted that she'd get the chance to free the pipe from its bag, little say play the first few notes she'd need. All her purse had was her makeup, some money and ID, her compact. . . .

Gaze fixed on the beast, she reached into her purse. The dog growled and took a step forward, then paused when it saw that all she took out was her compact. Without seeing him, she knew that the gruagagh was only moments from reaching the roof himself. That was why his creature kept her at bay—it was waiting for him. So she only had moments in which to work.

She didn't think for a moment that she could deal with the gruagagh himself—that needed a level of magery that she couldn't hope to match. But a trick, played on a gruagagh's shadow, that wasn't beyond the capabilities of a halfling Pook like herself.

She flipped open the compact and thrust the mirror towards the dog. Whether it looked with its own gaze as well as that of the gruagagh, or if it was only the gruagagh's gaze that was upon her, wouldn't matter. She whispered a brief phrase in an old tongue.

"*Gaoth an iar liom a comhnadh.*" Wind from the west, protect me.

She moved the mirror sun-wise in a quick circle, then spat at it and threw it at the dog.

It was only the smallest of spells. A charm, really. A call to the west wind who opened the doors between flesh and spirit. A deasil turn of the mirror to wake it and make it ready. Her saliva, a gift from her body.

The west wind touched her briefly. The mirror took her saliva and made of itself an image so that the dog saw Jemi attacking. It snarled, lunging up from the ground to confront the image, while Jemi bolted in the other direction. She counted the seconds as she ran.

One thousand and one, one thousand and two.

She reached the far side of the roof and swung herself over.

One thousand and three, one thousand and four.

Fingers and toes found the tiniest of perches as she went down the wall, moving like a spider, limbs outstretched.

One thousand and five, one thousand and six.

The black dog howled. It had seen through the mirror-charm. She tried to go faster, but even sidhe had their limits in such a situation. Especially halflings.

One thousand and seven, one thousand and eight.

She was past the halfway mark now, but there came a sound from the roof. Daring a glance up, she saw the gruagagh leaning over the side, looking down at her. The black dog hung like an aura about his head and shoulders. She continued her descent.

One thousand and nine, one thousand and ten.

As the gruagagh loosed the dog and tossed it down towards her, Jemi let herself drop.

It was some fifteen feet to the ground. Turf absorbed some of the impact, her bent knees some more, but it still jarred her enough to rattle her bones. Cat-like the sidhe could be, but she was out of shape.

She dared another glance up, saw the gruagagh's shadow dropping towards her, riding the air with wide bat wings, then she took off, running for all she was worth. She zigged and zagged her way across Nicholas Street, heading across it to where the land dipped towards the Rideau Canal, every sense strained to gauge the position of the creature. When she sensed it dropping towards her—a shift in the air currents warned her, an almost inaudible whisper of its shadowy wings—she threw herself to one side.

The creature swooped down to where she'd been, then angled back up once more. By then Jemi was on the grass verge at the far side of the street, coming out of a roll to slip and slide down the sharp incline towards the canal. The creature dove at her again, but she moved too quickly and it missed, rising up on its vast wings for a second time. Without hesitating, Jemi threw herself into the chilly waters of the canal and began to swim across.

Above her the creature seemed to come apart in the night air. It became one, three, a dozen airborne creatures, all swooping down at her. Jemi dove deep, still stroking strongly for the other side. When she came up for air, she half-expected to find that the gruagagh had given his shadow aquatic shapes, but the bat creatures were still in the air above her. They hovered in place with great sweeps of their wings, their attention no longer upon her as they gazed south.

Reaching the far side of the canal, Jemi hauled herself out of the water, teeth chattering. She wrinkled her nose at the smell of her wet clothes. The water of the canal wasn't exactly known for its purity. She reeked of algae and stagnant water. Getting to her feet, she looked up once more. The flock of bat creatures had become one again, its attention upon her, its voice ringing in her mind.

It seems that Bhruic's pet has returned to her lair, the creature said. *But don't fret, my ghostly Pook. There will be time for you later.*

Without another word, it bent its wings against the air and flew silently south.

Jemi leaned weakly against the metal rail that ran along the length of the canal and watched the creature go. She was safe. For now. But what had the gruagagh meant? Bhruic's pet. . . . And then she knew.

It was the new Jack. Her sister's murderer was after the new Jack, and why not? It made perfect sense. The Jack's responsibility was for the luck of Kinrowan. The gruagagh had been disturbing the fiaina rades, which was what the sidhe used to gather their luck. Of course he'd go after the Jack. Kinrowan's luck would be like a treasure feast compared to what he could steal from a sidhe rade.

She shivered from the chill of her wet clothes and ran a hand through her hair, pushing it back from her brow. Water puddled all around where she was standing.

It wasn't a name, she thought as she looked south, but it would have to be enough.

She took her pipe from its soggy bag and shook it free of water. Pulling out the reed, she blew through the hollow body of the instrument until it was as dry as she could get it. She held the reed up, studied it for a moment, then fit it back into the pipe's mouthpiece.

The first notes she blew had a ragged sound to them, but soon she was playing a calling-up tune faultlessly. The belling cry of her pipe was loud in the quiet air. She saw a light go on in one of the upper stories of the houses near the canal, then another. But if the tune was loud in the world that men knew, in Faerie it rang from one end of Kinrowan to the other and out into the borderlands, a piercing insistent music that no sidhe could ignore. For it was a calling-on tune, a skilly music. It was the sound of a Pook calling up her rade to lead her folk to war.

She played the tune through once again, and then a third time. Before the echo of the last notes died away, she'd thrust the pipe back into its wet bag and was running silently along the canal, south to where the Jack's Tower stood in Crowdie Wort's Bally.

The first bogan was the worst.

Jacky came upon him where the Rideau Canal made a sharp westward turn near the corner of the Queen Elizabeth Driveway and Waverley Street. He was a great hulking squat lump of a creature, reeking of stale sweat and old swamps. She stopped dead in her tracks at the sight of him, her knees knocking against each other. The little voice of reason in the back of her head came back, but now it was only crying getawaygetaway in an ascending panicked wail.

She was all set to do just that, but the creature merely nodded in greeting to her.

"I'd rather be eating than creeping, hot damn," he muttered to her.

Jacky remembered Finn's warning about how his stitcheries couldn't disguise their voices, and managed a rough assenting grunt.

"Spike 'em all," she added.

Her voice didn't have the right sort of deep grumble to her ears, but the bogan didn't appear to notice. She stilled the tiny voice wailing in the back of her head and stood a little straighter.

"Ho!" the bogan said. "I'd like to see you spike the droichan—a little toadsucker like you."

"Spike you, too," Jacky told him, growing braver.

It was the right thing to say. The bogan laughed and gave her a rough clap on the back before going on. She watched him go, breathing through her mouth until the air wasn't quite so filled with his reek, then headed on herself.

That wasn't so hard, she thought, her confidence boosted by

the encounter. Though, she had to admit, she didn't smell much better than he did.

She ran into more and more Unseelie creatures, the closer she got to the Tower, and no one seemed to pay her any more mind than they did to each other. Only the little creatures called gullywudes—that appeared to be nothing more than little stick and twig bundles held together by who knew what—eyed her strangely, plucking at her arms and legs. She got quite nervous until she saw that they did much the same with the other bogans, who merely clubbed them with their big fists when they got too near. She hit a few of the ones closest to her and they soon left her alone as well.

"Damn little shitheads," a bogan remarked to her as a new crowd came upon both of them on the street in front of the Tower. They both battered them away. "I'd eat the crowd of them, hot damn, if they didn't taste like toothpicks," he added.

Jacky nodded in agreement and followed him up onto the porch of the Tower and inside.

"Find anything?" a black-bearded duergar asked the first bogan when they stepped into the hallway.

The dwarf was two-thirds the bogan's height, but the bogan took a half-step back from him. Jacky wondered if he was an Unseelie skillyman by the way the bogan acted, then spotted the elder wand thrust in the dwarf's belt. By that she knew he was a gruagagh of sorts—what Finn called a widdyman. He had skilly abilities, but used them widdershins to work bad luck rather than good.

"Not a damn hair," the bogan replied.

"What about you?" the duergar demanded of Jacky.

She simply shook her head.

"Then what are you doing back here, you toadsuckers?" the widdyman demanded. "The boss said find her!"

"I look better with a full belly," the bogan told him.

"Nothing could make you look better, arsebreath."

"No, Greim. I mean—"

"I know what you meant," Greim replied, and shook his head wearily. He jerked a hand over his shoulder towards the kitchen. "See what you can find," he added, "but then get your arses back out there. You wouldn't like to see the boss get mad at you, now would you?"

Taking her cue from the bogan, Jacky shook her head as he

did and followed him into the kitchen, where a great crowd of creatures were milling about. The door to the fridge stood ajar and there was little left in it. Every bit of foodstuff had been pulled from the cupboards and the crowd was picking through the remains.

Gullywudes tugged and plucked indiscriminately at empty cereal boxes and the clothing of other creatures. A troll sat hunched in the kitchen nook, all nine feet of his length folded up so that his knees almost touched his brows as he popped chunks of bread into the maw of his mouth. He held the remainder of the loaf protectively under his arm and swung out at any creature that came near him. A hag stood by the sink and was pulling down cups and saucers. She dropped them one by one on the floor, where they shattered to the applause of a pair of goblins and some gullywudes that were standing around her. Two bogans were hacking at a frozen roast with their knives, cursing picturesquely as only bogans can.

Seeing that crowd of creatures, the mess that they were making of the kitchen and with their reek in the air, Jacky had to lean against the doorjamb for a moment. The mess almost broke her heart. When Kate saw this . . . Her collection of English cottage pictures smashed to the floor, her teacups and saucers all broken, her pride-and-joy teapot—a cow sitting on its haunches that poured tea from its mouth—lying in a dozen pieces right by Jacky's feet. . . .

Jacky blinked hard. She cast a quick look down the hall to where the widdyman Greim was berating a new set of arrivals, another look into the kitchen where everyone was too busy to notice anything she might do, then she slipped up the stairs.

Any moment she expected to hear the alarm go off, but she soon discovered that the upper floors of the Tower weren't off-limits. Through the open doors she passed, she saw more Unseelie creatures lounging about in the ruins of what had been Kate's and her own bedrooms. The reek was stronger up here as well, for there were sluagh drifting restlessly about. A pair passed her going downstairs and she almost cried out at the cold clammy touch of their misty bodies, the drowned faces that they turned towards her. The restless dead of the Unseelie Court probably scared Jacky more than all the others combined, giants included.

Shivering, she hurried up to the third floor. There, perhaps because of Bhruic's spell that made the room seem empty, she finally found herself alone. She'd half-expected the droichan to be in here, but she realized now that he must be out searching with the rest of them.

She moved quickly to the hollowed leg of the worktable and removed the wally-stanes, tying their bag to the belt that held up her jeans. This was going to be easier than she'd thought. Congratulating herself on her wisdom for going through with it, she went to the window.

There she hesitated, looking out on the broad nightscape of Kinrowan spread out before her. She was still a little nervous about this mode of transportation. Sure, it had worked once. She just wished she knew more about it. Maybe it would be smarter to go back downstairs and brave her way through the Unseelie creatures once more.

She started to turn, then shook her head. No, that was being a chickenshit. This was going to work.

She put her foot up on the sill and started to draw herself up, when the view disappeared. The window went black. She stumbled back, almost losing her balance. Catching hold of the sill, she drew closer, trying to look out through the sudden darkness. It was as though someone had dropped a curtain down in front of the window. She put out her hand and touched something cold and ghostly damp. Before she could withdraw, two red eyes blinked open and stared at her with a mocking expression in their depths.

Leaving so soon? a voice said in her mind.

Jacky recognized the droichan's voice. She stepped back from the window, her knees going all watery on her again. She thought of making a break for the door, but the droichan had foreseen that. A long, tentacle-like shadow arm lunged out from the deeper darkness beyond the window and slammed the door shut.

I thought you might be back, the droichan went on conversationally. *That's why I left a little safeguard on the door to warn me if you returned.* The amused gaze studied her again. *Not a bad disguise. Did you make it yourself, or did one of your little hob friends put it together for you?*

Jacky's fear was like a nail screeching on a chalkboard. Whatever courage she might have had shivered up and down her spine, then huddled cowering in some deep corner of her mind.

"What . . . what are you going to . . . to do with me?" she asked in a small voice.

Oh, we'll talk some, the droichan replied. *I have some distance to travel before I can be here with you in person, but then I'm sure we'll find some way to amuse ourselves. You might consider how you'll transfer Bhruic's power to me.*

"But I don't know . . . how. . . ."

The red eyes seemed to pin her soul. The droichan's voice, when it echoed in her mind again, went through her like shivers of ice.

We'll find a way, little Jack. Even if I have to take you apart, piece by piece. We'll find a way.

All the strength went out of Jacky's body and she sank to her knees on the hardwood floor. She slumped there, hardly hearing what the droichan was saying anymore as he rambled on. All she could do was wait for him to return to the Tower in person, numb with the realization that she'd blown it again.

How did you spell Jacky Rowan?

That was easy. S-T-U-P-I-D.

She didn't doubt that the droichan would find a way to get the information out of her—even if she didn't consciously know it herself. And then her friends—no, not just them, but all of Kinrowan—would be in the droichan's power.

Distantly, she heard a sound then, a faerie pipe playing a calling-on tune. The eyes of her captor closed, returning the window to a wall of blackness, and she knew that the droichan's shadow was looking outward, seeking the source of that sound. She thought of trying to escape while his attention was turned away, but before she could move, the red gaze was fixed on her once again.

The ghost of the Pook is calling up her rade, he informed her.

The *ghost* of the Pook? Well, why not?

I will have to see that a suitable welcome is waiting for her if she plans to ride on this Tower.

Jacky closed her eyes. Strangely enough, she didn't feel so frightened anymore. Something in that calling-on tune had heartened her. But when the droichan's gaze fixed on her once more, a bleakness settled over her and she just felt dead inside.

* * *

Finn and Gwi said their farewells on Wellington Street. The forester was mounted on a tall, golden steed—one of the Laird's own mounts that could claim a direct lineage from the huge White Horses of the old country who left their chalk outlines on the sides of hills when they died. Gwi, even with the stature that her troll blood gave her, looked like a doll perched on its back.

"At times like these," she said, "I wish we'd acquired the use of some human tools like a telephone."

"I'd use one," Finn said, "only who in Faerie could I call?"

A brief smile touched Gwi's lips. "Exactly. I'll be back in two days—with what word I can gather and a company of foresters. Don't do anything foolish until then, Finn."

"I'm not brave," Finn assured her.

"I'm not so sure—the line between the two's a thin one at the best of times."

"Take care," Finn said.

Gwi nodded and the hob slapped the horse's flank. Such was the animal's speed that before he could count to three, Gwi and her mount were long gone from sight. He hoped Gwi *would* take care. The Harvest Fair was at Ballymoresk and faerie from all over gathered to it. But near Ballymoresk was also the largest Unseelie Court in eastern Canada.

He sighed and started back from Gump's home, hoping that the trow and Kate would be back when he arrived. When he returned, all he found was Jacky's note.

"Oh, damn!" he muttered. "That foolish, well-meaning Jack."

He crumpled the note in his hand, was about to throw it away, then thought better of it and thrust it into his pocket. He'd have to gather up Gump and Kate and go back to the Tower with them. He only hoped they'd still find Jacky in one piece.

When he stepped outside, he smelled the darkness in the air—the darkness of Unseelie creatures loose and abroad. Oh, they were brave now with a droichan to boss them and most of the Court away to the Fair. And why shouldn't they be?

He shut the entrance to Gump's home with a softly-spoken word. Before he could take a step, though, he heard the faltering sound of a sidhe pipe finding its tune, then the ringing notes of a calling-up music. The sound came from close by and he started to jog in its direction, reaching its source just in time to see a bedraggled and wet Pook thrust her pipe into a bag hanging from her shoulder before she set off at a quick pace.

Oh, this was a bad night, no doubt of it. The Court away, a droichan loose, the Unseelie Court abroad and hunting, and now the sidhe gathering for a war rade.

As he ran after the Pook—the direction she'd taken was the same he needed to follow to find Gump and Kate—he hoped that there would be something left of Faerie when the sun finally turned its dawn face their way.

With her hob-stitched shoes, Kate was just able to keep up with Gump's pace-eating stride. After a few blocks, the trow took her on his shoulders to go more quickly and they reached the street they were looking for in record time.

"This has to be it," Kate said.

Gump crouched so that she could clamber down from her perch and then the two of them stared across the street, studying the building. The house stood in the middle of the block, empty windows staring darkly out onto the street. On the lawn of the two-storied structure was a sign that read:

ANOTHER RENOVATION BY
J. COURS AND SONS LTD.

A red maple, its leaves beginning to turn, and a clutch of cedars appeared to lean away from the house as though avoiding even its shadow. The lawn was somewhat unkempt, riddled with clumps of spike-leafed weeds.

Kate didn't like the look of the place, and now that they were here, she wasn't all that sure exactly what they were going to do. The house looked deserted, but there was a sense of something sentient about the way its windows looked out at the street, the drop of its roofline hanging over them like the low hairline of a browless troll. She glanced at Gump.

"What should we do?" she asked.

"We go in."

"That's what I was afraid you were going to say."

The trow patted her shoulder. "Don't be afraid, Kate. The droichan's not here—I'd sense him if he was. Now, come on."

He rose up like a small mountain standing at her side and started across the street. Kate sighed and followed in his wake.

"I was worrying more about what the droichan might have left behind," she muttered to Gump's back.

"Only one way to find out," Gump replied.

The porch creaked under his weight. The question of how they were going to get in died on Kate's lips as Gump struck the door with the flat side of his elbow. He hit it near the lock and tore the lock right out of the wood.

"They took more care in building doors in the old days," he remarked to Kate as he stepped into the darkened hallway. "I can remember a time when it took myself and a brother a good minute to break one down. Of course, every hall had its own skillyman in those days."

Kate kept close behind him, not really listening to what he was saying. She felt an all too real sensation of being watched as they moved slowly down the hall and stepped into the first room. To her surprise, the room was furnished. True, the sofa and chairs were old, the coffee table's surface scarred with deep scratches, the carpet threadbare and faded, the two pictures on the wall hanging askew with their glass broken on the floor below them, but it was still more than she'd expected.

"Can you sense someone in here with us?" she whispered to Gump.

The trow turned away from the fake mantelpiece and cocked his head, considering.

"Something," he admitted finally. "But it's more an echo than a presence, as though it's only a memory of something that *was* here and is now gone."

"The droichan?"

"Something with his kind of power—if not the droichan himself."

"Wonderful," Kate said. "The last thing we need now is two of him."

"It seems to be stronger upstairs," the trow said.

He moved back into the hallway, floorboards creaking ominously underfoot. Kate clutched at the bag that held Caraid, quite happy to let Gump take the lead again. The stairs sagged under the trow's weight, but that didn't seem to particularly concern him. Kate followed uneasily, sure that if some creature of the droichan's didn't get them, then the house would simply collapse about them and bury them in its basement.

She passed a light switch at the top of the stairs and gave it a try, but nothing happened. That made sense. Why would the electricity be on in a place like this? J. Cours and his sons had quite the job lined up for themselves in renovating it.

Her eyes were beginning to adjust to the dimness now, enough so that she thought she'd be able to read. Tugging Caraid free from its bag, she began to tell the book about the house and its condition.

"Any ideas where the droichan might have hidden his heart?" she asked when she was done.

She held the book up to a nearby window for better light.

Dear Kate, the book replied in Bhruic Dearg's clear script. *I told you before. You must know the droichan's mind before you can riddle the location of his heart.*

"Can't you even guess?" Kate asked.

I need something to base my guess on.

"Oh, come on," Kate said. "Guessing's just luck—that's all."

"Then perhaps we *should* have had Jacky accompany us," Gump said. "We could use a Jack's luck in this."

"This house had a grey aura when we saw it from the special window in the Tower," Kate said. "Doesn't that mean the droichan was here?"

It means something disrupted the flow of the Moon's luck in this place, Caraid replied. *It need not necessarily have been the droichan.*

"But it was the same grey as was in the places where he *did* work his magics," Kate said. "Doesn't that mean something? Or are we on a wild-goose chase?"

"I could use a goose," Gump said. "I'm feeling peckish."

Kate glanced at him, hoping his appetite didn't run to human women.

What you have postulated could be true, her book admitted. *The droichan could well have worked magics here. But that doesn't necessarily mean that his heart is hidden here. Or that it was ever hidden here.*

"Well, what magics could he have worked here? What did he need this place for?"

Magics are always stronger when worked in a place where moonroads meet.

Kate looked at the trow. "Oh, what are we going to do?"

"For one thing," Gump said, "we should finish looking through the house before we give up."

He set off again, making his way down the second-story hall to the first open door. Kate glanced at Caraid, but the book had nothing to add. She put it away in its bag, then left the window where she'd been standing to follow the trow. Gump was waiting for her in the second doorway down the hall.

"Here," he said. "Can you feel it?"

Kate squeezed in beside him and stood just inside the room. "I . . ." she began.

The feeling of being watched returned to her, stronger than ever. On top of that sensation lay the taste of old magics, used and discarded, only their echoes remaining.

"Yes," she said. "This is where he worked his magics. And he's left something behind"—she glanced at the trow—"hasn't he?"

The room was longer than it was wide. It had been someone's study once, but the bookshelves were all empty now. A table, that had once served as a desk, she guessed, stood by the window, a stained and tattered ink blotter and a scatter of pencil stubs and paper on its surface. A chair stood by the table. In the middle of the room were a few cardboard boxes.

"Just trash," Gump said as he looked through a box.

"Gump," Kate said. "You didn't answer me. He left something in here, didn't he?"

"I'm not sure," the trow replied. "When mages and grua-gaghs settle down to work their spells . . . *things* tend to gather, to watch them. That's what we're sensing, I think."

"Things? What kind of things?"

"I'm not really sure. I'm not a gruagagh, Kate. I've just heard the same stories that everyone knows. There were spirits in this land long before we reached its shores. They like to spy on our skillyfolk—some say to make sure that they work within allowed boundaries, but mostly it's thought that they do it simply out of curiosity."

"And that's what's here now?" Kate asked.

The trow nodded. "I think so. I hope so."

"And there's no droichan's heart?"

"I can't say yes or no, Kate. Someone worked powerful spells here. Maybe one such spell was the droichan hiding his heart."

Kate sighed. She went over to the table and pried about, moving to the boxes when she was sure there was nothing of interest on either it or its adjacent windowsill. She emptied the first box unceremoniously on the floor and pawed through its contents. Most of the papers had something to do with governmental statistics.

How boring, she thought.

As she started on another box, Gump left the room and went into the next one down the hall. Kate followed his progress by listening to his weight creaking the floorboards. She was bitterly disappointed at coming up with nothing in this house. The idea had seemed so perfect when it first came to her at Gump's home.

But that would have made things too easy, she realized now. And nothing was ever easy when it came to Faerie, and especially when it came to Faerie's skillyfolk like the gruagaghs.

When she was finished going through the boxes, she stood in the center of the room and made a slow turn, trying to *feel* where the magic echoes were the strongest, or where the hidden watchers were concealed. She felt a tug near the table and returned to it, wishing she'd had the foresight to bring a flashlight with her. Holding up papers to the window was all well and good, but it didn't do much for looking into crannies or finding hidey-holes.

She ran her fingers over the table, wishing she knew something about dowsing. That'd do the trick—just wave some stick over the table until it bent down at the required hiding place. But she didn't have a magical dowsing stick—didn't even know all that much about dowsing in the first place—and the table had no secrets to give up, or at least none that it was willing to give up. She turned away, defeated, to find Gump standing in the doorway.

"This is the only room with such strong echoes," he said.

Kate nodded glumly. She toyed with the buttons of her jacket, started across the room to join him, then remembered the rowan twigs sewn to the inside of her jacket.

"Wait a sec," she said.

Gump watched with interest as she unfastened the twigs from the inside of her jacket and tied them into a rough Y-shape.

"You know how to do that?" he asked as she stood with her makeshift divining rod in hand.

"Not really. But Finn seemed to think I could work magics if I studied hard. And this isn't really magic anyway, is it? Even humans can do it."

"If they have the skill."

"Oh, don't be such a poop," Kate told him. "Have a little faith."

The trow shrugged in agreement and sat by the door to watch, leaving Kate wondering if she'd bitten off more than she could chew. She'd read a book once on the Cambridge don Tom Lethbridge and his experience with dowsing. Having fully planned to immediately try it herself, she'd ended up distracted by something else and never really coming back to it. But she tended to remember everything she read, so she settled down now to concentrating on the task.

Keeping her mind empty of everything but the vague "something" that both she and the trow had sensed in the room, she made a slow circuit, her divining rod loosely gripped in her hands and held out before her. To her delight, the rowan twigs gave a definite tug in the direction of the table.

Without looking at Gump—though she was feeling very pleased with herself and dying to tell him, I told you so—she walked slowly over to the table, the makeshift rod increasing its tug against her fingers, the closer she came. Behind her, Gump lumbered to his feet and creaked his way across the floor after her. He towered over and watched as she made a circuit of the tabletop with the rod.

In the center of the table, closest to where she was standing, the rod jumped sharply downwards. The movement was so quick that Kate involuntarily held on tighter to the rod. Threads snapped and her divining rod fell to pieces.

Kate jumped back, startled, bumped into Gump, and almost screeched before she caught hold of her nerves and steadied herself. She took a deep breath and let it out again before turning to face the trow.

"It's right here," she said, pointing to where the twigs had fallen. "There's something right here, Gump."

She gathered up her twigs and stuck them in her pocket, moving aside so that Gump could have a look. The trow bent down until one big eye was level with the spot and he could study it.

"Something . . ." he agreed in a bemused voice.

He reached out a hand and moved it around the spot.

"Oh, look!" Kate cried unnecessarily since Gump's eye was still inches from the spot.

A vague outline was taking shape on the wooden tabletop, slightly luminous like the numbers on a digital watch which had a battery that was wearing down. Kate stared with rounded eyes as it became clearer. It was a round, slightly domed shape, with a flourish of intertwined ribbonwork encircling the central design, which appeared to be a pair of cow's horns.

"What is it?" she breathed.

"An echo of magic," Gump replied.

They both stared at it, trying to make sense of what it was. Before trying to touch it, Kate took out Caraid and held the book open overtop of it so that a copy of the design could be made on a blank page. Then she tried to touch it, but whatever it was, at the contact of her fingers, it simply dissolved away.

"Was that his heart?" Kate asked.

Gump shrugged. He looked from the table to where the design was now taking shape on Caraid's page.

"I don't know what it was," he said. "Perhaps his heart— more likely some magical object that he was imbuing with power."

I agree, Caraid wrote under the image on its page. *This is a droichan's work—there is no doubt of that. Notice the symbol of the broken crescent moon.*

And she'd thought they were cow's horns, Kate thought, glad that she hadn't said anything.

"We should show this to Finn," Gump said. "He might recog—"

The trow broke off as a distant music rang through Faerie. Only slightly aligned to the Seelie Court through his friendship with Finn, Gump felt the strong pull of the sidhe calling-up tune. He wanted to run out into the night and find the piper, to follow her anywhere.

A rade called up.

The thought of it filled him with an inexplicable joy.

"What's that sound?" Kate asked.

For a long moment, Gump said nothing, then he slowly shook his head. The hold of the tune on him lessened. He blinked and concentrated on ignoring the music as it continued to sound.

"The fiaina sidhe are being called up for a rade," he said.

"And you want to go?" Kate asked.

Gump nodded, surprised at her insight. "I don't need its luck, but I've been there, a time or two, following the winding pattern of a fiaina rade. It's not something you forget."

"I sort of feel like gathering with them myself," Kate said. "What does that make me?"

"A skilly mortal who's spent too much time in Faerie."

"You make it sound dangerous."

"Not dangerous," Gump said. "But it changes you. Faerie don't steal mortals—not so much anymore, at any rate—but the Middle Kingdom is still a chancy realm for mortals, Kate. Too long in it and you'll never want to leave."

"Then I've already been in it too long." She gave him a quick grin. "We should go back to your place and show Finn and Jacky what we've found."

The music had died away now, but there was a new sound in the air of Faerie. Gump paused, staring at the window, listening. Then Kate heard it, too. Part of the sound was the wind, rising at the call of the sidhe to mask the sound of their movement. But part of that sound was something else, a sound like dark wings cutting the night skies, of Unseelie creatures called to their own gathering.

"War," Gump said. "The Pook's calling up the sidhe to ride to war and the droichan's gathering his own army to meet her. Oh, this is a bad night for faerie, Kate." He sat down in a slump and leaned against an empty bookcase. "I don't like fighting. I don't like it, Kate. I'll stand up and do what needs doing, but I don't like it. It makes us all small—winners and losers alike."

Kate had a moment of thinking it was odd that such a big, gruff creature like the trow would feel this way, but then she remembered the beautiful mechanical birds she'd seen in his home and realized that she was being very small-minded. Just because Gump was a trow didn't mean he had to like hurting people. She sat down beside him and leaned her head against his arm.

"No one likes it," she said. "Not if they're at all decent."

Gump nodded unhappily. "I don't take sides, because I don't like being a part of what comes from taking sides. Unpleasantness. Fighting. But this . . . We'll all lose our luck if we allow the droichan to win."

Kate tried to think of something she could say to make it easier, but there was nothing. Just because something had to be done didn't make it any easier to do it. She stroked Gump's arm.

"I'll be fierce for both of us," she said. "You can—"

She broke off as she heard a sound downstairs. Someone had entered the house. She shot Gump a quick glance, then stood quickly and moved towards the door.

"Now it begins," the trow muttered.

He rose as well and took up a stance on the other side of the door. The floor creaked as he moved and Kate hoped that maybe the sound would drive the intruder away, but while the noise downstairs ceased when Gump moved, after he'd been still for a few moments, it began again. A stealthy movement up the stairs.

Gump lifted an arm so that it was raised above the doorway. He looked at Kate and gave her a smile, but it didn't reach his eyes. Kate tried to smile bravely back, but all she could think of was, What if it was the droichan? What could they possibly do against him?

The intruder paused at the top of the stairs, then moved to the first doorway, stopping abruptly when a floorboard creaked underfoot. Long moments of deathly silence followed. Kate thought she was going to collapse from holding her breath, but she didn't dare breathe. Then the intruder moved again, coming towards the doorway that they were guarding.

I should have grabbed a chair, Kate thought. Maybe a double-whammy—chair and trow-fist—would at least knock the droichan out long enough for them to make good their escape. Instead she was just standing here, hands closed into small fists, staring wide-eyed at the door and still holding her breath.

A figure moved into the doorway, Gump's big fist started to come down, then Kate lunged forward.

"No, Gump, don't!" she cried. "It's Finn."

The little hob froze at the sound of his name, then stepped hastily back as Gump's fist narrowly missed him. The trow lost his balance, but Kate managed to steer him against a wall where he caught hold of a bookcase and saved himself from falling. Finn stood shaking, looking as though he was ready to bolt at any moment. Slowly he regained his composure and glared at the pair of them.

"You should have called out," Kate said sweetly.

"There was a stink of magic about the place," Finn replied. "I should have realized that it was no more than that of a trow and his sweetheart playing hide-and-go-seek in the dark."

"We thought you were the droichan," Kate said.

"And I thought—oh, never mind. Listen closely now, for I—"

"Look," Kate broke in.

She thrust Caraid towards Finn, open to the page with the circular image on it.

"We dowsed and pried," she said, "until we got a magical echo to give up this much. What do you think it is, Finn?"

"Kate. You're not listening to me."

"Oh, don't be mad," she said. "We didn't know it was you, and you didn't know it was us. It was an honest mistake."

"I'm not talking about that," Finn said. He caught hold of her arm. "Jacky left Gump's home and has gone to the Tower by herself. I'm afraid the droichan's captured her again."

All the blood drained from Kate's face.

"Oh, no," she said in a small voice. "What are we going to do?"

Gump straightened up at her side.

"Rescue her," he said.

Johnny woke with a start to find that he'd dozed off on the couch. Mactire was standing over him, shaking him awake.

"Huwzzat?" he mumbled, sitting up and rubbing his eyes.

"Listen," the wild boy said.

"But I don't hear anything . . ." Johnny began, then his voice trailed off.

There was no mistaking that sound, nor its urgency. It was

Jemi's pipe, its music ringing through all of Faerie. The tune went coursing through him until it seemed that his every cell vibrated to its call. He sat dumbfounded by the intensity it awoke in him, sat there long after its last notes died away.

"What . . . that tune . . . ?"

"It's the calling-up music of the fiaina sidhe," Mactire told him.

He caught hold of Johnny's arm and hauled him to his feet.

"But—"

"We mustn't delay. She calls the sidhe to war. That means she knows the name of our enemy."

Johnny looked down the hall to where Henk was sleeping.

"But," he started again.

Mactire shook his head. "There's no time. Are you coming, or do I leave you behind?"

"No. I . . ."

Still fuzzy with sleep, and dazed from what the music had woken in him, Johnny finally started to move. He grabbed his jacket and started for the door.

"Your fiddle," Mactire said.

Johnny went back for it.

"Jemi's going to be okay, isn't she?" he asked as he started for the door again, fiddle case in hand this time.

"Not if we don't hurry," the wolf boy said.

Outside he set off at a lope that Johnny was hard put to keep up with, but keep up he did. Down Bank Street they went and over the Lansdowne Bridge into Ottawa South. In the Middle Kingdom they had another name for this place, Johnny remembered from talking to Jemi. They called it Crowdie Wort's Bally. It was there that the Tower of the Jack of Kinrowan stood, and on the grassy park south of that Tower, the sidhe were hosting tonight.

Behind, in Johnny's apartment, Henk awoke in time to hear them leave. He'd fallen asleep on the bed fully dressed, so that when he reached the door and saw Johnny and the wild boy hurrying off down the street, he had time to snatch his own jacket from where it lay on a chair, and set off into the night, following them.

His night fears scurried up and down his spine, but this time he was determined to ignore them. Unsure of where they were going, he still knew he had to follow. Just before he'd woken, he'd been dreaming. Nothing remained of that dream, not one image; only a haunting music that had called him up from sleep to find Johnny and his strange companion leaving the apartment.

As he ran in their wake, he wondered what was so important that it had sent them hurrying out into the night as they had.

CHAPTER
15

The droichan's shadow had congealed on the floor between Jacky and the window, crouching there in the shape of a large black dog. It stared at her with its hot-coal eyes, silent now.

Jacky wouldn't look at it. She couldn't. She sat on her haunches, chin against her chest, and stared at the floor. The noise of a large commotion downstairs rose up through the floorboards, but it didn't really register. It wasn't until she heard a certain footfall coming up the stairs, until the door opened, that she lifted her head and slowly turned.

The droichan had returned.

He filled the doorway, his brown cloak hanging in loose folds to the floor, its hood thrown back to show his handsome features. The fire from his shadow-creature's eyes flickered in his own gaze as he regarded her.

"Sweet Jack," he said. "The time for kindness is past."

Jacky couldn't suppress an involuntary shiver at the sound of his voice. The strength to get up just wasn't in her, so she sat where she was, staring back at him.

"What . . . what do you *want* from me?" she asked.

"Everything."

"But I never hurt you. Why would you want to—"

The droichan made a sudden gesture with one hand and she was jerked roughly to her feet by an invisible force.

"Nothing?" he asked softly. "You stuck a knife in my heart, sweet Jack."

"But you—"

"Enough."

He made another gesture. Jacky heard a roaring of storm winds in her ears. The unseen force took her and slammed her against a wall, spread-eagled. She hung there, a foot or so from the floor. Helpless. Unable to move.

The droichan stepped slowly across the room until he was a foot or so away from her.

"It's time to end this," he said. "I want the luck of this Tower, sweet Jack. I want what Bhruic left you. It's as simple as that. A sidhe army is hosting behind the Tower. Perhaps my bullyboys—unruly rabble that they are—can defeat them, perhaps not, but why should I bide the outcome? I want what Kinrowan has to offer me—every drop of its luck, sweet Jack. Nothing less will do."

"But . . . they . . . can't . . . hurt you . . ." Jacky mumbled through taut jaws.

"Not forever, no. But they could conceivably best the Unseelie army that I can field at this moment. They could catch me and cut me to pieces. I wouldn't die, no. But think how long it would take me to become whole once more. I won't have that. I will *not* allow it. This Tower is the key to Kinrowan, and you are my key to the Tower, sweet Jack. You will unlock Bhruic's secrets for me. I will brook no more argument."

"But I don't *know* how to unlock—"

Invisible hands drew her back from the wall and slammed her into it again.

"No argument," the droichan repeated softly.

Fires glimmered wickedly in his eyes. He made a gesture with his hand in front of her face, fingers moving in an odd pattern, and cobwebs covered her features. They clung thickly to her skin, letting her only see the world through their grey gauze. She moved her head back and forth, trying to dislodge them, but they stuck to her like a second skin.

"When my kind dies," the droichan said, "*truly* dies, this is where we go."

One by one, Jacky's senses deserted her. Sight went first—from a gauzy veil to nothingness. Her other senses compensated, becoming more acute.

She heard her own raspy breathing, the droichan's light

breaths. In the Tower itself, the cries of the bogans and other creatures readying for war. The sound of them issuing forth from the Tower to the park behind, gathering under an Unseelie banner—a flag with the image of a crucified swan-man encircled by briars upon it.

Then her hearing went.

Now she could smell the sharpness of her own fear, the earthy smell of the droichan. The open window of the Tower brought in the scents of autumn, mingled with a bog-reek of sluagh and bogans.

Smell went.

She could taste her fear now—a raw vomit sour in her throat. The salty sweat that beaded her lips.

Taste went.

There was nothing left but touch. The hard wall at her back. The vague kiss of a breeze on her skin. Then her nerve ends began to tingle and go numb. Limb by limb, feeling withdrew until she was devoid of all sensation.

No outside stimuli entered her. She might as well have been immersed in a sensory-deprivation tank. But there was no peace to be found in this. No rest. No solace. She hadn't chosen to withdraw from the world to capture some inner harmony. She'd had her senses stolen from her by a monster and been cast adrift in a bleak void of his making.

There was no way to measure time.

A moment could have passed and it could have been forever. An eternity slipped by in a scurry of seconds. Blank, utter panic came gibbering up from the back of her mind and flooded her brain.

Had he left her here?

Could anything exist in such emptiness?

She tried to call up comforting images in her mind's eye, but they were slow to come. She managed a small candle, its flame spluttering.

The flame went out.

A residue of its light remained as a faint nimbus. She built that into a spark of light—just one tiny star that she could focus on.

The star went out.

The void encircled it. Choked it. Swallowed it.

Her panic worsened.

She was here forever.

She might already have been here forever.

Escape was impossible. Without the droichan's help, she couldn't return to the world.

Give him what he wants, her panic told her.

But I don't know, she wailed. I can't give him what I don't know how to give.

Give it to him. Giveittohim. Give. It. To. Him.

No, she told that voice. Even if she could, she wouldn't.

She clung to that thought, repeated it, used it to force the panic away. The Tower had been her responsibility. It was already half-fallen to the enemy, and for that she had to pay. But she wouldn't give the droichan any more. He could leave her here forever, if that was what it took, but she wouldn't give in to him.

Her terror receded fractionally.

The spark she'd tried to call up suddenly burst into the image of a full moon, hanging swollen in the bleak night skies of her mind.

It flickered and was gone.

A woman stood in its place, regarding her. She was silver-haired and round-faced, full-lipped and dark-eyed, generous body wrapped in a tattered cloak of moss and leaves and twigs. Mushrooms grew from her shoulders. Fungus glimmered palely in amidst the dark debris that made up her cloak. She smiled at Jacky—a warm smile, the kind a mother would give to a child who had pleased her. Then the image was gone and the void returned.

But the fear didn't return with it.

That must have been the Moon, Jacky thought. The Moonmother Arn, herself. She came to me. She came and looked at me, with her luck in her eyes.

It wasn't much, she realized, floating there in the void. She hadn't been offered freedom, or revenge. Merely a look of pride. But it would have to be enough. She'd have to hold that memory forever, because she wasn't going to have anything else. She'd—

Her senses returned to her in a choking flood.

Sight and sound. The droichan's face, eyes mocking her; the heaving rasp of her own breathing.

Smell. The stink of her fear and the bog-reek of the Unseelie Court.

Taste and touch. The sour bile in her throat; the ache of her back and shoulder muscles pulled tight against the wall.

She drank in their return, ignoring the droichan. Her resolve to stand firm faltered as she savoured sensation. Even fear and bile and pain were something. Anything was better than the void, wasn't it?

The droichan let loose his invisible bonds and she slumped to a boneless heap on the floor.

"That is where we go when we die," he said. "I can send you there, if you don't give me what I want. Into that bleak eternity. Or you can give me the key to the Tower and when you die you'll walk the green fields of the Region of the Summer Stars, perhaps even to be born again.

"There is no escape from that void. No rescue is possible."

Jacky slowly lifted her head to look up at him. She wanted, she so desperately wanted to be able to say, Just you go to hell, you bastard, but she couldn't imagine returning to that emptiness. Just thinking of it made her hard-won resolve drain away.

"Which is it to be?" the droichan asked.

"I . . ."

Her voice came out like a frog's croak. Slowly she pushed herself up along the wall until she was half-sitting, half-leaning against it. She wanted to be standing when she answered him. Maybe that would lend her bravery. Lying at his feet, she could only give in. She clawed at the wall, struggling to find purchase, but her fingers kept slipping. She tried to find the Moon's face inside her again—that strange woman in her foresty cloak, with the luck in her eyes.

I want to be strong, she told that memory. But I can't be strong, just lying here.

She tried again.

The droichan stood back, watching her efforts with a half-smile on his lips.

Damn him. He could be so patient. He was just drinking in her pain, stealing her luck. That was why she was so weak. He had to be sucking the life right out of her.

But she wouldn't give in. She'd get to her feet and spit in his face and damn the consequences. But not if she lay here. Lying here, she just wanted to give up. She just wanted to say, I don't know what the key is, but you're welcome to it, only don't send me back to that place.

The droichan made a gesture with his hand, and invisible fingers plucked at her shirt, lifting her a few inches, before letting her fall again.

"Do you want a hand up?" he asked.

Jacky didn't bother to answer. She concentrated on forcing her limp body to do what it was told. She brought Bhruic's face to her mind's eyes and was surprised at how easily it came. She called up Kate then, and Finn. Eilian, the son of Dunlogan's Laird. The big trow, Gump. Sly Kerevan, the trickster with his fiddle in a bag, hanging from his shoulder.

Calling them all up, feeling the weight of their gazes upon her, she found the strength she needed. They were faerie—and faerie, Kinrowan's faerie, depended on her.

She made a slow, faltering progress, but she clawed herself to a standing position, supported herself against the wall, and looked at the droichan.

"Well done, sweet Jack," he said. "You've more strength than I gave you credit for. But are you wise as well? Which have you chosen? The void, or to aid me?"

"I . . . I'll give you the key," she croaked.

The droichan smiled as she reached into the pouch hanging at her belt, but the smile faltered as she drew out a wally-stane. The fires, just glimmering in his eyes, woke into a raging blaze.

"You—" he began, a hand rising to shape a gesture in the air between them, but Jacky moved more quickly.

"No, you!" she cried as she broke the wally-stane against her own chest.

A sparkle of crystal dust exploded from between Jacky's fingers like a puffball's spores floating free from a kick. The droichan stepped back from her and continued to make a spell with the twisting gesture of his hands. When he loosened the magic, Jacky stood in front of him, unaffected.

"You can't touch me," she said.

She moved towards him. From the droichan's feet, his shadow reared up in dog shape and lunged for her throat. Before it could reach her, it slid sideways as though it had run up against an invisible wall. It tried again, and again, to get at her, but it too couldn't reach her.

"I've made myself safe from widdy spells," she said. "Do you know any kindly magics? You might try one of them."

The droichan's hands fell to his sides.

"Clever Jack," he said. "You knew not even a magic could kill me, so you turned your spell on yourself."

"A mouse could kill you," Jacky replied. "All it needs to do is take a bite from your heart."

"But first it must find that heart."

"You can't stop me from looking for it—and I'll tell you now, I'll never give up."

The droichan shook his head in admiration. "What a droichan you would make, sweet Jack. But you forgot something."

He moved towards her, edging her into a corner away from both the window and the door. Nervously, Jacky eyed him, unsure of what he was up to. She racked her brain, trying to think of what she'd forgotten when she spelled the wally-stane. It wasn't until he lunged at her that the truth dawned.

She was safe from widdyshin magics—his or another's, oh, yes. But not from physical harm.

She tried to knee him in the groin, but he moved too quickly. He twisted to one side, grabbed her by the shoulder, and spun her around. Before she could recover her balance, the flat of his shoe hit her in the small of her back and she went pinwheeling against the wall. She hit hard, slumping to the floor. He was upon her immediately, knees on her back, grinding her against the hardwood floor, hands at her throat.

"You've played your last trick, sweet Jack," he said. "Now give me what I want, or I'll snap your neck."

She was safe from his spells, but the trick had backfired. As usual, she'd blown it. A smart person would have been out that window so fast it would have made the droichan's head spin, but not Jacky Rowan. Oh, no. She was the Jack of Kinrowan, wasn't she just, and oh so clever. Rather than do the smart thing, she'd stuck around to rub the droichan's face into his failure, never bothering to think things through.

But at least he couldn't send her back into the void. And she might die, but that was all the satisfaction he was going to get from her. The Tower's secret was safe because she couldn't give it to him even if she wanted to.

Somehow, none of that brought her any consolation.

Because now, helpless under his weight, with his hands at her throat, she was still going to pay.

"I've been all around," Finn said when he rejoined Kate and Gump, "and there's no sign of her."

He'd left the pair of them hidden in the backyard of the house across the street from the Tower while he made a circuit of its grounds in his bogan disguise. He'd found sluagh and real bogans and all manner of Unseelie creatures in great numbers, but not even a rumour of Jacky.

"She's gone inside, then," Gump said.

Kate looked at the Tower and shivered. After just a day, it already looked different. There was a veil of corruption about the Tower, just like there had been at the house in the Glebe that she and Gump had investigated. The trees were beginning to lean away from its walls, the garden taking on an air of decay. Malevolence hung thick from its gables and walls.

"How can we fight so many?" she asked.

Finn gave her a wan smile. "With a Jack's trick. A hob and the makings of a skillywoman, that would make them sit up and blink. But who would notice a pair of bogans in the company of a trow?"

"It'll never work," Kate said.

"It has so far."

"There's some that might know me in there," Gump said.

"Then you'll have to be convincing when you tell them of your change of heart," Finn said. "Are you with us?"

Gump nodded.

"Then let's get to it," the hob said.

Kate had the sudden urge to look in a mirror, just to be sure that her disguise really *was* working, but Finn had already set off towards the front of the house. When they crossed the street, two bogans were preceding a trow to the front door of the Tower. No one gave them a second glance until they entered the Tower itself and they were stopped by a black-bearded, duergar widdyman. He eyed Kate and Finn for a long moment, then turned to the trow.

"I didn't think to find you in our company again, Gump," he said.

The trow shrugged. "Times change, Greim. I've heard about the new boss. Word is, if you're not with him, then you're against him. I never liked to take sides, but this time it seems I have no choice."

"A pretty tale," Greim said. "And I might half-believe you, if it wasn't for the stink of skilly magic on your friends. I've learned to see through this trick."

Kate swallowed thickly, ready to bolt, but before she could decide which way to run, before the widdyman could call up an alarm or toss a spell, Gump hit the dwarf. He brought a meaty fist down on the top of Greim's head and the widdyman collapsed on the floor, sprawled out like a wet rag. Finn shot a quick glance down the hall to the kitchen, where they could hear the voices of other Unseelie creatures, but no one seemed to have noticed.

"Is he dead?" Kate asked.

Gump shook his head. "Though he deserves to be. He's an evil little creature, have no doubt of that."

"Up the stairs," Finn said. "Quickly!"

Kate took the lead. Gump followed, carrying the limp dwarf under one arm. It didn't seem wise to leave him where he could be discovered.

"We're just lucky this isn't a true Unseelie hall," Finn said, taking up the rear, "or our disguises would never have taken us even this far."

Kate nodded. Skilly spells didn't work in an Unseelie Hall.

"But how did he see through our disguises?" she asked.

Finn sighed. "You heard him yourself. He'd seen the trick before."

Seen the trick before, Kate repeated to herself, then she shivered. Seen it when they caught Jacky is what that had to mean.

Gump deposited Greim's limp form in Jacky's bedroom. The second floor was empty now. Looking out the window onto the park, they could see the Unseelie Host gathering in a motley array. Trolls and bogans, sluagh, hags, and goblins. Bands of capering gullywudes. Spriggans who puffed themselves up to troll size, shrank again, then grew once more.

Kate turned away when she caught sight of their banner. The swan-man depicted on it reminded her too much of Jacky's friend Eilian.

There was no sign of the sidhe rade.

Kate turned to ask Finn about the fiaina when they all heard a shriek that came from the third floor. It dissolved into a long, aching moan that woke goosebumps on her arms.

"Oh, God," she said, white-faced. "That must be Jacky. The droichan's hurting her."

Gump nodded and started for the door, but Kate got there first. The sound of Jacky's moaning fired her worry to such an extent that she forgot to be afraid. She ran towards the stairs going up, but before she could take the first step, Gump caught hold of her arm and pulled her back.

"Wait," he said.

"We need a plan," Finn added. "We can't just rush in there against the droichan."

"But Jacky's probably dying—"

The moaning ceased abruptly and they heard a soft thump, like a body hitting the floor. Kate looked at Finn, then at Gump, a pleading in her eyes.

"We've got to do *something*."

Finn nodded. "Yes, but—"

Kate pulled herself free from Gump's grip and sprinted out of reach, up the stairs. She paused at the door to look back. Gump reached her side first, Finn, brow furiously wrinkled in thought, right behind him. They could hear voices—Jacky's and another's. The droichan's.

Relief ran through Kate. Jacky was still alive.

"When we go in," Finn whispered, "we split up immediately. No matter how strong the droichan is, he can't aim spells at three different moving figures."

"Then we crush him," Gump said.

He opened his big hands and then closed them into fists, a grim look on his face.

Finn shook his head. "We need his heart for that. No, the best thing would be to keep him off-balance. Throw him out the window perhaps—while he's concentrating on breaking his fall, we can try to escape."

"Or we could jump through the window," Kate said, remembering what Jacky had told them about its odd properties.

"That will still leave things as they are," Gump protested.

"Do *you* know where his heart is hidden?" Finn asked the trow.

Gump said nothing for a long moment, then slowly shook his head.

"This way we might win free to keep searching for it," the hob said.

Kate plucked at both their arms.

"We've got to go in now," she said, only just remembering to keep her voice pitched as low as theirs.

They could hear the sounds of a struggle from the other side of the door.

"What if there's more than just the droichan in there?" Finn wondered aloud.

But Gump was through with waiting. He bent low, put his shoulder to the door, and smashed it in. There was no more time for plans or second thoughts.

They went in, Kate darting to the right, Finn to the left, Gump charging straight through, rising to his full height once he was in the room. They saw Jacky pinned under the droichan in a corner of the room—the corner nearest to Kate. A moment's hesitation on their part was all the droichan needed.

"Can't spell you," he muttered to Jacky as he woke his shadow. "But what about your friends?"

Finn had it wrong. The droichan was quite able to throw more than a spell at a time. His shadow-creature lunged at Gump. An invisible force lifted Kate from her feet and slammed her against the bookcases. As he turned his attention on Finn, Jacky lunged from under him, throwing him off-balance.

The hob charged the droichan, but Colorc recovered quickly. He batted Jacky aside with one arm. Before Finn could reach him, the droichan's shadow-creature split into two, one pinning Gump to the floor, the other bowling the little hob over and trapping him as well.

"Don't even think of it," Colorc told Jacky as she pulled another wally-stane from its pouch.

But Jacky could only hear Kate's moaning from where she was pinned up against the bookcase. She could see Kate's wide-open eyes—only the whites showing, because they were rolled back in her head. Kate was staring into the void.

Jacky remembered that bleak place all too well. Kate was lost there. Trapped in its emptiness. Death, with its promise of the Summer Country, was far preferable to that. Death for herself, for Finn, for any of them, rather than letting even one of them spend eternity in that place.

She placed her will in the wally-stane and threw it, straight and true, across the room where it struck Kate and exploded into a shower of crystal dust. Kate's eyes rolled down, seeing this world once more. The invisible bonds holding her against the bookcase lost their power over her and she fell to the floor in a crumpled heap. Only then did Jacky turn back to the droichan.

Colorc towered over her, the fire in his eyes burning like a torched countryside. His cloak fell from his shoulders and pooled on the floor. The night skies outside the room went darker still. Thunder rumbled directly overhead. Rain exploded against the Tower's roof. Lightning seared across the sky in sheets of icy fire.

"This has gone too far," Colorc said.

His voice was quiet, almost conversational, but cold as a winter sky. He swept over Jacky, and before she could move, he'd grabbed the front of her shirt and hoisted her up, smacking her up against the wall again.

"Do you see your friends?" he said. "You've saved one, but my darkness will feed on the souls of the others. It will tear their bodies open and spill their entrails on the floor. It will suck the juices of their brains and make bracelets of their bones."

Jacky had hit her head on the wall when the droichan threw her against it. Sparks danced before her eyes. She found it hard to breathe with his hand pulling the throat of her shirt tight across her windpipe. But she could see the droichan's shadow-creatures crouched over Finn and Gump.

The side of the trow's throat was bleeding where the skin had already been broken. The shadow holding him was lapping at the blood with a black tongue while the trow struggled uselessly against the creature's superior strength. Finn was almost swallowed by the one on him. It lay across his body like a loathsome cloak, wet with the boggy reek of the sluagh. Kate was the only one not trapped, but she lay very still where she had fallen.

Colorc pulled Jacky from the wall and slammed her against it again. She tried to fight him, but his sheer strength was just too much for her. She clawed at his chest, tearing open his shirt, breaking the skin with her nails, but the droichan ignored her efforts. The unnatural storm continued to rage outside, counterpoint to the fires in his eyes.

"Give me what I want!" he shouted at her, spittle showering her face.

He pulled her back again, driving her against the wall with so much force that she thought she could feel her bones rattling against each other.

"Your friends will die," Colorc told her. "One by one, torn apart before your eyes, and then, then I'll take you apart with my own hands and feed your flesh to the night."

Thunder boomed, punctuating his words with an earth-shattering crack that shook the Tower to its foundations.

Jacky could hardly see the droichan now. Her eyes were blurred with tears of frustration and pain. She desperately needed air. She tried to focus on him, but she saw merely a blur.

There was the dark of his torn shirt, and the lighter hue of his skin. The red fire in his eyes. A gleam of brass or bronze hanging from his neck, hidden until she'd torn his shirt. The white gleam of his teeth as he drew back his lips, snarling at her.

He slammed her against the wall a fourth time, and then even those blurry sights were driven away by a new shower of dancing sparks.

"Give me the key!" the droichan roared, but his voice seemed to come from very far away now.

The scene was like something out of an old Hollywood western, Johnny thought as he and Mactire reached the park.

They entered off Bank Street, right near Billings Bridge. Spread in a long line along the bank of the river was the rade of the sidhe, ready for war as they had been when he and Jemi had called them up earlier tonight. If they were the Indians, then the Unseelie Host were the white-eyes. They were a disorganized swirl of creatures—bogans and gullywudes, trolls and goblins, things for which Johnny had no name.

"Jesus," he breathed as he and Mactire stopped to reconnoiter. "We haven't got a chance."

The Unseelie Host outnumbered the fiana sidhe, three to one.

Mactire frowned, also taking in their number.

"I hadn't thought there were so many left after the Jack destroyed their Court last year," he said. "But still. We have no choice. We must—"

The sound of someone calling Johnny's name made the wolf boy pause. They turned to see Henk running up to them. When he reached Johnny's side, he bent half over, clutching his side and breathing hard through his mouth.

"Henk. What're you doing here?"

Henk straightened slowly. "I wanted to see what you were up to . . ." His voice trailed off as he took in the scene before them. "Oh, Christ. Tell me I'm dreaming."

Touched by faerie, he could see into the Middle Kingdom now.

"You'd better go," Johnny said.

"No way. I'm staying right here with you."

"You don't know what you're getting into."

"I know enough," Henk replied. He pointed out Loireag and Dohinney Tuir near the center of the long line of sidhe. "Those two—they're the ones I met by the river when I was looking for you."

Johnny followed the line of Henk's vision, but his gaze went further to the small figure that the kelpie and hob were talking to.

"Jemi!" he cried.

Without looking to see what the others did, he ran along the line of sidhe to where she was.

She looked up at his approach, a faint welcoming smile appearing briefly on her lips before her features went grim once more. She was sitting astride a small shaggy pony and looked wet and bedraggled. Her hair was mostly plastered to her skull, except for the odd pink tuft near the back that was dry. As he got closer to her, a vague marshy smell came to his nostrils.

"What happened to you?" he asked.

"I had a swim in the canal."

She slipped from the back of the pony to give him a quick hug. Stepping back, she touched the back of her hand to his cheek.

"I'm so glad you're here, Johnny. I was afraid you wouldn't hear the call, but there was no time to go by your place. I just had to hope that you'd hear—that you'd understand what it meant and come."

"Well, I'm here. But Jesus, Jemi."

He turned to look at the Unseelie Host. They were jeering and catcalling the sidhe, but kept to their unruly ranks.

"This is going to be a slaughter," Johnny said.

Jemi shook her head. "Only if we don't kill the droichan."

"The what?"

"Droichan—it's a kind of gruagagh, but worse. Way worse. He's the one who's been behind all of what's been going on. I ran into him in Sandy Hill while I was fetching this."

She pulled the little bone flute pendant from under her shirt where it was hanging and showed it to him. Johnny felt a spark flicker inside himself at the sight of it. He put his hand in his pocket and closed his fingers about his fiddle charm. It was hot to the touch.

He tried to concentrate on what Jemi was telling him about the droichan—how his shadow could run free and kill people for him, how he was deathless, except he could be killed, but only if his heart was found first—but his attention kept wandering to the colour of her eyes, the line of her chin, the shape of her ear. He shook his head. There was no time for that kind of thing right now.

"I'm going into the Tower," she said, finishing up her explanation. "Johnny, will you lead the rade for me?"

Johnny shook his head again. "I'm going with you."

"But the rade needs a mortal to lead it—we'll be stronger then."

"I can't let you go in there alone."

"You don't think I can handle it?"

"I'm sure you can handle anything you set your mind to, Jemi. I just can't handle being out here and not knowing what's happening to you."

Jemi sighed, but before she could argue anymore, Henk stepped up.

"I'll do it," he said. "If it's the kind of thing that anyone can do, not just Johnny."

"You?" Jemi said, surprised to see him there. She'd only had eyes for Johnny.

Loireag moved closer. Henk flinched at the sight of her looming over him, but he stood his ground.

"Has this tadpole suddenly found teeth?" she asked, looking Henk over.

"Loireag," Tuir warned.

"Don't worry, Tuir. I'm saving my anger for the bogans. I just want to test the mettle of this tadpole, that's all." She turned her attention back to Henk. "Can you lead us against that?" she asked, pointing at the Unseelie Host. "Or will you run off with your tail between your legs halfway through the first charge?"

Johnny started to speak, but Jemi caught his arm and shook her head.

Henk's throat felt too tight. He swallowed, Adam's apple bobbing, and looked at the Host. He'd thought the sidhe had been his nightmares come to life, but he'd been wrong, he realized as he looked on the creatures of the Unseelie Court. He tried to imagine leading a charge against that monstrous, unholy crowd, and couldn't. But he knew that if he didn't, the dark would continue to haunt him for the rest of his life.

"I'm scared shitless," he said, looking back at the kelpie. She started to nod knowingly, until he added, "But I'll do it."

Their gazes met and held for long moments, then Loireag nodded.

"So be it," she said. "I think the Moon can ride you."

"Lend him your fiddle," Tuir said to Johnny.

"He can't," Jemi said. "He'll need that for where we're going."

"I can't play one anyway," Henk said. "My instrument's the concertina."

"Anglo or English?" Loireag asked.

Henk blinked. "Uh, English."

Loireag sent word up and down the line of the sidhe until a small hob trotted up on his pony and handed Henk an instrument. It was a beautiful old Wheatstone, its silver gleaming, its wood dark, its leather bellows worn but still strong.

"It was my father's," the hob said. "Play the Moon fierce in it."

Before Henk could thank him, the hob turned his mount and returned to his place in the ranks.

Henk hefted the instrument. "I'm not so sure I understand," he said. "We're going up against those things with music?"

"Oh, no," Tuir assured him. "The music's there to call up the rade and aim its strength like an arrow against our foes."

"Any particular music?" Henk asked.

"I think a march would do the trick," Jemi said. "Something fierce."

" 'O'Neill's Cavalcade'?" Johnny suggested.

"That would do," Jemi agreed.

"Okay," Henk said. "When do I start playing?"

"Now!" Loireag cried, but Jemi quickly shook her head.

"Wait for them to make the first move," she said. "If we haven't lose all our luck, Johnny and I will have put an end to the droichan and there'll be no need for this war. The Host will quickly lose heart without a chief to lead them."

"I want blood," Loireag said. "Someone has to pay for all we've lost."

"Tuir, please?" Jemi asked, turning to the hob. "Hold back until you've no other choice?"

"Different words from what you asked of us earlier tonight," the kelpie complained.

"I didn't know then what I know now," Jemi replied.

"If I've got to start it," Henk said, "I'll make sure we wait."

Loireag and Jemi both shot him looks, the one angry, the other grateful.

"Thank you," Jemi said.

Leaving her pony for Henk, she led Johnny past the ranked sidhe, back to Bank Street. From there they doubled up Riverdale, turning down Belmont to come up to the Tower by the front. There were few Unseelie creatures abroad now, most having gathered in the park to face the hosted sidhe.

"Have you got a plan?" Johnny asked as they crept near the Tower.

Jemi nodded. "But it means me going in and you staying out."

"I don't want that."

"Listen to me, Johnny. At least hear me out."

Reluctantly, Johnny did. When he heard what she had planned, he had to agree that he couldn't accompany her.

"But only if the front door's guarded," he said.

"That's a bargain."

And an easy one to keep, Jemi thought as they closed in on the Tower. She'd already spied bogans and a tall trollish figure in its doorway. They appeared to be looking for someone or something. She led Johnny quickly by until they were standing by the front of the Tower. Johnny looked up and shook his head.

"You can climb that?" he asked.

Jemi nodded.

"What are you—part monkey, too?"

"Just a Pook, Johnny—and a halfling at that."

"And you're sure the droichan's heart is in there?"

"I've met him," she explained again. "He's the kind that needs it close at hand—probably even on his person. Will you play the tune, Johnny?"

"Sure."

He opened his case and took out fiddle and bow. Tightening the frog until the bow's hairs were taut, he started to put the instrument under his chin, then paused.

"Jemi?"

She looked at him, then leaned close for a kiss.

"If we lose," she said softly, "I'll look for you in the Summer Country."

Johnny swallowed dryly. "Yeah. But we're not going to lose, right?"

"Right."

Fiddle under his chin, Johnny drew the bow across its strings and began to play the tune that Jemi had requested of him. It was an instrumental version of the traditional Breton folk song "Kimiad"—a sly music that fit into the sounds of the night so that the Unseelie Host would ignore it, but a music that would call down the Moon's strength for Jemi to borrow. She needed her own hands free for the climb.

"The Gruagagh had a window there, on the third floor," she'd told him. "A window through which he could see all of Kinrowan and some of the borderlands as well. It's there that the droichan will be. Like a spider in its web, hoping to catch a fly. But this fly will come in through the window, not by the door. I'll need that moment's edge, Johnny. I'll need the edge and the Moon's strength that your music will borrow for me. Luck in every note, liquid as her light, Johnny."

So he played the tune and called down the Moon as he could, watching with open-mouthed amazement as Jemi went up the side of the house, finding finger- and toeholds in between the bricks where there shouldn't have been any. He didn't know if the Moon was answering his call, but he felt a quickening inside him that had nothing to do with the rush of adrenaline that danger had called up in his body.

He could hear bagpipes in the music and harping, a hundred fiddles, and the sound of Jemi's own pipe. The music was a soaring chorus, but at the same time, it was filled with the sounds of leaf rustlings and wind, tree boughs groaning, houses settling, distant traffic.

"Don't let her be hurt," he whispered against the music that his bow drew from his grandfather's fiddle.

She had just reached the halfway point between the second and third floors when the sky suddenly went dark.

Christ, Johnny thought, forcing himself to concentrate on his music. I sure hope this isn't a sign from the Moon that she's got better things to do than help us.

Hard on the heels of the darkness, thunder boomed directly above him and the vast set of cloud that had appeared to darken the sky loosed a downfall of rain. In moments, Johnny found it impossible to see more than a foot in front of himself. The wet hairs of his bow slid against the strings and the music faltered, then died. He tried to peer through the rain, up to where he'd last seen Jemi, but his eyes filled with water faster than he could clear them. A sheet of lightning tore across the sky. In that instant he saw that she had almost reached the third-floor windowsill that she'd been aiming for, then the darkness fell again.

"Screw this," he said.

Fiddle and bow still in hand, he raced for the front door, damn the consequences. He got into the hall when a strange little creature that seemed to be made all of twigs ran up to him. Johnny kicked at it and it fell to pieces as his boot connected with it. A grunt came from down the hall and a bogan peered out of a room and spied him.

Johnny bolted up the stairs. Behind him, he could hear the bogan scrabbling around the corner and starting up after him.

When the sky darkened and the rain hit, Jemi echoed Johnny's thoughts, but for a different reason. The blast of rain very nearly succeeded in knocking her from her precarious

perch. For long moments it was all she could do to hold on,
little say continue up the side of the Tower.

But she refused to give in. Inside was her sister's murderer.
Inside was a creature determined to drain Faerie of its luck and
leave a wasteland behind it as it moved on to yet another Court.
Well, he was going to be stopped, she vowed, and stopped
here.

Squeezing her eyes shut against the downpour, she lifted a
hand, found a minuscule hold for it, and drew herself up
another few precious inches. One bare foot went up, found a
hold, then the other. She pulled herself carefully up, flung out
a hand, and could have kissed a bogan, for it closed on the
windowsill she'd sought.

Cautiously, she went through the whole process with her feet
once more, first one, then the other. She started to pull herself
the rest of the way, moved too fast, and her hand started to slip.
She didn't even think of what she did next. As the one hand
slipped, she concentrated on maintaining her balance, hugged
the wall, and caught a firmer grip with her other hand.

Then it started to slip.

She tensed her hand and her grip held. A moment later she
got her other hand into position and pulled herself the rest of
the way up until she was crouched, wet and bedraggled, on the
sill.

She peered down, trying to spot Johnny, but she couldn't see
far enough. She listened for his music, but the rain drowned it
out if he was still playing.

Oh, don't get brave and rush in after me, she prayed. Bad
enough that one of us is probably going to die—don't you get
hurt too, Johnny.

Then she turned her attention to the inside of the room.
She'd moved with the utmost quiet—and had been helped by
the downpour—so she wasn't surprised that no one inside had
noticed her. Now that she was looking in, she understood why.

A trow and a hob were being held to the floor by a pair of
the shadow-creatures that pursued her. A young woman with
curly hair lay by one wall, a book clutched in her hand. And
then, as Jemi turned her head, she saw the droichan, slamming
another woman against the wall.

Jemi wanted to help the woman the droichan was attacking,
but she had to think first. Where would his heart be hidden?

She'd get just the one try—if she was lucky—and no more. So where? On him, probably, but what would it look like? Would it be a ring, a charm, a pendant, a coin in his pocket, a button on his shirt, a thread in his cloak? Or would it be hidden somewhere in this room?

She looked around again, saw that the woman clutching the book was sitting up now, eyes wide as she saw Jemi perched outside the window. Jemi put a finger to her lips, but the woman merely opened her book and held it out so that Jemi could see the curious drawing on the page. When she shrugged her shoulders, the woman touched the drawing, then pointed at the droichan.

Jemi's teeth bared in a sudden grin.

Arn above, she thought as she swung into the room. She'd just been given the droichan's secret.

Henk sat uneasily on his borrowed pony. He had the concertina resting on one knee and he stroked the pony's shaggy mane while he stared across the park at the gathered Host of the Unseelie Court. Nothing seemed real. At the same time, everything seemed more real than anything he'd ever experienced before.

"They make an awesome sight, don't they?" Dohinney Tuir said quietly, edging his own pony closer to Henk's.

Henk glanced briefly at him, then returned his attention to the Host.

"They're my night fears,"he said. "I thought your friend the kelpie was one, but now that I can see those creatures I know I was wrong. I've never really faced them before. I'm not always scared of them—hardly ever, really—but they still come back to me, just like that"—he snapped his fingers— "and when they do, they cripple me. Now that I know they're real . . . I'm not any less scared of them, but somehow it makes it easier to face them. To know that I wasn't crazy all those years."

"We might all die," Tuir said.

Henk nodded. "I know. But it beats getting run over by a truck. At least this means something."

"Does it?" Loireag asked, stepping closer to his left side. She smiled as he glanced at her but he wasn't sure if the bared teeth were mocking him, or if she just generally wore a sardonic air.

"To me it'll mean something," he said.

Before Loireag could reply, the sky went dark. Thunder cracked above them, impossibly close, and a sheet of rain engulfed the park, immediately drenching them. Lightning flickered like snakes' tongues through the dark.

"This is it," Loireag said. "They'll attack under cover of the rain."

Henk started to lift the concertina, wondering how he could play it in this kind of weather, but the little hob on the other side of him touched his arm. When Henk looked at him, Tuir shook his head.

"Not yet," he said. "This is some working of the droichan's—his rage manifesting itself in the weather. It means he's angry. Perhaps Jemi's reached him."

"He can cause this just by getting angry?" Henk asked.

"When you speak of droichan, you speak of power," the hob replied. "But they pay a price for such displays. They lose their souls, Henk. They lose the chance of all the lives that are to come. And, in the end, they lose the green promise of the Region of the Summer Stars."

"Uh, right."

"They can live forever, unless their heart is destroyed. But destroy it, and they no longer exist—not on any plane of existence."

Loireag pawed at the ground with one hoof, the rain waking a dark sheen on her skin.

"I want his blood," she hissed into the night. "For all our kin that he slew. For Jenna. I want his blood."

"Patience," the hob said. His voice worked like a salve on her, reining in her anger. "You will get your desire all too soon."

Henk looked from one to the other, then shivered. He was soaked to the bone, cold and scared. He couldn't see the enemy anymore and that just made things worse. He thought of the creatures and the hellish banner unfurled above their ranks. The Host could be creeping up on them right now. They were already outnumbered.

His fingers touched the buttons of the concertina without pressing down on them, recalling the opening bars of

"O'Neill's Cavalcade." Would the instrument still play in the rain? Would some enchantment make it work?

"How will we know when it's time?" he asked, his voice sounding weak and high-pitched to his ears.

"We'll know," the hob said grimly at his side. "Don't fret, Henk. We'll know."

"But what are they waiting for?"

Tuir shrugged. "The droichan's word? Some chief to lead them? I don't know. Perhaps they wait for courage."

"But they outnumber us three to one."

"To an Unseelie creature," Loireag said, "those are poor odds. They prefer the sure thing."

Henk shivered again and settled down to wait with the silent ranks of the sidhe. The kelpie might feel that the Host facing them was afraid, but he didn't have any such false hopes. He'd seen the creatures for himself. There was no way monsters like that could be scared of an army that was just a third of their own size.

"Christ, I hate waiting," he muttered.

Neither of his companions replied. He hunched his neck between his shoulders, uselessly trying to keep out the rain. He didn't know why he bothered. He was already as wet as it was humanly possible to get.

"Christ," he muttered again, then fell silent as well.

All he could do was wait.

CHAPTER
16

When Jacky freed Kate from the machinations of Colorc's spell and brought her back from the void, some part of that empty place stayed inside her. Colorc's invisible grip lost its hold on her and she was dropped to the floor, but once freed, Kate's muscles were all slack and rubbery. She couldn't lift her head. She couldn't even open her eyes.

Memory of that empty place lodged inside her like a dark needle stuck straight through her heart. She wasn't relieved at her escape. She didn't feel anything; only a bleakness that was made worse by the sudden sensory overload as sound and smell and feeling all returned to her in a rush. She curled herself around Caraid, trying to escape it—memory of that place and the return of her senses—all to no avail.

She squeezed her eyes shut, willing her surroundings to disappear, but they flickered open almost of their own volition. Her nostrils stung with the reek of sluagh and other Unseelie creatures. Sound was worse. The sound of Jacky's struggle with the droichan. The whispering hiss and snick of the droichan's shadow-creatures. The rough rasp of a tongue against Gump's skin. Finn's moans.

But when she opened her eyes, she saw none of that. Her gaze settled on the window overlooking Kinrowan to see a wet, pink-haired figure balancing on its sill.

Slowly, Kate sat up. Her every bone and muscle ached at the movement, but she knew she had to help the newcomer. One look in the bedraggled figure's eyes told her that this was no creature of the droichan, nor one of the Unseelie Court. She opened Caraid to the page showing the curious image that she and Gump had found in that house in the Glebe, and showed it to the small woman in the window.

The woman shrugged, so Kate pointed at the drawing, then at the droichan. Understanding woke in the woman's eyes and she grinned fiercely, swinging down from the sill.

Kate leaned weakly against the wall, not really sure what the symbol meant to the woman, only that it meant something. That had to be enough, didn't it? But the void still fingered her heart, threatening to overcome her again with its empty bleakness.

The woman moved across the room towards the droichan, whose back was towards them. Kate watched her go. What did the symbol mean? What would the woman do? And suddenly Kate—fueled by the fear of what lay inside her, what the droichan had put inside her—felt that the knowledge she'd passed on wouldn't be enough. She got to her feet.

"No," she whispered to the woman.

Jemi froze at the sound of Kate's voice. The whispered word rang loud in her ears—too loud. It sounded above the tumult of the storm outside. The droichan paused, too, turning with Jacky still held upright by one arm. He saw the Pook.

"You," he said.

"My God!" Kate cried. "He's wearing it around his neck."

The droichan blanched. His free hand went to the medallion hanging from his throat, but he didn't move quickly enough. Jacky yanked what she saw as only a bright blur of metal on his chest and gave a sharp tug that broke it free of its chain. With what strength she had left, she tossed it towards Kate, but Jemi reached up and snatched it from the air.

The droichan threw Jacky aside and woke a spell. Invisible fingers plucked at Jemi's body and started to lift her into the air. And then Johnny came thundering up the last few stairs and burst into the room.

"Jesus Christ!" he said as he took in the scene.

His appearance distracted the droichan. It took only a fraction of a second for him to turn to see who it was, then return his attention to the Pook, but that was all the time Jemi had needed. She slipped free of his invisible grip with a sidhe sidestep—into the world of men, back into Faerie—and then she dropped the medallion onto the floor and ground it under her heel.

It had the look and feel of old gold, brassy and worn, but it was the droichan's heart and under the stamp of her heel it splattered as a human organ would have. The sting of its blood and bursting tissue burned the bottom of Jemi's foot and the floor hissed and smoked where the fragments landed. But Jemi could endure the pain. She had only to think of her sister and all those the droichan had killed. She had only to look at his anguished features.

A wail of despair left his mouth, then all the years he'd stolen fell upon him in a rush. His flesh grew lined, hard, brittle. It flaked and turned to dust. In moments, an empty sack of clothing fell to the hardwood floor in a shower of dust. The storm outside the Tower ceased as abruptly as it had begun.

Kate leaned back against the wall and slid weakly to the floor. The droichan's death had come too suddenly, looked too much like the last reel of an old B horror flick to seem true. Real beings, magical droichan or not, didn't just dissolve into dust, did they? But the sliver of the void was gone from her heart and while the blood still thundered in her veins, the realization hit home that the cause for all their terror was gone.

She looked slowly around. A strange young man with a fiddle and bow in one hand was crossing the room to hold the pink-haired woman. The shadow-creatures were gone and both Finn and Gump were sitting up, the trow clutching the side of his neck, blood leaking through his fingers. A bogan came barreling into the room, but Gump knocked it senseless with one blow of his free hand. Jacky lay against the wall where the droichan had thrown her, weakly trying to rise.

"Is . . . is it really over?" Kate asked.

The pink-haired woman shook her head.

"The droichan's gone," she said. "But there's still a war to be won."

The bogan Groot was the proud bearer of the Unseelie Court's standard. He held it aloft, grinning as it flapped in the wind, still grinning when the rain came and it clung wetly to its shaft.

Such a standard. A widdyman hob had stitched it over long

nights, sewn every stitch widdershins. Such an unsainly emblem to lead them. And the droichan. He promised to be a better leader than any Big Man, hot damn. Kinrowan would bleed under their heels. But first there was the sidhe host to feed on.

He could see only their vague outline through the rain and wondered how long it would be before either Greim or the new boss himself would send word for the charge. He could already taste sidhe flesh. Just thinking of the toadsuckers made his mouth water.

"Come on, come on," a troll muttered beside him. "Spike 'em—what's taking so long?"

Groot nodded. Maybe he should lead the charge himself. He had the banner. The Host would follow. Wouldn't the boss reward him, hot damn, at the victory Groot would give him?

But then Groot frowned. Maybe not. The new boss demanded utter obedience—a hard thing for a bogan to buckle under—but he promised much to those who served him well. Human flesh, as well as Seelie. Though human flesh was luckless, it was sweet. Could he risk the boss's wrath?

"Whadaya think?" Lunt asked, joining him at the front of the Host.

"Think about what?" Groot asked the other bogan.

"Is Greim going to send the word, or did he run off and get spiked?"

"Don't talk like that," Groot warned. "Not unless you want to spend the rest of your life as a heap of shit."

"Bah!" Lunt spat in the muddying sod. "I think—"

Groot never got to hear what he thought. From the Tower behind them came a piercing wail, and then the storm suddenly stopped. The night seemed almost bright as the clouds vanished from above. Groot stared across the field at the long grim line of borderfolk, and an uncertain shiver went through him. It didn't matter that his own army outnumbered the sidhe three to one. It didn't matter that the Unseelie Host had a droichan leading them.

Something was wrong.

"What was that?" Lunt said.

"Guess the boss spiked that Jack," a voice said from the crowd.

"I'd like a bite of her myself," someone else added to a general laugh.

"I don't think that was it," Groot said. "There's a bad feeling in the air right now."

A moment later a shout came from the Tower.

"The boss is dead!"

Pandemonium broke loose in the unruly ranks of the Unseelie Host.

When the rain ceased, a stir of anticipation went through the long line of the waiting sidhe. They were wet and cold. Hands and backs were stiff from the unfamiliar weight of weapons and armour. It had been a long time since they'd gone to war. But with the rain gone now, they could see the ranks of their foe once more and backs straightened from slumped postures, weapons were readied again. Their gazes drifted from the Unseelie Host to the mortal who would lead them when the time was right.

Henk was uncomfortably aware of their attention. He could sense Loireag's tension beside him as she pawed the muddy ground. On his other side, Tuir sat glum on his small pony, knowing what was to come and regretting it. Mactire, resting in wolf shape near the hooves of Henk's pony, rose to his feet.

"What are we waiting for?" Loireag demanded.

Henk stirred and glanced at her.

"It's not time yet," Tuir told her.

"Damn time and damn waiting," Loireag returned sharply. "I'm sick to death of them both."

Just then they heard the cry making the rounds of the Unseelie army. The droichan was dead.

"By the stag's own heart," Tuir murmured. "She did it." He turned to Henk, grinning. "Jemi did it!"

"Now let's finish the night's work," Loireag said.

"No need," the hob replied. "They'll disperse soon enough on their own."

Henk wanted to agree with Tuir, but he was looking at the house that they all called the Tower. Rising up from behind it—impossibly huge, at the wrong time in its cycle—was an enormous full moon. As he looked at it, something jumped inside Henk. Some part of him recognized that there was more to that orb than a dead asteroid floating in orbit around a blue-green planet. It was the wrong time of the night for that moon to rise. It shouldn't have been that full at this time of the month. So he knew that what he saw now was the Moon of Faerie.

And it was calling to him.

He touched the wet concertina on his lap and found that it was dry. He put his hands into both of its side straps. The Moon filled his sight, touched places inside him that he'd never known existed before. He wet his lips. He glanced at Loireag, urging him to play them to war, at Tuir, pleading for peace. Then at the Moon again.

It mourned the loss of its Pook.

It mourned the loss of so many of the borderfolk.

"Awake the music," Loireag hissed. "Send us to war."

"I beg you," Tuir said in the same breath. "Don't."

But Henk put his fingers to the buttons of his instrument and the music spilled forth.

Loireag gave a cry of joy. Tuir bent his head across his pony's neck in defeat. But the music Henk played was what neither of them had expected. He played the tune that the Moon woke in him, the music to call down her luck for the thirsty sidhe to drink, the liquid light of her luck that they'd been denied for so long.

As the music grew in strength, the Unseelie army began to moan. The bogan holding the unsainly banner with its crucified swan-man dropped the flag onto the muddy grass and fled. The whole of the Host broke their ranks and fled in all directions. Underfoot, radiating out from the Tower, grew a webwork of gleaming moonlight ribbons. The Tower was their center, like the center of a spider's web, and the moonroads spun out, through Kinrowan and out into the borderlands.

One by one, the fiaina sidhe dropped their weapons and armour on the wet green grass. They looked to Henk. He stared at the swollen Moon that hung over the Jack's Tower, then dropped his gaze to the field before them. The Host was gone. Only the banner remained, trampled into the mud. The Moon spoke to him and gave him the secret pattern of its luck.

Still playing the music, Henk put his heels to the sides of his pony and led the sidhe out onto their rade.

The borderfolk fell in behind him as he took a moonroad that led away from the Tower, into the lands that were their own.

They went, hobs and skinwalkers, a tall troll and waterfolk, little twig-men and tall willowy women, all the sidhe, until only Loireag and Tuir were left.

The hob looked at Loireag, but didn't speak. Loireag frowned. She tried to deny the tug and pull of the music and the Moon's rade, but she couldn't. At last she sighed and nodded to Tuir.

"This is the right way," she said. "We went back and forth, Jemi and I—first the one of us raising the banner, then the other—but it took a tadpole to stop the war."

She gazed after the last figures of the rade, almost lost from sight now.

"I'll still miss her," she added in a gruff voice.

"How could you not miss Jenna?" Tuir asked.

Tears brimmed in his eyes. He touched Loireag's shoulder, then touched heels to his pony and set off after the rade. Loireag waited a moment longer.

"Goodbye, Jenna," she whispered to that swollen Moon.

Then she took the shape of a dark horse and together the kelpie and hob joined the rade that Henk led through the borderlands in a pattern that the Moon had taught him when she moved inside him.

"You have faced your fears," Arn had told him as he first woke the music. "Now is the time to heal the scars they left behind. The night is for the strong and you have earned the right to take joy in its shadows."

As he led the winding column of the sidhe along a complicated pattern of moonroads, Henk understood what the Moon had meant. Whatever else this night left him, he would always look forward to the hours between dusk and dawn.

Jemi and Johnny stood at the window of the Tower's third-floor study and looked out over Kinrowan and its borderlands. It was Finn who had dissuaded the Pook from leading the sidhe into a charge against the Unseelie army.

"There'll be no need," he'd told her simply.

And, as they watched the Unseelie Host disperse in panic at the death of their leader and the waking of the Moon's music, as they saw Henk lead the sidhe away on the first rade the borderfolk had known for many a month, she had understood.

So she stood by the window now, her arm around Johnny, his around her, and watched a quiet fall across Kinrowan.

In the room behind them, Bhruic's study had appeared once more between the four barren walls. The bogan that Gump had knocked down had woken and, after one look at the droichan's empty clothes, fled both the room and the Tower. Gump sat by the door, a bandage around his neck. Finn perched on the worktable, his legs swinging in the air. By the reading chairs, Jacky and Kate were sitting on the floor. They were both bruised and shaken, Jacky more so than Kate. They sat with their arms around each other, needing the comfort of their friendship to heal the fading memories of the void and everything that they'd so recently gone through.

It wasn't time to talk it through yet. It was just time to know that the other was there.

After a while, Jemi sighed and turned from the window.

Kate looked up. "When I warned you," she began. "When I said no . . ."

"I know," Jemi said. "The picture alone wouldn't have been enough. But the Moon was with us."

Finn nodded. "She has her own ways of dealing with droichan. I can see now that she used each one of us to do the task for her."

"Do you have a broom?" Jemi asked.

Kate nodded. "In the kitchen closet," she said, "If the bogans haven't eaten it. Why?"

"I thought I'd sweep up that mess," Jemi said, pointing with her chin at the heap of clothing and dust that lay in the middle of the room.

CHAPTER
17

A month or so later, All Kindly Toes was playing a combination Halloween/farewell dance at the Glebe Community Centre. The four younger members of the band were finding that they needed more time for their university studies, Greg already had a new project lined up for the winter, and Jemi Pook had plans of her own. There was talk of re-forming in the spring—something similar had happened the previous autumn—but for now it was a time of playing their very best, because who knew when they'd all play together again? So the band was in fine form, running through their favorites. "Shoo-de-poo-poo," "Mr. Big Stuff," "Love You Anyway," "B-A-B-Y," "Poison Ivy." . . . One tune followed the other, and the dance floor stayed packed.

Henk and Johnny were both there, Johnny standing on the sidelines, Henk dancing with Jacky or Kate, though more often the three of them danced together. Johnny just enjoyed watching them move and taking in the band—especially the pink-haired sax player who kept shooting him grins from the stage. When the long night finally wound down, the four of them helped the bank pack up, collected Jemi, then they walked south down Bank Street to the Tower.

Gwi Kayleigh had returned from Ballymoresk in a day and a half, rather than the two she'd promised Finn, with a company of Seelie foresters in tow. She was relieved to find them all well and the threat over, though somewhat chagrined that she'd missed it all. She and the Laird's foresters were busy for a week or so, driving the last few Unseelie creatures from Kinrowan, but thereafter things settled down.

Once again it was possible to walk the streets of Kinrowan without spying a bogan or sluagh, though they all knew that wouldn't remain so. The Unseelie Court never changed. Sooner or later another boss would rise from their ranks, and they'd be dogging the folk of Kinrowan once more. But for now, it was quiet.

The damage to the Tower had been mended, though it was weeks before the boggy stench of sluagh and bogans was entirely erased. The trees in its yard snuggled close to its walls once more and the browning of its garden was due to the season now, rather than the presence of unsainly creatures.

When the five of them reached the Tower, Kate went to make tea for them all, while Jacky put on a Kate Bush record and they all made themselves comfortable. Just as Kate was bringing in the tea, Finn arrived, so she had to go back for another cup and dig up some donuts for the hob's sweet tooth.

"So you're really going?" Kate asked Jemi when they all had their tea.

The Pook nodded. "The sidhe have Henk to lead them on their rade and I never really wanted that anyway. I've lived most of my life outside of Faerie and I'm just as happy doing that."

"But looking for the Bucca?" Jacky asked. "That seems like it'll just take you deeper into Faerie."

"Maybe. But it's something I have to do." She touched a bone flute that hung in the hollow of her throat. "I want to ask him about these charms. Tell him about what happened to Jenna. And Johnny's coming with me, so what more could I want?"

"Jemi's promised to show me the fairer side of the borderlands on this trip," Johnny added. "And I want to learn more about what music can do in Faerie—how it fits in, and why."

Jemi grinned. "I'll make a Fiddle Wit out of him yet. Or if I don't, you can bet Salamon will."

"I almost wish I could go with you," Jacky said. "It sounds like it'll be fun." She shot Kate a quick glance. "If you should happen to run into Kerevan or Bhruic . . ."

"We'll give them all the news," Jemi said. "Shall I tell them you've got plans to become a skillywoman?"

Jacky laughed. "Not likely. I had three wally-stanes left after that night and I ended up wasting one trying to make myself a book like Kate's Caraid, only all my book does is tell me stories and try to play the odd trick on me. I guess I'm stuck being a Jack. But that's okay. Every Court needs one. Still you can tell them that Kate'll be a gruagagh before you know it."

"I've wondered about those wally-stanes," Henk said. "They seem . . . Well, I know if you've got a certain head-set, *all* of Faerie seems impossible. But once you get into it, it begins to make a certain sense. Except for the wally-stanes. If they can do just about anything . . . ?"

"Hardly," Jacky said. "You should try using one."

"They're a rare magic," Finn explained, "and make for the basis of all those fairy tales of three wishes and the like. You won't find many these days, though. The nine that Jacky won from Kerevan are the first I've seen in a hundred years."

"Did you ever think of using one to wish for a hundred more wishes?" Henk asked.

Kate and Jacky laughed.

"God, no!" Jacky said. "Who knows what would happen if we did. They backfire enough as it is. If we tried that, they'd probably backfire a hundred times worse."

The record ended and Jacky replaced it with an Ian Tamblyn cassette.

"When will you be going?" she asked Jemi as she sat down again.

"Tonight." The Pook drank down what was left of her tea. "Now."

Johnny stood up with her. "We've our packs to collect and that's it. Thanks for letting me store Tom's stuff here. I couldn't think of a better place for those books."

"We collect books," Kate said.

"And hey," Jacky added. "We sure needed the furniture."

They said their goodbyes then, Henk leaving with Jemi Pook and Johnny. He was going to see them on their way as far as the Ottawa River. Finn left a little later, but not before reminding Kate to be on time for her skilly lessons.

When they were all gone, Jacky and Kate stood out in the backyard of the Tower and looked at the sky for a while.

"You don't think it was just the bone charms that brought Jemi and Johnny together, do you?" Jacky asked after a bit.

"What does it matter?" Kate replied. "They're happy enough now."

"Oh, I don't know. It'd just be nicer if it was only true love, that's all."

"God, you're such a romantic, Jacky."

"I guess." She turned to Kate. "We should go on a quest ourselves."

"What for?"

"Boyfriends."

"I take it back," Kate said. "You're not a romantic. You're just an incorrigible flirt."

Jacky gave her a slight punch on the arm, then sighed. "Maybe. But when you see something work the way it does for them, it kinda makes you want to have that for yourself, too—doesn't it?"

"Are you thinking of Eilian?"

Jacky nodded. "I'm not being very fair to him, am I? It's on-again, off-again, until neither of us knows what's going on. I keep getting afraid that one day I'll know for sure that he's the right one, but that by then it'll be too late. He'll have gotten himself married off to some Laird's daughter."

"So why don't you talk to him about it?"

"It's hard, Kate. My brain gets all tangled up and muddy when I try."

"Good things never come easy."

Jacky shook her head. "Trust you to come up with such an original thought."

She paused, looking as if she had more to say, but then stayed silent.

"But?" Kate prompted her.

Jacky gave her back a grin. "But I'll give it a try all the same."

"That's my Jacky," Kate said. "Ready to go in now?"

"Um-hmm."

Arm in arm, the two of them went back into the Tower to clean up the tea mugs and then to their respective beds. Above the gable peaks of the Tower, the Moon traveled west across the sky, and all of Kinrowan, and the Borderlands beyond, drank the bright luck of her light.